Grace

Mark Batey

Clink
Street

Published by Clink Street Publishing 2022

Copyright © Mark Batey 2022

First edition.

Painting on cover originally by CJ Staniland.

ISBN:
978-1-914498-37-4 - paperback
978-1-914498-38-1 - ebook

To my mother and father

Knivestone

Lighthouse · Longstone

Big
Hawker

North Wamses · Clove Car

South Wamses · Little
Hawker

Brownsman

Megstone · Gun Rock · Staple Island

Crumstone

Staple Sound

Fang

Knoxes Reef

Little Scarcar

Inner Farne · Wideopens

Farne Islands

Bamburgh ○

North
Sea

Seahouses ○
(North Sunderland harbour)

Farne Islands impression
by Wham Media

Contents

Prologue: Pre-history   11

1   Loading the *Forfarshire*   15

2   Longstone   21

3   The metal jungle   27

4   Cuddy   33

5   The captain's table   39

6   The lantern room   45

7   A gift for Annie   51

8   Bamburgh Castle   55

9   Boiling point   67

10   Memories of winter and *Autumn*   73

11   Last attempt   77

12   First watch   83

13   Off Berwick Bay   87

14   Mercury falling   93

15   First impact   97

16   Spotting the stricken ship   105

17   Second impact   109

18   The vicious sea   123

19   On Big Hawker rock   131

20   The woman with the wind-blown hair   137

21 In the quarter-boat 143

22 Off Big Hawker rock 147

23 The Castle Agent 151

24 A crowded home 157

25 The Half Moon 161

26 The first inquest 169

27 Circus Royal 177

28 National treasure 183

29 The artist and the smugglers 193

30 In the eye of a storm 199

31 *Rosa Victoriana* *209*

32 The Edinburgh debacle 215

33 A dragon reawakens 221

34 Alnwick Castle 227

35 The lucky charm 241

36 Dickson, Archer & Thorp 245

37 Meeting Jane 253

38 The trustees convene 261

39 The Aberdeen Angus breed 269

40 Coquet Island 273

41 Consumption 281

42 Shine bright, my angel 291

Epilogue: Aftermath 301

Author's Note 305

About the author 307

Prologue: Pre-history

It began 360 million years ago, long, long before the dinosaurs of the Jurassic era roamed the Earth.

This was a planet utterly alien from the one we inhabit today. Further fiery movements of the tectonic plates at the Earth's crust would occur before a recognisable layout of continental landmasses even began to emerge on the surface.

With a warm, humid climate, the atmosphere was sticky. Land and sea melded into one another. The earliest primitive human beings, standing on two legs, would not evolve until many more millions of years had elapsed. And yet the wild forests shrouding so much of the low-lying marshlands were far from silent: they made slithering, crawling homes for a glut of giant insects.

By now, the dense trees had developed the ability to grow protective bark. But the seawater that flooded these ancient swamps, into which naturally decaying shrubs, moss, ferns and trees collapsed, did not yet contain the bacteria that would help such vegetation to decompose.

Layer upon layer of fossilised plant fibre was heavily compressed as, over millions of years, successive layers of soils, clays, sands and rocks fell on top. The compacted plant fibre formed peat which eventually, as the Earth slowly cooled, turned into rich seams of coal.

It is known as the global Carboniferous – coal-bearing – era because the vast deposits of coal discovered underground in the lush landmasses of Britain, parts of Europe, Asia and America too, date back to this formative period. Whilst the timeframes of pre-historic ages inevitably defy precise measurement, the

Carboniferous era is deemed to span sixty million years, lasting until three hundred million years B.C.

Aeons later, much of the power that gave rise to mechanised manufacturing processes in the Industrial Revolution of the late eighteenth and early nineteenth centuries A.D. was carbon-based. Pit heads and colliery heaps became trademark features of north-east England and other regions, while an expanding network of railways linked mines with seaports. As more and more citizens turned to industry to make their living, farms expanded into villages, villages into towns. And so, the mighty geological upheaval that defined the Carboniferous era would also, three hundred million years later, help to shape human destiny.

Towards the end of the Carboniferous period, stretching motions in the Earth's restless crust caused huge volumes of magma – molten rock – to rise, under intense pressure and at searing heat, from deep inside the Earth. Nearly all of today's Earth surface, and its unique life-sustaining atmosphere, are a consequence of magma eruptions.

Not all the magma penetrated the surface. Much of it remained injected between the buckling strata of the Earth's core. Over the ensuing millions of years, the magma cooled and crystallised. One upshot is that a vast subterranean sheet of hard, black, igneous rock – dolerite – some seventy-five miles long and up to seventy metres thick formed, and lies still, beneath swathes of north-east England.

In Northumberland, England's most northerly county, known today for the sweeping views across its undulating countryside and alluring coastline, many distinctive features arise directly from this dolerite complex, which is aptly named the Great Whin Sill. Among local quarrymen, 'whin' meant unmalleable rock; 'sill' is a geological term for a flat-lying layer of rock.

The famous Northumbrian castles at Bamburgh, Dunstanburgh and Holy Island all take strategic advantage of high cliffs formed by the Great Whin Sill. Central segments of Hadrian's Wall, constructed early in the second century as the Roman Empire's northern frontier against marauding Picts, were laid along the line of the sill.

Thick dolerite is extremely tough, resistant to erosion. But today, after so many millennia of buffeting by wind and rain, rocky slivers of the sill protrude above the rugged surface.

The Farnes, a chain of small, dolerite islands lying between one and five miles into the North Sea off Bamburgh, are the easternmost outcrop of the Great Whin Sill. There are twenty-eight low-lying islets, split into inner and outer clusters by the mile-wide Staple Sound. They are irregular wedge-shaped rocks, mostly barren and treeless.

Their original name, the *Fern* Islands, stemmed from the Celtic for *land*. Yet as many as half of them lurk entirely submerged at high tide.

Few people have ever lived there. Smaller-scale maps, by not even revealing their existence, keep the secret. The islands are best known as a domain not for mankind but for seals and seabirds. An abundance of gulls, puffins, eider-ducks and more colonise the Farnes' remote ledges.

When gales blow in, seawater pummels the face of the islands so violently that the towering plumes of white foam are visible from miles along the mainland shore. The tides that swirl and gush around the Farnes can all too rapidly switch direction and force. At any time of year, they can be treacherous.

Through the ages, many ships have floundered on these rocks; many terrified, shivering souls have been lost. The ominous names of some of the islets, such as Knivestone, Gun Rock and Fang, attest to their ability to shred hulls. The notoriety of the Farne Islands as a mortal hazard to navigation – a ships' graveyard – endures.

Let me assure you – I've been in the area long enough to know – it is a reputation well earned.

— 1 —

Loading the *Forfarshire*

"Magnificent, isn't she?" declared the man facing her.

A brown rat sneaked past his right leg and edged behind a tower of crates, where it gnawed on some discarded cabbage leaves and raw carrots.

Forty minutes to cast-off.

With the gnarled fingers of his left hand, the man traced a line in the air from bow to stern along the gleaming coal-black vessel moored at the quayside. "The pride of Dundee, no less, on her maiden voyage a couple of years ago."

His voice was deep and commanding but not unkind. The distinctive north-east accent spiked his vowels with an upbeat inflection. He straightened the black cap above his high forehead – it made him look like a soldier – and clasped his hands behind his back. Undeniably, he exuded a quiet authority, a calm presence standing his ground among all the bustle and racket on Hull's hectic quayside.

But the precocious girl, perhaps five years old, blonde curls spilling over her shoulders, was paying no attention to him. Nor to her mother and brother. Her upward gaze was held transfixed by the twin vertical rows of shiny buttons adorning his blue blazer. What were they made of? Where had they come from? What might they be worth?

The man smiled at her mother. This made his long, dark sideburns collide with the upturned corners of his mouth, which bulged with warm yellow teeth. As a courtesy, her mother gave the *Forfarshire* a second fleeting glance, but to no positive effect. She had never seen a ship like it. But with its wooden masts, tall funnel stack and the huge circular casings for the paddle wheels that protruded ten feet to each side, it looked rather an ungainly beast.

"Really, Mrs Dawson," the man said before her mother could speak, the velvety tones swelling in his voice, "the *Forfarshire* is as powerful and luxurious as any ship on the coastal route. Marvellous as they are, steam engines are quite a recent innovation, and some fine tuning is only to be anticipated, eh?"

He paused momentarily to draw breath as a short man in braces heaving a barrow-load of sugar sacks clattered past. There were now two rats nibbling vegetables at the crates. One had glistening wet fur and had lost a section of its tail. No one took a blind bit of notice.

"Her boilers were cast and assembled at the Tay Foundry – some excellent engineers there – and they've been inspected today by our local experts, the Barretts. Any trace of a leak, they'll have closed it up as a matter of routine, nothing more, nothing less. There's no cause for alarm – is there, my dear?"

At his side, his wife Annie was dressed tastefully in a long-flowing crimson skirt which she liked because it made her look taller. Her outfit was complemented by a pair of coral drop earrings.

On cue she addressed Mrs Dawson: "My husband is a most experienced master mariner and, I'm pleased to say, not inclined to take careless risks. His record is faultless. He has sailed the *Forfarshire* up to Dundee and back many times. As it transpires," she finished, looking Mrs Dawson in the eye, "I'll be on board myself for this trip."

The captain nodded his approval while Mrs Dawson turned her gaze to a caterpillar of crewmen lugging crates, barrels and more sacks up a sagging gangplank into the heart of the great ship. Everywhere you looked, something was going on.

With a brusque command, a cart laden with machine tools and spare pipes was drawn away from the quayside by a pair of dappled horses. Three stout men had squeezed on to the raised bench in the front of the cart. A painted sign dangling from the backplate read: Barrett & Sons.

Mrs Dawson reflected, made her decision. "Very well, thank you, captain. Mrs Humble, too. I was bothered when I heard talk of a leak – more like shouting, really – I couldn't help but overhear. But you've set my mind at ease. We'll wait for my husband to finish work, then come on board, I hope very soon."

Mrs Dawson's husband, Jesse, had found work as a labourer in Hull, where he was putting in full daylight shifts mowing and trenching, although he was born and bred in Dundee.

"Splendid," said the captain. "I'll look forward to seeing you all on the ship."

Less than thirty-five minutes to cast-off.

A flock of white gulls with black wingtips soared overhead, screeching to each other as they followed the serpentine river to the sea.

Mrs Dawson clutched her daughter, Matilda, and her son, James. He had been standing quietly behind her throughout her conversation, chewing something tasty and observing a stray dog as it sniffed for scraps. Perhaps it had caught the scent of the rats.

She led them off towards the entrance to the quay. Not only did her tight grip on their small hands transmit feelings of love and security to them, but it also made a sense of fulfilment swell within her. Feeling soothed, she banished from her mind any lingering doubts about the ship's engine.

Come to think of it, was she even sure that she'd heard correctly what the mysterious Irishman had been saying? Who was he and anyway, how did he know what he was yelling about?

The captain watched them go, his right arm poised to wave if any of them looked back. My guess is they didn't. He only half-realised it but Annie's eyes were drilling into him, trying to decipher his thoughts.

His attention was attracted by a woman dragging a small brown valise that was much too heavy. She switched it from hand to hand, strained to lift it with both hands. He indicated to Annie and they crossed the quay. He introduced himself to the woman, noticing but not commenting on her elfin face, and asked whether she would like a porter.

The woman looked startled, caught out. "Oh no, thank you, sir, I can manage." The valise on the ground beside her, she rubbed her slim hands and looked furtively about.

"Very well. But if I can be of any assistance…"

Leaving the sentence dangling, he strode arm in arm with Annie towards the ship.

He later learned from a steward that this woman – Miss Evelyn Martin – picked one of the *Forfarshire's* superlative cabins, which had mahogany furniture and exquisite Axminster rugs. When purchasing her ticket, she was the only passenger who tendered two gold sovereigns.

Half an hour later, at six-thirty that evening, Wednesday 5 September 1838, the steamship *Forfarshire* slipped away from the Hull quayside, bound for Dundee. At least two other ships, the *Pegasus* and the *Innisfail*, cast off at the same time, likewise taking advantage of the ebb tide. The *Forfarshire* had to weave a delicate course through the array of vessels, most much smaller than she, choking the port.

The captain, John Humble, stood on the forecastle, deep in conversation with his first mate, an efficient, confident Scotsman named James Duncan. Every Wednesday, they set off on the *Forfarshire* northbound from Hull, and every Saturday they left Dundee on the return leg, about 220 nautical miles each way.

Captain Humble, who did his best to welcome the passengers on board before every departure, had always felt that the sea was in his blood. He was born in Shields, a fast-growing fishing town at the mouth of the Tyne, downstream from the city of Newcastle where we'll spend some time later in the story. Shields even had its own member of parliament, although, as I'm sure you'll know, it took until the twentieth century for women, and many men, to be enfranchised.

Humble's first berth was on a collier trading between Shields and Newcastle. He enjoyed it, tried to learn the tasks that every crew hand carried out. After that, he worked on a tugboat, the *Target*, but his ambition was not sated. He progressed to the *Neptune*, an early steamer travelling between Newcastle and Hull, and then, in his fifties, was made master of the *Forfarshire*.

The skilled workforce at Thomas Anderson's Seagate yard in Dundee built the *Forfarshire* in 1834 to carry passengers and cargo for the Dundee & Hull Steam Packet Company. At a cost of £20,000, she was seen as a huge vote of confidence in steam power on the burgeoning coastal route. With a length of 132 feet and a twenty-foot beam, she was big – the biggest vessel yet to come from Dundee which, like many coastal towns, had a thriving port. The *Forfarshire* was completed, trialled and registered, sailing in service from May 1836.

In that happy year, too, Captain Humble's married daughter gave birth to a son, named John after him, delivering a second reason for Annie and him to feel proud. Baby John had been colicky, but thankfully the symptoms had cleared up and he was fine.

As he'd advised Mrs Dawson, steam-powered ships were a relatively new mode of transport. The engines needed to be tended with care. Like other steamers at the time, the *Forfarshire* still had masts for sails, one fore, the other aft, on either side of the now billowing funnel. A crew hand had roped triangular flags to the mast tops, and they flapped with gusto.

Novel it may have been, but the new-fangled propulsion technology was advancing rapidly. As Humble knew, paddle steamers were increasingly familiar sights on rivers and around coastlines. Only recently, he'd read about the startling designs of Isambard Kingdom Brunel.

And in 1838 alone, no fewer than three British companies began their transatlantic services on paddle steamers from London to New York. In many ways it was a landmark year and I expect he felt thrilled to be a part of it.

Humble wondered how far, how fast engineering would have developed by the time his grandson, John, had reached his fifties in another half-century. It seemed such a long time ahead, and yet in the wider scheme of things, the merest blip.

His line of thought was snapped by the first mate, informing him that the ship's stewards were starting to collect fares from the passengers: one pound five shillings for a main cabin, fifteen shillings for a fore cabin and seven shillings and sixpence for a steerage place on deck. Covered accommodation on benches, albeit often crowded, was available towards the bow for the deck passengers to rest at night. Sometimes Humble joined the stewards in collecting fares, but not today: with his wife aboard, he preferred to spend the time with her.

As the *Forfarshire* chugged sedately away, Humble surveyed the port of Hull's waterfront landmarks. He blinked to clear his eyes – was his vision less sharp than it used to be? After the pilot office, there were two shipbuilders' yards, a social club, various taverns that appeared to be thronging, and a grand hotel at the entrance to Queen Street. The Holy Trinity church steeple rose majestically in the distance.

The many sloops, schooners and tugs moored on the river, some with sails hoisted, bobbed up and down in the wake of the *Forfarshire*, nodding in deference.

Humble descended the iron stairway from the fo'c'sle and headed for his cabin where he hoped Annie would be settling in comfortably before dinner. The summer's warmth was fast evaporating, the light would soon fade behind the blanket of cloud. It was twenty-five miles through flat countryside to Spurn Point at the mouth of the mighty Humber, where the *Forfarshire* would enter the German Ocean or North Sea. Part of the larger Atlantic Ocean, it was one of the coldest seas in the world.

So it began, like any other journey.

But let me tell you, no one on board could ever have imagined how the next few days would play out, or how far into the future the shock waves would resonate.

— 2 —

Longstone

Home sweet home.

At the same time as the SS *Forfarshire* was leaving Hull, a much smaller craft arrived on the eastern tip of Longstone, the outermost of the twisting chain of Farne Islands off the Northumberland coast. The craft was a wooden coble, twenty-one feet long.

The twenty-two-year-old woman who stepped out and tethered it by the little boatshed had luxuriant reddish-brown hair, parted in the centre and gathered in a bun. A few loose curls danced at her temples, she twisted them away. She had a clear complexion, her mother's gentle brown eyes and a chin as firm as her father's. She stood a mite over five feet tall. Even in her loose-fitting shawl, she looked slim, although her upper arms were strong – thanks, I'm sure, to her frequent coble-rowing.

She walked up the rocky incline towards the lighthouse carrying a panier of eggs and earthy potatoes. She stooped to pick up a creamy white whelk shell, which she turned over in her palm before dropping it into the basket. As she skipped past the oil store and up the stone steps to the heavy door, she could not resist craning her neck to take in the full height of the tower.

Stretching nearly a hundred feet into the sky, this lighthouse never failed to impress her. Some of her most vivid childhood memories were of its construction.

She was just nine when, back in March 1825, a man named Joseph Nelson came to survey the site for a new light on Longstone Island. He arrived in a sleek yacht belonging to Trinity House, the organisation that protected sailors around the British Isles. Clever and softly spoken, Nelson was an architect and engineer in their employ.

Incorporated in Henry VIII's reign, Trinity House was granted powers to set up beacons to help ships find safer passage into harbours. Gradually it bought up existing, privately funded lighthouses, maintained them well and expanded the chain with new ones. By an act of parliament in 1836, Trinity House became Britain's official lighthouse authority – which it still is today.

Her paternal, Scots-born grandfather, Robert, was appointed the first lighthouse keeper on Brownsman Island, one of the Outer Farnes, back in 1795. This was twenty years before her birth. She never knew Robert or his wife, Elizabeth: both had died, and were buried in the mainland village of Belford, before she was born.

The first one was a forty-foot tower on the north side of Brownsman that burned timber, coal, and – later – oil, in a fire basket on the roof. A new lighthouse was built there in 1810 and her father, William, was promoted from assistant to principal keeper when Robert died. While she had been born and baptised – by Reverend Andrew Boult – in Bamburgh, a picturesque mainland village, the Brownsman lighthouse had been her family home since she was taken there at three weeks old.

But there was a problem. You see, the light on Brownsman was not ideally placed. It proved to be too close to shore to prevent ships from striking the outermost Farnes. In the deep winters of 1823 and '24, hundreds perished in the shipwrecks on the jagged Knivestone, Megstone and Crumstone islets, while the brig *George & Mary* came to grief on Brownsman itself with the horrifying loss of all hands. As sea traffic proliferated, the risk of disaster on the Farnes was only going to rise, wasn't it? For centuries, the islands had been a blackspot and now, more than ever, Trinity House was determined to intervene.

Having completed his survey, Joseph Nelson reported back, confirming that the only feasible site for a new light was on Longstone. It was a world apart from Brownsman, where the soil allowed for some crops and poultry. Longstone, by contrast, was barren, inhospitable. No one – and nothing, bar some seaweeds – lived there. No animal could breed – the sea would wash their eggs away.

Nelson planned first to erect stone barracks to house the workmen. He measured out grooves to be cut into the Longstone rock for the lighthouse foundations. To withstand the assault from the North Sea gales and hold the structure steady, the base would be enormous. He made it cylindrical to resist storm-lashings from any direction.

During construction, Nelson and his foreman, Thomas Wade, stayed with her family on Brownsman. Nelson's regional twang revealed him to be a Yorkshireman. Now aged forty-eight, he had already been involved in the building of northerly lighthouses, including two early examples on the Inner Farne island, so he was the ideal person for the job. Later, he would design others at Berwick-upon-Tweed and Burnham-on-Sea.

The construction phase lasted almost a year. Work was particularly complicated because Longstone stayed only a few feet above water at high tide, even in flat-calm conditions. The huge coarse granite blocks which formed the tapered tower were carted from a quarry at Bramley Fell in Yorkshire, then carried on sloops along the Humber and up the coast. From the Northumberland mainland they were brought over to Longstone on an armada of specially hired small boats. Her father had given her rides in the coble back and forth on many of these crossings in that exciting summer of 1825.

Just to say, I mention the route of the granite blocks because it exemplifies what a hazardous, painstaking process it was to build this lighthouse.

She would also never forget the visit by the Duke of Northumberland, from his ancestral castle in the town of Alnwick, when the construction neared completion. It was on 29 September. Tall and suave, the duke breezed in on his private craft, the *Mermaid*, with his own skipper and a mate. Among his other commitments, the duke was Vice-Admiral of the Coast of Northumberland, and he was fascinated by the scientific advances in the new lighthouse and its state-of-the-art lantern. He introduced himself as Hugh, Hugh Percy, and was unfailingly affable and good-humoured. She felt instinctively that he warmed to her father's gracious welcome. Later on, the Percys will play a momentous role in our story.

On 17 December 1825, three men arrived to install the lantern. One of them, an eighteen-year-old Newcastle lad named Jack Weldon, took a shine to her. When he learned that she'd only recently celebrated her tenth birthday – on 24 November – he sang sea shanties inserting her name into the lyrics. This embarrassed her, made her painfully self-conscious, yet she could also remember her secret excitement when Jack worked on over Christmas and crooned a fresh ballad to her each day.

The lighthouse was finished off with iron railings around the lantern gallery. The light itself was lit for the first time on Wednesday 15 February 1826. By all accounts, Trinity House was delighted and ordered the old light on Brownsman to be extinguished permanently.

The Longstone light was operated with cutting-edge technology. You'll appreciate, throughout this story, that I love to know how things work. Why they are the way they are. I admire the inventors of devices and services that improve the lives of others, and in the early nineteenth century many of the foundation blocks of our modern way of life were laid down. So, I'll try to shade in a bit of context as we go along – please keep with me on the ride.

Designed by the Swiss physicist Ami Argand, the Longstone lamps were lit by twelve oil burners, backed by gleaming brass parabolic reflectors twenty-one inches in diameter. They magnified and projected the light beam far out to sea, representing a big improvement on earlier lamps. The reflectors were mounted on a clockwork platform, wound by heavy pendulums suspended in metal tubes, which ran the full height of the lighthouse walls.

The Longstone light could be seen, so her father had assured her, more than ten miles offshore, far enough to cover the busiest coastal shipping lanes of the day. The light was so expensive that its cost stuck in her father's memory: it alone accounted for one-third of the building bill of £4,771.

Whatever had been spent, to the young woman now standing at the threshold of the Longstone lighthouse, this building was priceless. She had grown accustomed to, and comfortable with, an unpretentious life with a high degree of privacy. The lighthouse was more than just her family home. It was her safe haven, her retreat, her sanctuary, and she derived enormous strength from it.

The iron bolts on the inside of the door should still be open. Good, yes, they were. She turned the smooth handle on the black rim lock and stepped inside.

Her name was Grace Horsley Darling.

— 3 —

The metal jungle

The shock of white hair.

That was the first thing everybody noticed about him – they just couldn't help it. But there was much more to the man – he had an exceptional knack for visualising mechanical processes and how different materials would react in different conditions.

Allan Stewart, chief engineer on the SS *Forfarshire* for the last eleven months, was a tall, stout Scotsman whose mane of thick white hair was obviously a distinguishing feature. He had just taken off a tight-fitting blue cap, which left a groove around the sides and back of the mane. His long moustache joined the ends of his sideburns, forming a bushy white frame with his blue eyes in the middle. The moustache had overgrown his top lip and seemed to fill both nostrils.

When he spoke, his voice was deep, gravelly and necessarily loud. "Don't lean over! Make space for everyone!" I'd say it was not a voice to be ignored.

And moments later: "The engine is deep inside the ship, but she's a big beastie, ye'll all have a line of sight."

The engine room, extending the full beam of the *Forfarshire*, was not fully enclosed. Below the bridge and the fo'c'sle lay a promenade deck which incorporated a large hatch. Surrounded by railings, the hatch overlooked the central section of the engine room. A long passageway led into and straight out of the open room, well below decks. There were no doors, just a low guard rail with a gate, but there was a difference in level, the engine room floor being a step lower than the parquet corridor.

Stewart stood against the railings on one side of the hatch. His presence seemed to occupy the entire width, without him stretching out his arms. Along the other three sides were clustered a dozen or more passengers, parents or guardians with children, whom they let stand in front.

A few more passengers had grouped in the corridor down below, outside the confines of the engine room but with a clear view inside. Stewart could see the top of Valentine Scott's bald head. A passenger from Dundee, Scott was holding the hand of his seven-year-old son.

Facing Stewart from across the hatch, Arthur Ellison, a cabin passenger, squeezed the shoulders of his son, Albert, and grinned at him when he looked up. Albert was worried. He was uncertain whether lions lived in Scotland but this man, Mr Stewart, standing there ready to pounce, appeared to be descended from one. His two canine teeth were longer than the little row of incisors in between them and their sharp tips convinced Albert that they were fangs, protruding from a furry lip.

As soon as the *Forfarshire* was unshackled from the Hull quayside, these passengers had scrambled to secure a vantage point with a view of the mechanical marvel that was the steam engine in operation. Reputedly this machine was transforming travel around the whole world. What did it look like? How did it work?

Although the *Forfarshire* was moving slowly along the Humber, it was already clear that steam engines made for hot work. The engine room was a metal jungle, high and wide, crammed with inter-connecting pipes, twisting tubes, quivering dials and three huge metal containers, each held together by rows of stud rivets.

From deep within the jungle rose a cacophony of clanking, clattering, pounding and hissing. It would get louder still when the *Forfarshire* gathered speed on the open sea. The engine room assaulted every human sense, and the Lion knew from the line of faces that the passengers were spell-bound. I'm not really certain whether this Lion should have a capital L, but I think I'd better give him one.

"Ladies and gentlemen, steam propulsion is the century's greatest advance," the Lion roared above the rumble. A man after my own heart, he sounded utterly convincing. "Ye may think that the engine before you is incredibly sophisticated. Ye'd not be wrong. But what the engine is doing, the task it's performing, is essentially straight-forward."

The Lion slackened the red-and-white Stewart tartan scarf that he was wearing under his blue overalls. Embroidered in white on the breast was the name, the Dundee & Hull Steam Packet Company.

"Ye will observe that the engine is situated precisely in between the two great wooden paddle-wheels, encased on either side of the ship. The three large containers are boilers full of water, each with a coal-fired furnace."

As if on cue, would you believe it, two crewmen emerged from the jungle shadows, bearing shovels laden with coal. In turn, they opened a door in the front of the port-side and starboard-side boilers and, with well-practised ease, flipped the coal inside. Several passengers observed for the first time, as the two men strode about, that the engine room floor was coated in a film of water.

"Mr Kidd and Mr Nicholson there, are two of our firemen, who load the coal they've received from the trimmers into the furnaces. The trimmers make sure that the coal heaped in our hold stays level, so it never causes the ship to tilt."

Across the Humber another departing ship's bell clanged. A tugboat passed the *Forfarshire* on its way back to port.

"The burning coal heats the water, which vaporises into steam. The steam is piped under high pressure into a cylinder." The Lion, in his element, pointed over the railing to a gleaming cylinder deep below.

"The cylinder contains a piston," he continued. "That's a metal plunger, ye ken, which moves up and down with the flow of the steam. The motion of the plunger turns a rod – a crank shaft – which is connected to the axle at the centre of the paddlewheel. And that is how, ultimately by using water, clean and limitless, the *Forfarshire* is powered."

Having hoped for wonder and awe, the audience was not disappointed. Spontaneous applause rippled among the passengers. The Lion was used to such a reaction, it happened on practically every trip. He realised that the ovation was for the feat of engineering rather than his address, but still he gave a small bow. Showmanship mattered. He carried a half-bottle of gin in his overalls and he would treat himself to a wee nip in his tiny cabin later.

I gather that, in these presentations, Stewart sometimes mentioned his fellow Scotsman, the late James Watt, who had built an efficient steam engine fifty years ago. Audiences enjoyed the tale of Watt – allegedly – drawing inspiration to harness the power of steam from watching the lid flipping off a boiling kettle. On this occasion it was probably getting a bit late for the younger members of the crowd, so he left it out.

In the fading light of the evening sky, a flock of sandwich terns soared overhead. Soon they would embark on their migration from the north-east coast to the Earth's southern hemisphere, where they would find another summer.

Down in the engine room, as the passengers had dispersed, a crewman entered. It may have been Bill Douthy, I can't be sure. Whoever, he checked the reading on a pressure valve, hoicked up a horizontal lever and wiped a sleeve across his brow. He glanced at the hot water sloshing around his boots and decided it was no worse than when he had last checked, so he went on his way, leaving a trail of wet boot prints.

Arthur Ellison steered his son around the hatch towards the Lion. Young Albert's eyes registered panic but his father's grip tightened on his shoulders.

"Thank you for that," Arthur said to the Lion. "May I ask how fast the *Forfarshire* can go?"

"A good nine knots out at sea." The Lion bared all his front teeth when he smiled. "The engine's output is ninety horsepower."

"Logic suggests that as the coal is burned up, the ship gets lighter and rises, so the paddles can't dip so deeply into the water. Is that true and, if so, does it affect the speed she can achieve as the journey goes on?"

The Lion nodded approvingly. "Well done, sir. Aye, we do find that with steamships in general. But given the size of the *Forfarshire*, it's no problem. Between them, the paddles will give us a quick, smooth ride all the way."

"And the boilers? How do you find them? I've heard talk that, even with low water pressure, they can leak? Or explode?"

"Don't ye worry, sir," growled the Lion, relooping his scarf and wafting away the question. "The metal plates around the boiler flues are three-eighths of an inch thick." He emphasised the solidity with his thumb and forefinger. "We have the boilers cleaned out every other voyage – ye know, descaled, desludged. And the joints and rivets are maintained in good order. The *Forfarshire*'s a dependable young lady. If she's prone occasionally to be a wee bit temperamental, well, which of us can genuinely say we blame her?"

Cuddy

Grace Darling leant back.

She felt the familiar carved wood contours of the inside of the lighthouse door and satisfied herself that it was properly closed. Then she greeted her mother, who looked up and broke into a broad grin.

"Hello, angel."

Even in adulthood, you see, Grace remained her mother's 'angel'.

Returning the smile, Grace put down her basket and crossed the floor to the fire crackling in the hearth. The heat she felt on her face and hands seemed to thicken the air in the whole room.

The ground floor of the lighthouse was one large circular space, open plan we might now call it, more than twenty feet in diameter.

By the fireplace was a stove, above which Grace's father, William, had fixed shelves for kettles, pastry cutters, copper moulds. There were hooks for pots, pans and ladles. A dresser contained apples, onions, sugar, a few cherries, jars of tea leaves and coffee beans, and a block of butter. This kitchen area had a long, oak table surrounded by an assortment of stools and benches which the family had used for meals since they moved in twelve years ago in 1826.

The rest of the room was living accommodation. Worn rugs covered the flagstones. Four easy chairs, each coated with chequered knitted blankets, pointed in different directions. A side-table bore a pair of Staffordshire pottery dalmatians, bookending well-thumbed copies of the bible and *A Help &*

Guide to Christian Families, to whose 200 pages she remembered her father referring regularly.

Set into the floor opposite the door, and below a muslin-curtained window, was a pump head. This was connected to an underground tank – 'the well' – where supposedly sweet-tasting rainwater was collected to drink and use about the lighthouse. But the sea must have long since penetrated it because the water often tasted briny – *yuck!* – and they would ferry barrels of clean water over from the mainland.

Close to the well, on a cushioned wooden chair, sat Thomasina, Grace's mother. As ever, she was at her spinning wheel, an oil lamp burning by her side. Even when she looked up, her right foot maintained a consistent rhythm on the treadle. Pure instinct. The twisted yarn passed smoothly through her fingers and coiled around the bobbin. Infused into every spin and every stitch was Thomasina's love.

Thomasina Darling (née Horsley) was sixty-four yet looked much younger. She was thirty-one on her wedding day – 1 July 1805 – while her bridegroom, William, was merely nineteen. Grace now understood that, when they married, their twelve-year age gap had provoked gossip on the mainland. Why had William proposed to Thomasina when there were other eligible women nearer his own age, including Thomasina's three younger sisters?

Finding the very thought of such intrusive scuttlebutt to be unsettling, Grace banished it from her mind. Unlikely as the union may have seemed to some, it had led to a happy marriage, already more than three decades long.

"I will love you for eternity, if you'll let me," Thomasina had said to him on the night he proposed. He did, and she did too.

"We will take care of one another, you and I, always."

Grace's eyes swept the big room, occupied only by her mother and herself. In keeping with the social norm, her devoted parents had produced a large family. Thomasina spent more than five years of her life pregnant. She carried nine children, of whom Grace was the seventh, all raised in the cottage attached to the lighthouse on Brownsman, before the

Longstone tower was built. They'd worn the same baby dresses, handed down, until they were about five.

Ten months after William and Thomasina's marriage came their first-born, William – 'Laddie' to them all, so I'll use that name for him here.

Two years later, in August 1808, twin girls arrived safely, Thomasin, who had a cleft lip, and Mary Ann.

Just after Christmas 1810 came number four, named Job Horsley Darling after his maternal grandfather.

Next, Elizabeth – 'Betsy' – was born in August 1812 and another son, Robert, in March 1814.

Grace came into the world in November 1815, followed finally in August 1819 by twin boys, George Alexander and William Brooks Darling.

That all nine babies survived childhood was due in no small measure, I reckon, to the competence of the family's physician, Dr Thomas Fender, and the qualified midwife resident in Bamburgh.

That said, the family suffered a devastating tragedy eight years ago, in 1830. Job Horsley Darling caught a sudden fever and died in the prosperous, coal-rich city of Newcastle – 'canny Newcassel', where he was an apprentice joiner – just three weeks short of his twentieth birthday. He had written to his parents saying how happy he was and of course they'd treasured the letter ever since.

Illness, even premature death, were not uncommon in youth. Still, the anniversary of Job's death, 6 December, was a cripplingly sad occasion, especially for Thomasina, whom Grace was sure to comfort when she found her aching alone, weeping quietly into a handkerchief.

Grace had always known a supportive home, lively and healthy. She felt her family members were devoted to each other, however spartan their lives on Brownsman may have been. When she was born, Laddie, her eldest sibling, was nine years her senior. He'd spent hours on end looking after her while her parents were occupied. Now his mind was set on his own family – last year, Laddie married his sweetheart, Ann Cobb, in Belford.

Growing up, Grace forged the closest bonds with her big sister, Thomasin, seven years older than she, and her younger brother, William Brooks. As you'll see, both remained close figures throughout her life.

But by the time the Longstone lighthouse opened, most of her siblings had already flown the nest. Laddie left the family on Brownsman soon after his sixteenth birthday to become an apprentice joiner in Alnwick. Poor Job had been trying to follow in his big brother's footsteps when the fever wrenched him away.

Thomasina taught all her daughters the skills of spinning and sewing. In the weeks before Christmas, they would take turns at making bedsheets, pillows and eiderdowns, which would be distributed as gifts to grateful relatives and friends.

Thomasin, Grace's sister, excelled at needlework. She had been the one who repaired all their clothes. Now she'd made it a profession and opened her own dress making house in Bamburgh.

Thomasin's twin, Mary Ann, also opted to live in Bamburgh instead of moving to Longstone. Six years ago, in November 1832, she had married George Dixon Carr, a nice lad. But of their five children, I believe that, sadly, only the fifth survived infancy.

Betsy, who at first bunked with Grace on Longstone, took a job on the mainland as a maid. She too was now married, to John Maule, who worked as a draper near to North Sunderland fishing harbour, south of Bamburgh.

Robert and George both left to take up apprenticeships: Robert, age seventeen, as a stonemason in Belford; George, age fourteen, as a ship's carpenter in Newcastle.

The upshot of the family growing up: George's twin, William Brooks, was the only one of Grace's siblings still living on Longstone. As it happened, that very morning he had gone ashore to North Sunderland, eager to help his friends on their fishing smacks.

Demand for fresh herring was rising, but Grace knew North Sunderland harbour to be a rank-smelling place where the fish curing never stopped. Neither did the heat emanating from the lime kilns, situated near to the harbour for easy loading. Lime putty was used by builders, while slaked lime boosted soil fertility.

Many times, Grace and William Brooks had accompanied their father to catch herring from the coble or rock pools on the shore. They would let them dry out on the rocks before selling off the catch they didn't need for eight shillings a barrel.

When William Brooks was ashore, Grace had to admit that she missed him. His aquiline nose and floppy brown fringe suited his beguiling personality. He'd been born with mischief in his eyes. Even his twin brother George called him 'daft as a brush'. When he hit adolescence, he was the one who tested behavioural boundaries in ways, and at inopportune moments, that most irked their parents. But to Grace he felt like a friend as much as a brother.

Perhaps her mother had read her thoughts as she chose that very moment to halt the spinning wheel.

"How were things on Brownsman, angel?" she asked. "What about the birds? Any changes?"

"One new thing." Grace's eyes lit up. "They were so beautiful, Mama, you'd have loved them. A pair of fledgling petrels – I watched them for a while and they took flight, I think for the first time."

"They were nice and plump?"

Grace nodded. "And their down had a bluey grey tint. The signs looked good."

Every May, fulmar petrels laid their large white eggs on several of the Farne Islands' cliff ledges. The parents would incubate the eggs for up to two months, then feed the hatchlings by regurgitating semi-digested fish into their beaks for a further two months. Usually by September, the young were ready to leave their parents' protection and fend for themselves in the open air.

Thomasina appreciated how deeply her daughter loved nature, especially the many species of birds with which she'd been familiar since she first learned to walk on rocky Brownsman Island. Out of all her children, Grace had most keenly observed and studied the birds, season by season.

When she was six or seven, Grace befriended a brown-feathered eider duck which built a nest out of seaweed and coarse grass close to the lighthouse on the north side of Brownsman. The eider became so accustomed to Grace, who brought titbits of raw fish, that she would let her – only her – approach, cooing softly, without any apparent qualms.

Grace nicknamed her 'Cuddy'. I gather the breed was a staunch favourite of Cuthbert, the early Christian bishop and saint who spent ten years in seclusion on the Farnes in the mid-seventh century. Resolute soul.

Cuddy laid four olive-green eggs that June and incubated them for exactly twenty-eight days. As far as Grace could tell, Cuddy never left her nest in all that time, living off her body fat. As soon as they'd all hatched, Grace watched spellbound as Cuddy escorted her quartet of down-coated fledglings into the sea.

They bobbed along on the swell in single file, Cuddy diving occasionally for mussels or crabs or to avoid gulls. It was Cuddy who made Grace realise how strong the bond of a family was, not only in people but throughout the natural world.

Brownsman upheld a wonderful variety of seabirds. Its soil enabled the family to grow potatoes and other veg in a net-covered walled garden. Trinity House permitted them to retain the garden and their few sheep, goats and hens when they left for Longstone. This required frequent mile-long trips in the coble to check on the animals' welfare, milk the goats, collect the eggs and, not forgetting, pull up the weeds.

Thomasina adjusted her flimsy mop hat, which had slipped too close to her tired eyes, and pressed her right foot flat on the spinning wheel's treadle.

"Well," she said, "I'm pleased you enjoyed today's visit. Now, angel, why don't you go upstairs to see your father? He must be about to light the lantern."

— 5 —

The captain's table

"In so many ways, Britain's destiny is shaped by the sea."

Captain Humble set his knife and fork down on the empty china plate and relaxed into his well-padded chair. He liked to hold court whilst dining with the passengers once on each voyage; on this occasion it was just a couple of hours after the *Forfarshire* left Hull.

Two years old, the dining room looked brand new. It smelled new, too, scents of wax polish, leather and fresh flowers tempering the aromas of hot food. Meals were served on bespoke 'Steamer *Forfarshire*' crockery, rims decorated with floral patterns encircling a starboard-broadside image of the ship, steam clouds billowing from the funnel. Printed on the base was 'Dundee & Hull Steam Packet Company'.

On the clean walls, both Captain and Mrs Humble most admired the West Highlands watercolours by Horatio McCulloch, fast becoming Scotland's finest landscape painter. I viewed his artworks – his dramatic sense of scale must have perfectly complemented the size and sophistication of the *Forfarshire* itself.

"Incidentally, that was delicious. I hope you thought so too?"

Humble glanced around the table, seeking approval. Alongside his wife was John Robb, ordained two years ago as a minister of the ancient Celtic parish of Dunkeld and Dowally. He was based at Dunkeld Cathedral, whisperingly close to the Highlands. Seemed a thoroughly decent sort, someone to have as a friend. Yet he looked skeletal, older than his thirty-nine years, and Humble noticed that he left most of his baked lemon haddock. Instead, the Reverend inhaled a pinch of snuff, laid on his hand from a tiny box tucked in a pocket.

Reverend Robb was the last passenger to board at Hull, having just arrived on the *Yeoman Warder*, a packet steamer from London. He had spent a few restorative – or so he'd hoped – days ambling around churches, visiting the zoo, strolling along the Thames. At that time, though, the river was thickly polluted and foul-smelling.

Four years earlier, in October 1834, the medieval Palace of Westminster – the riverside home of parliament – had burned down. Construction of the new parliament building had not yet started, but Robb hoped it would incorporate Westminster Hall, the one part of the old palace which he observed was intact. Note: It did.

Next to Reverend Robb sat Kitty Patrick. Well dressed, well spoken. Travelling alone, she was married to another master mariner, the captain of the *Clara*. Humble thought he detected a scent of the vinegar with which she washed her hair: it was the same variety as Annie used.

The table was completed by two other cabin passengers, Wilfrid Baxter and Conrad Brown, both of whom nodded vigorously to confirm their satisfaction with the repast.

"Splendid," said Humble with a sigh. "Mr Tickett, our head chef, will be delighted. If any of you has a sweet tooth, I recommend his bread-and-butter pudding, nourishing to the nth degree. Now, as I was saying…"

Annie recognised the slick shift back into a speech which, she assumed, he delivered in similarly mellow tones on every voyage. Somehow, he managed to make the patter sound spontaneous.

"…Successive invasions by the Romans, Normans and Scandinavians brought to our shores new peoples, new languages, new customs. Today the oceans offer us a route out to every corner of the globe for pleasure, for commerce. Our cities and factories are being transformed by steam power, aren't they?"

Wilfrid Baxter's eye was caught by the under-rim of his plate as a steward took it away. "How long has the Dundee & Hull company existed, captain?"

"Oh, three-and-a-half years," Humble replied, sipping water from a glass tumbler. No wine on duty. "Founded in March 1835, to link the producers and farmers along the Tay with the customers on the Humber. We were the first operator to unite those two great rivers. That's a fine thing, isn't it?"

They all agreed, naturally enough.

"Who'd like a drop more wine? If you please," Humble signalled to a passing steward. "Yes, trade on our route is as extensive as any outside London and the Thames. Steam power makes it so much quicker, more efficient. There are times when you feel the engines have truly conquered the tide and the wind."

Humble missed the slightly raised eyebrow on his wife's face.

"I was wondering what you make of railway transportation." Baxter revealed the sharper point underlying his opening question. "After all, the Stockton to Darlington and the Liverpool to Manchester steam railways have been operating for a few years – they're already carrying the post, instead of horse-drawn carriages, aren't they?" A fleeting pause while a diner from the next table squeezed past behind him. Breathe in! "As of last year, London has a terminus at Euston. Just a few months ago, I attended the inauguration of the Newcastle to Carlisle railway. As you know, the line runs straight across the country on a direct route, which surely gives it an advantage over ships, no?"

Captain Humble did not miss a beat. "Steam-powered shipping is the lifeblood of our nation. The *Forfarshire* has been so successful that the company's expanding. It's an exciting time to be on a ship like this, with its speed and dependability. Brunel's stupendous steamer, the *Great Western*, was launched in Bristol last summer. She can cross the Atlantic in a fortnight! Amazing, isn't it?"

Feeling he'd regained the initiative, he pressed on. "I'm what I think is called a technological optimist." He might have been a bit ahead of his time with that phrase, but we know what he meant. He glanced around the table, letting the expression sink in. "If people end up with a choice of ways to travel, that can only be good, yes? To my mind, the one complements the other. Steamships have a prosperous future, whatever happens with our burgeoning railway network."

Conrad Brown had been pondering an earlier remark by the captain. "You don't really think this ship can defy Mother Nature, do you?" He scratched his nose. "I mean, isn't that idea rather dangerous? 'Conquer the tide and the wind', I think you said, but surely no matter what, the sea is always in charge?"

"Well, provided the weather conditions permit, we really do have the power to cut through," Humble replied gently, his eyes fixed on Brown. "That simply wasn't possible before steam propulsion."

Brown fell silent, supped his robust Portuguese red.

"How much cargo is on board?" Kitty Patrick asked.

"We left Hull fully loaded," Humble answered, not wanting to be outshone by the *Clara*. "Our cargo capacity is more than four hundred tons. We're carrying boilerplates, spinning equipment, purifying soap and reams of the finest cloth."

"What about livestock?" interjected Reverend Robb, whose parish contained a spread of rural properties.

"Not on this voyage. But the *Forfarshire* has space in her hold for horses and cattle, as our clients require." Humble gazed at the selection of English cheeses being offered to him on a marble board garnished with black grapes. "To that end, the Dundee-Hull company has negotiated an agreement with the Humber Union Steamship Company. We transport cattle from Scotland to Hull on the *Forfarshire*, then they take them the rest of the way down to London. We always ensure they're placed in excellent pasture until the onward vessel is ready," he added wisely, given that his wife was an animal lover.

"And how many passengers are in your care?" Reverend Robb got this question out just before, to his embarrassment, a coughing fit overcame him. He raised his handkerchief to his forehead, wiping away beads of sweat.

"Well, Reverend, I was told just as I came to dinner that we number sixty-three souls on board. Merchants, tourists, families, many returning home to Scotland. Let me see, twenty cabin passengers plus nineteen tickets bought for steerage – that is our deck accommodation – plus my wife and I and my full complement of twenty-two crew, without whom…"

Humble left that sentence hanging and began another. "My crew comprises three stewards, who are on duty this evening, seven men at the engine – four firemen, two trimmers and my chief engineer – and twelve others, including my first and second mates, excellent, well-trusted men, every one of them."

Wilfrid Baxter cleared his throat and helped himself to a second portion of Stilton. Well, no one likes to see good food wasted, do they?

"The steam engine on this ship," he said so softly that his fellow diners leaned in to hear. "What shape is it in?"

The lantern room

At full pelt Grace hared up the spiralling staircase two steps at a time.

She passed her bedroom on the third floor, heading straight for the lantern. She swept her curls behind her ears, smoothed her hair, straightened her blouse.

The man who greeted her, setting down the cloth with which he was polishing the reflectors for the second time that day, was tall, clean-shaven, long-legged and smart. At fifty-two, his hair was turning grey, but his solid black eyebrows put up a fierce resistance.

Let me introduce you to William Darling.

He had lived in the north Northumberland town of Belford, where he was born in 1786, until he was nine. Then his parents, Robert and Elizabeth, moved out to the Farne Islands. His father was excited – as they all were – to be taking up his appointment by Trinity House Corporation as keeper of the new lighthouse on Brownsman.

After a spell working as a labourer in Bamburgh, William was made assistant keeper. He and his new bride, Thomasina, started a family of their own on Brownsman, where William himself became keeper on the death of his father in September 1815. This was two months before his seventh child, Grace, was born. Unsurprisingly, in their Brownsman cottage the family found that space was at a premium.

Robert and William carried out many rescues, saving sailors from stricken ships on the rugged outer islands. From the off, they built a covetable reputation with Trinity House.

On Longstone, William was paid an annual salary of £70 plus a £10 bonus for satisfactory service. Extra performance-related bonuses were available for specific actions: being the first to reach a ship in distress; saving lives; recovering bodies; and, the lowest priority, salvaging cargo. Overall, it provided for a comfortable, reliable income.

Despite his face and hands being weather-beaten, to Grace he was more than a caring father. You see, he was her teacher and mentor, her inspiration and best friend. He was her hero.

While her siblings were encouraged to forge their own paths, to take up the best offers of apprenticeships, occupations, service or marriage, there was no such talk regarding Grace. It seemed William and Thomasina had always intended – expected, even? – that she would remain on Longstone, helping to run the household and the lighthouse, to look after visitors and rescued sailors.

In many ways, Grace resembled her father: courteous and self-effacing; thoughtful and disciplined; honest and respectful – never more so, in William's case, than when communicating with Trinity House. They lived in the here and now, neither of them a daydreamer. Scratch the surface, though, and they possessed deep reserves of strength and stamina. Neither would easily give up a task once begun.

The Darlings may have lived in isolation on Brownsman and more especially on Longstone, but Grace never doubted that her life had good purpose. The familiar structure of her busy days was itself comforting –I'm sure many of us can relate to that. Rebellion was neither in her genes nor in her character.

She kept in touch with her brothers and sisters and diligently supported her father's work. She felt fulfilled. In practice, of course, the feelings were mutual: William valued all of Grace's productive assistance as much as she appreciated his.

The duties of a lighthouse keeper employed by Trinity House were to ensure that the lamp shone clearly and brightly from sunset to sunrise, and to keep nightly vigil in two shifts changing over at midnight. All the equipment, floors and windows had to be kept spotless and maintained with the utmost precision, which necessitated hours of toil. Even the wicks that burned the oil had to be trimmed every three hours.

William taught Grace to manage all these obligations, although he never left her to cope alone. He took a quiet pride in the accuracy and completeness of his records. He kept a series of logbooks, noting the hourly rise and fall of the tides all year, for which he used an eight-foot staff marked in inches; the times when the submerged sections of the Farnes were exposed; and the rate at which the tides coursed through the various guts between the islands.

The guts were narrow channels of water, close to the coastline, which were prone to strong tidal currents abruptly changing direction. Just to alert you – they still are.

One October night a few years earlier, a small Scottish sloop travelling south to Newcastle ran into the black rock of Little Hawker, one of the Outer Farnes, in a harsh north-easterly. William rowed the coble out from Longstone and pushed the sloop off the rock with the eight-foot staff.

The skipper, his wife and two children, the only people on board, had been effusively grateful for the personal risk he took to save them. William, though, restricted his logbook account of the incident to two matter of fact, unemotional sentences. It was Grace, back at Longstone, who understood his wonderful achievement that night and congratulated him heartily.

The lantern room on top of the Longstone lighthouse had doubled for years as the classroom where William taught his children. He knew the general provision of education was haphazard. For poorer children there were church schools, and other establishments endowed by charities and private benefactors. Teaching might be left in the hands of the older or abler pupils, who would have a lesson early in the morning and later deliver it, by rote, to younger classes – can you imagine! In fee-paying, private schools, religious studies, Latin, classics and sports tended to be the focus, while boarding school life was dreaded by some for its brutality.

William had heard of voices, in and out of parliament, calling for the lot of children to be improved. Instead of being sent, age six, to work in factories, on farms or down mines, schooling should be expanded and made compulsory, at least up to the age of ten. But surely, he surmised, while supporting this step, such fundamental change would be a long time coming?

Grace Darling never went to school. But William knew from when she was very young that she possessed an agile, enquiring mind and could articulate her own thoughts. Of course she could hold her own, being the seventh of nine!

He had taught her to read and write to the best of his ability. He talked about the natural world of plants and animals, a subject Grace adored. He had given her a wad of foolscap exercise pads with Trinity House printed on the covers and was delighted when she wrote detailed notes, as if compiling her own logbooks.

As you'd imagine, seafaring was an important topic in her education.

"If there's one point you always remember, Grace, let it be this. The sea is unpredictable." He drilled it into her. "Respect it, never let your guard down."

He shared his knowledge of the tides and weather formations, and the many kinds of ship that plied their trade past the Farnes. They listened to the sounds of the sea.

They discussed the present machine age. It was evident that steamships were displacing sailing boats – and yet, in some walks of life, mechanisation was strangely slow to effect change.

Many countryside dwellers provided food by tilling their own soil. Even when labour-saving, steam-powered machinery was introduced to farms, replacing the wooden and iron tools of yesteryear, living conditions seemed to stay as cramped as ever. Villages comprised farmers and labourers with smallholdings of poorly drained land, sustaining some crops and cattle. There were shops and craftspeople – saddlers, smiths, weavers, coopers, tanners, wheelwrights. Thomasin joined their ranks in Bamburgh as a dressmaker. Each village kept a hierarchy, from the land-owning squire all the way down to the casual labourer.

Now a dab more history – you'll soon see where it's heading. At the Battle of Waterloo in June 1815, Emperor Napoleon's

Grand Army was defeated by the allied Prussians and British, commanded by Arthur Wellesley, the Duke of Wellington – who will figure later in our story. The battle marked a turning point in Europe, bringing to a bloody close the decades of fighting for supremacy between Britain and France. Whereas France had long been the world's superpower, Wellington's victory helped to ensure that Britain wore this mantle in the nineteenth century.

Having finally abdicated, Napoleon was exiled to the remote, British-held isle of St. Helena in the South Atlantic in October 1815. There he wrote his memoirs and died, age fifty-one, in May 1821. Britain was faced with a dilemma after so many years of war in Europe: whether, and how, to stay an isolated island nation or to pursue new alliances. History does repeat itself, doesn't it?

Meanwhile, the wars had required the accumulation of a colossal national debt. This, and a sequence of poor harvests and relatively low levels of imports, conspired to keep the price of grain high. Inevitably, as William discussed with Grace, this affected the fare on kitchen tables the length and breadth of the country.

William had accumulated shelves full of books, spilling over to side-tables and windowsills. In addition to various editions of the bible, there were anthologies of poetry, which Grace loved him reading – performing, really – aloud. Rabbie Burns, the previous century's bard of Ayrshire, was a favourite:

> *"The best laid schemes o' mice and men*
> *Gang aft a-gley*
> *An' lea'e us nought but grief and pain*
> *For promis'd joy."*

William had been given a threadbare copy of the *Ecclesiastical History of the English Nation*, originally penned in the eighth century in a Northumbrian monastery by the scholar, Bede. Later valued as the father of English history, Bede was the first writer in medieval times to chronicle the development of the church.

There were copies of more recent novels by Walter Scott and Jane Austen, and *The Pickwick Papers*, a serial by Charles Dickens. But William had little time for escapist romances: as a man for whom risking his life was part of his chosen occupation, he was more concerned with day-to-day responsibilities. "Real life is a thrilling adventure, Grace," he would say. "There's no need to withdraw from it." Sadly, these words came back to haunt him.

There was plenty of time for amusement as well as work. Grace fondly recalled the occasions when William took out his violin and led his train of children on a merry march from top to bottom of the lighthouse, all whistling and singing at the tops of their joyful voices. He would play tunes for the sailors they rescued and brought to their hearth for a warm night. He knew many songs by heart but always had his cherished book of scores near at hand.

Now William handed a burning candle to Grace, indicating that she should light the wicks of the great oil-fuelled lantern. The room grew brighter. Soon the brilliant beam was reflected far into the distance across the inky sea.

"Thank you, Grace—"

He was cut off by a shockingly loud crash against the outside of the window. There were high-pitched shrieks, flashes of eyes and beaks and claws, and violent flapping. The lighthouse seemed to shake as if struck by a mighty wind.

"What—?"

They spun on their heels and stared. A huge flock of cormorants – guillemots, too, both large seabirds that would dive into the water and catch fish in their bills – had flown too close, too fast, to the tower and clattered into it. Nasty. Had they been disorientated by the sudden appearance of the brilliant light? Or what?

William took a cold, hard look at the evening sky. His face was set in a frown as he reached for the wall behind Grace and grabbed his long-barrelled, percussion-ignition shotgun.

— 7 —

A gift for Annie

The cold cream she had applied to her hands was waxy and took a lot of rubbing in.

In the captain's cabin on the *Forfarshire*, John Humble addressed Annie softly as she climbed into bed. "My dear, you know I'm duty-bound to deliver our passengers and cargo into Dundee on schedule. The company expects me to do my job." Yes, that was the long and short of it.

The iron bedframe supported a cotton mattress. There were two thin, hard pillows which Annie tried to plump with marginal success.

"The truth is that the boilers are not perfect," he persevered, "we all realise that, but the *Forfarshire* has the best there is. When metal sheets are riveted together, there's bound to be weakness at the joints. And when the pressure builds, well, sometimes they leak. Maybe one day, the design and construction and testing will be different. Until then…"

He shrugged and took off his brass-buttoned blazer, brushing its shoulders and hanging it in the wardrobe by his wife's crimson dress. Little did they know, she would never wear it again.

Next to the wardrobe stood a chest of six drawers, fastened to the wall. He opened the second drawer, reached under his leather-bound logbook, and pulled forward a wooden box. Lined with blue velvet, it had three trays. The first contained a tie pin, fashioned from eighteen-carat gold. Into the empty second compartment he placed the gold cufflinks he had been wearing on his white shirtsleeves. Despite his coarse fingers smothering the clasps, he was so well practised that he could put them on and take them off purely by feel.

The last tray contained a tiny giftbox with a red ribbon bow. He smiled, tried not to show it. In the box was a pendant locket with a floral motif. The shop salesman had assured him that symbols of freshness and renewal were the height of fashion since Victoria, age eighteen, had succeeded her uncle as monarch in June last year. Her coronation had taken place in Westminster Abbey in June this year, 1838, although I gather by all accounts it was under-rehearsed, a bit of a shambles.

The locket was a surprise for Annie on their wedding anniversary, just around the corner. He'd invited her to join him so that he could make a special presentation on the ship. He'd rehearsed his little speech over and over.

Annie had begun to collect jewellery: women were overtaking men as the primary wearers of jewellery for the first time. In previous eras, sailors pierced their ears with hoops of silver or gold, enough to pay for a proper burial. Now, increasingly, men wore jewellery that served a function, as Humble's cufflinks did, and was not simply decorative.

John Humble had not always made anything of their anniversary. But their infant grandson, named after him, had softened his heart in ways that he had not expected. He'd reappraised his own life as never before. He had a wife who, to him, had always been elegant and beautiful, and he counted his blessings to have met her.

He'd been fortunate, too, to have spent so much time at sea. Through travel, he'd come to realise, you accumulated experiences of life, places, people. It was not merely a journey from A to B. Wise man. He so hoped that Annie would look back on this journey with the love and affection he felt for her.

He finished undressing and climbed into his bed, a twin to Annie's, separated by a table with a glass jug of water and two tumblers. On the wall above their heads hung subtly lit paintings by Londoner, Mary Moser, of a floral bouquet, and Scouse-born George Stubbs of two horses pulling a haycart.

The beautiful images were most precisely in focus when he squinted, but if his eyesight was fading as he aged, he was sure it wasn't affecting his ability to read or work. At least, not yet. He lay on his back, arms folded, and exhaled deeply to relax. In the quiet he could feel the rhythmic pounding of the ship's paddles, and it comforted him.

"Goodnight, love," he said. "See you in the morning."

"Mmm… Sleep tight. No snoring."

After dinner, Annie had retired to the cabin to read, while he stayed in the saloon to chat to more passengers.

Thomas Woodrow, a tea merchant from Yorkshire, had recognised his accent and informed him proudly that his teenage son, Harry, was gainfully employed in a glass factory in the west end of Newcastle. "Did you know, sir, that more glass is manufactured on the Tyne than in all of France?"

Woodrow himself had seemed astounded. But his statement was true. As well as coal, the raw ingredients of construction such as tiles, bricks, lead and glass were among Newcastle's biggest exports.

In turn, Captain Humble sought to impress Woodrow with his knowledge of the global nature of maritime trade, which he recalled from a circular sent by his employer quoting *Lloyd's Register of Shipping*. At a time when Britain's navy was contracting, wooden warships being scrapped in the wake of the Napoleonic wars, her merchant fleet was expanding beyond anyone's dreams. It presently numbered 25,000 vessels, no less, nearly ten times as many as a century ago.

Humble left Woodrow, clearly impressed, and was making for his cabin further aft when he encountered Sarah Dawson walking in the opposite direction towards the ship's central lobby and washrooms.

He greeted her warmly, hoped her family was enjoying the journey. She told him regretfully that her husband, Jesse, had not finished work in time to join them at Hull after all, and only she had boarded with James and Matilda.

Having rounded Spurn Point, the *Forfarshire* was now in the North Sea, with the Yorkshire coastline three miles to her port side.

Some thirty miles north of Hull, past Scarborough and near to Bridlington, they would alter course to circumnavigate a distinctive promontory, about eight miles long, where the tides tended to switch direction. Had it been daylight, Humble would have drawn his telescope and relished one of the most spectacular sights on the whole journey. It was Flamborough Head. Sparkling sandy beaches at the base; chalky white cliffs, pocked with caves that were home to oystercatchers and gulls, towering four hundred feet above. Out of the untamed moorland on top sprouted a lighthouse, maintained by Trinity House, about a mile from Flamborough village.

Just as John Humble was drifting off to sleep, he became aware of heavy feet racing along the corridor. Closer and closer they came to the cabin…

Yes, this was real, he wasn't dozing. The running boots slowed as they approached. Then, a thunderous battering on the door. What the–? Now he was wide awake.

As he regained his composure and rubbed his eyes, he saw that Annie was already sitting bolt upright in bed.

"Who's there?"

— 8 —

Bamburgh Castle

"Be careful, Papa!"

With great heed, as if it were extremely fragile, William Darling carried his shotgun down the stairs winding around the lighthouse walls to the ground floor.

Grace waited until he had safely disappeared. Then she returned the rod, can of oil and cloths, with which he had cleaned the gun, to their shelf in the lantern room, alongside the diary in which he noted when the gun was fired. On Brownsman, he'd shot rabbits and birds, perhaps sixty mallards per season. Like it or not, no room for sentimentality with a growing, ever-hungry family to feed.

Thomasina had finished her sewing soon after Grace returned from Brownsman and was relaxing with a mug of warm milk. While her father locked the gun in its cupboard and cut himself a slice of ham, Grace showed her mother the whelk shell she'd picked up outside. Thomasina had collected shells with her children for as long as Grace could remember. Numerous windowsills overflowed with the family's most treasured exhibits from the sea which was the constant backdrop to their lives.

They chatted about the Atlantic grey seals which inhabited the Farnes in their thousands. This always gave them a child-like rush of joy, and they wallowed in it.

The grey seals spent most of their time out at sea, gorging on fish, but would haul out on the rocks and beaches to let their food digest. They were astonishingly well equipped with long white whiskers to detect fish wakes from far away.

The females came ashore to give birth, normally clustered in vociferous colonies. Their fluffy white pups were born in the autumn, but this September Grace had spotted no new arrivals. Yet. The pups remained on land until the spring when their white coats moulted. By then, they had trebled their bodyweight and could hunt for themselves.

Grace loved watching the adult seals – six feet long, she rightly estimated – throughout the year, identifying some individuals from the pattern of blotches on their furry skin.

"Their ears aren't visible, which adds to their playful look," her mother had once cautioned, "but looks can be deceptive. The males are merciless fighters – see the bite marks on their necks – don't forget, angel, those charmers are predators."

The warning had been issued before Grace went swimming with the seals, which she'd done during most summers. For all their wariness on land, in the water they were inquisitive, nimble, balletic, bewitching.

Grace bade her parents goodnight and sauntered up to her room. She said her regular prayers by candlelight, then climbed the rest of the stairs to the lantern, where she was to take the evening's first watch. As was her habit, she walked a full circuit of the lantern before settling down in her wicker chair.

There was sufficient light, some from the moon, some reflected from the lighthouse beam, to make out the largest local landmarks. Their very familiarity renewed her sense of security and contentment.

She could discern the outline of Cheviot which, at almost 2,700 feet, was the highest summit in the range of hills called the Cheviots. They stretched through Northumberland to the Tweed valley in the Scottish Borders. The stump of a pre-historic volcano, Cheviot itself was surrounded for miles by undulating moorland, dotted with occasional farms, cattle and sheep.

Farther round the lantern, but closer to hand, she gazed at the spectacular bulk of Bamburgh Castle. It dominated the view up the shore. Some lights still glowed in the windows and Grace could make out the blades of the windmill at the castle's west side. The corn it ground was sold off cheaply to the people of the village – Grace's own birthplace – that had developed in the castle's shadow. The granary occupied much of the top floor.

It was apparently in the sixth century A.D. that the founder of the Northumbrian regal dynasty, King Ida, selected Bamburgh as the location of the royal capital. Northumbria was the largest of the seven kingdoms into which the medieval country was divided.

Bamburgh is a small village, but its history is amazing. Let's rediscover it, just for a few moments.

Back then, Northumbria reached from the Humber estuary to the Firth of Forth. The site of the royal fortress had a long, narrow escarpment, towering 147 feet above a pristine sandy beach and the North Sea. The finished fortress looked as if it was a seamless extension of its exposed rocky base, rather than a building put on top of it.

In the year 635, at the bidding of Northumbria's King Oswald, an Irish monk named Aidan came to Bamburgh from the Hebridean islet of Iona. His mission: to convert the pagan people to the Christian faith.

Aidan based himself on Lindisfarne Island, which resembled his beloved Iona, north of the Farnes. He founded a monastery and served as its first bishop. He toured Northumbria extensively, and with much success, teaching the principles of Christianity each evening to local crowds. Oswald sometimes accompanied him and assisted with the Saxon dialect.

Many churches and schools were established in Aidan's name, including one, which Grace knew, just outside the castle wall in Bamburgh. It was in this very church that Aidan died, age sixty, in August 651.

His Christian tradition was preserved by Cuthbert, a farmer's son who rose to be Bishop of Hexham and later of Lindisfarne. He too travelled widely, spreading the gospel, but he also spent years in seclusion at a private oratory on the Inner Farne island. Like Aidan, Cuthbert sought the solitude for contemplation and prayer. A biography of Cuthbert, written by Bede, became a seminal text as Christianity took root in England.

When teaching their children, William and Thomasina Darling encouraged them to follow the essential example of these local champions of the cross: to be loving, humble and unselfish. Grace found Bamburgh Castle an awe-inspiring place; during her life it was a protective influence and, as we'll see, in adulthood she went there many times.

At the end of the tenth century, Viking invaders ransacked Bamburgh. The great castle fell into disrepair. A century later, it was renovated by Norman invaders as a stronghold for their warring forays into Scotland. By this time, the old kingdom of Northumbria was dissolved, its lands absorbed into northern England. The Normans endowed the castle with a massive square keep, walls up to eleven feet thick.

The castle remained a royal residence until the seventeenth century, when it fell again into disrepair. With the English and Scottish thrones united, the border's strategic significance diminished, and King James I decided to give away the castle to its last keeper in recognition of his many years of loyal service. He was Claudius Forster.

In 1701, after generations in the Forster family, the neglected castle passed to the final heir, Dorothy Forster. She married the distinguished third Bishop of Durham, Lord Nathaniel Crewe, a property owner, independently wealthy. When Lord Crewe died in 1721, he left Bamburgh Castle and his entire fortune in trust in his wife's memory. The effects of this legacy were far-reaching and transformational.

The stated aims of the newly formed Lord Crewe Trust were to restore the dilapidated castle and support the local people. One of the charity's most pro-active trustees was Dr John Sharp, a Cambridge University graduate who came from a large, ecclesiastical family and was himself an archdeacon of Northumberland.

In the mid-eighteenth century, Dr Sharp set about putting the Trust's plentiful funds to good use. He arranged for sections of the castle to be refurbished and installed a library. He and his fellow trustees bequeathed their own books, expanding the range and subject matter of the collection.

Within the castle walls, Dr Sharp built a state-of-the-art infirmary. In this endeavour I believe he was guided by his brother, a surgeon at St. Bartholomew's Hospital in London. Treatment was provided to shipwrecked sailors as well as local citizens.

He founded a school, too. The poorest parishioners' children, principally girls, were fed and clothed there, and taught by two schoolmistresses in writing, arithmetic, sewing and knitting until the age of sixteen. Usually, they would then be given an outfit and, like many women, placed in domestic service as housemaids.

An agent for the trustees was available to discuss any matter with the villagers. He would select the girls for the thirty or so school places, and he was required to improve safety along the Bamburgh coast. I'll introduce you to the agent in Grace's time later.

Grace had been fascinated to learn that Dr Sharp devised one of the first coastguard systems in the world at Bamburgh Castle, and she eagerly absorbed the details of his scheme. Here goes:

In stormy weather, a look-out with a loud bell was stationed on the castle's east turret, and two horseback riders patrolled for miles along the coast. If any ship was observed in distress, one rider would gallop back to the castle to summon help while the other stayed, keeping the stricken vessel in sight. A nine-pounder gun would be fired from the ramparts and a bright flag hoisted to signal to survivors that they had been sighted and relief was on its way. Apparatus stored at the castle included long iron chains and a spare coble.

Having been born in her grandfather's cottage in Bamburgh, Grace visited him – Grandpa Job Horsley – throughout her childhood. One of her mother's sisters, Aunt Mary, had had three children in rapid succession, all about the same age as Grace, born either in Bamburgh or nearby Beadnell, and there were times when Grandpa Job's little home had felt full to bursting with her brothers, sisters and cousins. Their merry family gatherings involved listening to stories, playing marbles and card games, and chasing dogs and rabbits outside.

Grandpa Job was employed as a gardener at the castle. At his side, Grace learned more about flowers and horticulture, how to sow seeds, catch slugs and earwigs. She loved him. The apricots and peaches that he grew looked and tasted so exotic.

One September Sunday – Grace must have been about eight – her father and Laddie rowed her across to Bamburgh. Her errand was simply to return a blue trowel to Grandpa Job; it held some sentimental, as well as practical, value and as soon as the family had finished with it in their garden on Brownsman, he'd asked for it back.

St. Aidan's Feast was in full swing. During this annual festival, the triangular village green was bedecked with striped tents selling Northumbrian cakes, gingerbread and all manner of sweets and fruits. Crowded stalls lined the surrounding cinder paths, too.

Picture the scene with me. A party of southern sailors, who had made a port of call in nearby Warenquay, danced in a corner of the green with village girls clad in pinafores, while a trio of fiddle players kept to metronomic time. They competed – not without irritation, I bet – against a pair of handbell ringers, who skipped circuits around the green's perimeter.

Popular entertainments included a wheel of fortune, skittles and quoits – although Grace's brothers insisted that the rounds of rope slipped off the scoring pegs far too easily for it to be coincidental. Circus performers dressed as jesters led pony rides, the plumed animals zigzagging sedately through a course of brightly painted tar barrels.

In a rickety shelter across a path from the green, a farrier, Elias Liddell, demonstrated hoof trimming and how to fit a horseshoe, ably assisted by his teenage son, Ben. The queues for the Liddells' demonstrations mixed with those for the slides. They snaked around a clump of trees, while peddlers pitched roasted hazelnuts.

Poor Grace had never experienced such a commotion. A border terrier scampered up to her, its ears pricked as if it recognised a friend, then it did an about-turn and vanished through the legs of the multitude. Although the festival was outdoors, she felt suddenly surrounded, trapped, frightened.

Desperate to get clear, she broke into a run and headed for the winding path that led up the steep embankment to the castle. The evergreen flower beds on each side were perfectly tended and Grace slowed to a walk to admire them. She began to feel calmer. To her right, over the wall, the jagged chain of Farne Islands stretched into the distance. Beyond Longstone, a collier sailed south towards Newcastle, riding so high that she must be empty.

Grace was halted in her tracks by a *thwack* and a hail of squeals. She realised, heaving a sigh, that the source was a Punch and Judy show below her on the green and made headway.

She reached the castle's inner bailey through a passage hacked from solid rock. She looked for her grandpa; no one was about. Was this usual, she speculated? She took a few minutes to walk all the way around the Norman keep in the centre of the inner bailey.

Still no one in sight. Her nerves crept back. Where was everybody? Had they gone revelling at the feast?

Four cannons pointing out to sea did not look as though they had seen battle recently. Glancing westwards, in faraway fields, a gang of boys picked hops, gathered firewood, rounded up straying cattle.

Grace followed a flagstone path that curved towards a chapel on the north side of the castle. To her right was a parade of stone edifices – a guard room, kitchen, armoury, great hall – with turrets high up on the walls behind them. She strode through an archway into a corridor and followed the fingerboards pointing to the great hall.

"Hello!" she called. An echo bounced along the gloomy corridor.

It was chilly and smelled so musty that the rank taste of it clung to her mouth and nose. Were there bats in this place?

The corridor divided and Grace forked left. At the end was a wooden door, the largest she had ever seen. Even the bolts on its hinges must have been two feet long. As she approached, she noticed that a standard-sized door had been cut within the huge wooden block. She looked behind her – deserted! – then knocked on the inner door. It felt thick, immovable, hurt her knuckles. No response.

Grace knocked again, louder, and this time tried the oval handle. The door swung open surprisingly easily. She stepped inside.

The great hall lived up to its name. One wall was shrouded in ornate tapestries. An exceedingly long wooden dining table filled the centre of the room. It was bare except for three silver candlesticks. There was a pair of high-backed chairs at the far end, below cross-mounted thrusting spears on the wall next to a framed portrait of a grand man in church robes.

Two more portraits, larger still, one of a man, the other a woman considerably younger than him, were mounted over a stone fireplace so that the subjects faced each other. Clearly the paintings had been commissioned as a pair. Oil lamps stood on various side-tables, none was lit. The only natural light seeped in through medieval arrow-slit windows, dozens of them, running the length of one wall which–

"Can I help you?"

Gulp. It was a woman's voice, strict and urgent. Grace wheeled around to face the newcomer. She was standing in the doorway, leaning on a stick which she clutched with the long, bony fingers of both hands. Just as Grace saw through the dim light that she was confronting an elderly woman, sixty at least, so too the woman recognised that this was a child.

Grace stayed frozen to the spot, silent. She kept a tight grip on the precious trowel. Who was this woman?

Hobbling towards Grace, the woman addressed her more gently. "What is your name, young lady?"

At first Grace's shyness got the better of her, prevented her from speaking. A few agonising moments passed, when only a choking sound emerged. Then she managed: "Grace Darling, ma'am."

The stern woman smiled. She was missing at least one tooth in her top row.

"What are you doing here, Grace Darling?" Liking the sound of the girl's name, she shuffled nearer.

"I – I've come to hand this to my grandpa," Grace answered, standing her ground, holding aloft the trowel.

The woman squinted at it. "What is your grandfather's name? How do you know he's here?"

"He works here." A deep breath. "He's Grandpa Job – Job Horsley."

The woman visibly relaxed. She exhaled and seemed to deflate before Grace's eyes.

"Ah, well, in that case, I think I can help you, Grace Darling. I know your grandfather, and if you come with me, I'll take you to him. You might have to walk slowly, though, I'm not as agile as I used to be."

Bless her, Grace too relaxed a little, but still did not loosen her grip on the trowel. She followed the woman as she walked towards another door in the far corner. Suddenly she halted and turned to Grace.

"Goodness me, I haven't introduced myself. My name is Mrs Wansbeck, Bess Wansbeck. My father was a trustee of the Lord Crewe Trust which made many improvements to this place. I work in an office here, helping the trustees' castle agent. Do you see that portrait?" Bess waved her stick at the man in the church robes. "That is Dr John Sharp, a leading light of the board of trustees. Have you heard of him?"

Grace gave a little nod, having been taught not long ago how Bamburgh Castle held a pivotal place, over many centuries, in the story of Northumbria and England. Her father had promised that her errand visit to Grandpa Job would be a reward for her concentration and learning.

"A great man, Dr Sharp. He died thirty years ago," Bess informed her. "We've just passed his sedan chair, he found it extremely comfortable. And those two over there," she waved at the pair of paintings over the fireplace, "are Lord and Lady

Crewe, Nathaniel and Dorothy, whose munificence made Dr Sharp's deeds possible."

They had reached the door they would take out of the great hall. Grace followed Bess up a flight of stone steps whose front edges were worn away in the middle. Half-way up, below a small window which cast a triangle of light on it, was a vivid painting of smugglers hoarding their contraband. It was an early work by the Newcastle-based artist, Henry Perlee Parker, and Grace preferred it to any of the portraits in the hall.

They ascended cautiously into another fusty corridor.

"Have you ever set foot in this castle before, Grace Darling?"

Grace shook her head solemnly.

"Well then, let me show you in here. I think you might be impressed."

Bess nudged a wooden door open with her stick and led the way in. At least this room was better lit, with broader windows, and Grace saw that it was a library. Row upon row of books stretched from floor to ceiling, an extremely high ceiling she realised as she peered up and along all four sides. There were desks and chairs in the middle of the floor, some draped in grey cloth.

"As you can see, this is the castle's library, founded by Dr Sharp," Bess said, propping herself against one of the desks. "Go on, have a guess how many books are here."

Grace looked around the room. Myriad, multi-coloured spines eyeballed her.

"I'll spare you the bother," Bess grinned. "Fourteen thousand, more or less. History, theology, common law, the classics. Up there are the atlases, over there some Italian and French literature, and you'll notice around the door a collection of periodicals. I love coming in here, it's inspiring of course, but a little challenging too. What do you make of it?"

Grace remained tongue-tied.

"Exactly!" Bess exclaimed and tip-tapped her way back into the corridor. "I have one more thing to show you, then we'll find your grandfather. I'm not making you late, am I?"

Grace shrugged, shook her head.

A man in a twill suit strolled past, whistling to himself. I've never been able to confirm who he was. He grunted a hasty "Hello" to Bess and continued on his way.

At the end of the corridor, Bess announced: "Here we are. Come and see this."

Grace stood on the threshold of the wide-open door. A similar size to the library, this was an infirmary, divided into three areas. The first contained two rows of cast iron beds, nine or ten to a row. There were shelves piled with pestles and mortars, bottles of medical ingredients, bellows for resuscitation, lots of gleaming metal instruments. Grace shuddered: how must it feel to be operated on with those?

The central area, much smaller, was an apothecary for dispensing ointments and preparations. Several chairs with cushions faced the counter, which had been left rather untidy.

The third section was for bathing. Half a dozen tin and copper tubs were lined up against a wall. Each one had a pipe emerging from the floor and bracketed to the wall so that the open end of the pipe would release water into the tub from about six feet above it. All the pipes were rimmed with limescale.

"The infirmary was installed years ago, decades ago in fact, by Dr Sharp," Bess explained ruefully. "It was very well used in its heyday. Thousands came every year – gashes, sprains, respiratory disorders, biliousness – not so many now. The facilities haven't changed, they're just as they have always been. We could never do much for the poor souls with typhoid or cholera – still can't."

A woman in an apron entered, bearing a pile of bedsheets. She turned on her heels and exited swiftly when she saw that Bess was there with a young guest. Grace was too dazzled by the bathing area to pay her any attention.

"You see those pipes on the wall?" Bess went on. "They can deliver sea water, or cold water from a deep well beneath the castle, or hot water from a steam boiler in the adjacent room. One thing we discovered is that by boiling instruments you can make them cleaner. And a douche of water is beneficial for everyone, whether they're a labourer with a fever or a shipwrecked sailor."

Bess thought for a moment and added: "There's a lot to be said for good sanitation. You'd be amazed, I think, what nasty infections can be avoided simply by washing, by keeping your face and hands clean." Amen to that.

She smiled. "Have you seen enough, Grace Darling? Come along, I really think I should take you to your grandfather."

They found him in a refectory drinking tea with a colleague. Job Horsley, a balding, hoary fellow with poor posture, embraced his granddaughter, thanked her heartily for returning the trowel and expressed his gratitude also to Bess Wansbeck for looking after her. Bess seemed impressed to learn from Job that Grace lived on the Farnes, where her father was a lighthouse keeper.

Job explained that the castle was unusually quiet, even for a Sunday, as the annual feast had proved to be a compelling diversion. "Last year it poured with rain, and the year before come to think of it, so this time everyone's determined to make the most of it."

Up in the lantern room on Longstone, the twenty-two-year-old adult Grace projected her recollections on to the glass windows. Grandpa Job – his wrinkly face grinning in her mind's eye – had passed away some years since, by which time he liked to tell everyone that he was as old as the sea itself. He tilled soil assiduously until close to the end.

Many of the lights in the windows of Bamburgh Castle had now been extinguished. Grace sat on her wicker chair, watched a brig go by, settled in for the next few hours of vigil.

Barely twenty minutes had passed when she sprang up and grabbed one of the brass telescopes supplied by Trinity House. Was that a ship's mainsail, detached from its mast, thrashing about loosely like a demented kite in the bitter night air?

— 9 —

Boiling point

Not far north of Flamborough Head, the *Forfarshire* ran into choppy seas.

Whipped by a strong easterly, the waves became shallow and short. The paddle blades could not provide the same smooth ride as they had done out of Hull and on her previous trip south from Dundee a few days earlier. If I'd been a passenger, and hadn't travelled on steamships much before, I'm sure I'd have found it unnerving.

Captain Humble was immediately aware of the *Forfarshire*'s jerky motion – the last thing he needed. But it should not be enough, he reasoned, to keep any passenger awake. He'd been summoned from his cabin by the first mate, James Duncan, who sounded sufficiently concerned when he rapped on the door for Humble to get dressed quickly, urged on by Annie, and to join a conference taking place in the engine room.

The air was so hot, so clammy, in the bowels of the ship that Humble felt sweat on his collar. Grimacing, he ran a finger around it, inside and out. The steam hissing from all three boilers made it impossible to see clearly and the clanking of the moving parts sounded oh so laboured.

Six men were present. As well as Humble and Duncan, his second mate, John Matson – young, bright, occasionally a little hot-headed – was there. On duty, too, were two firemen, John Nicholson and John Kidd, and a coal trimmer, James – known as 'Jas' – Hall.

Humble was relieved when his chief engineer, Allan Stewart, joined them, although the floor was uncomfortably cramped. Jas was doing his best to mop up, but parts of the room remained awash.

"Gentlemen," said Humble as calmly as he could, "what exactly are we facing and what decisions need to be taken now?"

"We should return to Spurn Point, sir, and get this lot properly repaired," the second mate called out in exasperation before a glare from the first mate silenced him. He stared at his hands, imagined a day off relaxing on a sunny beach, and swallowed his outburst.

Humble was sceptical. "Allan, what's your view?"

Allan Stewart removed his tartan scarf and stuffed it into the pocket with his half-bottle of gin.

"Well, sir, it's like this. The engine has deteriorated since our departure. There's turbulence ahead, and as things stand, we don't have the capacity to go faster than five, maybe six knots."

Under normal circumstances, Humble would expect a top speed of at least nine. He began a mental calculation to determine how late they'd now arrive in Dundee.

Allan Stewart was detailing the multiple failures. "The pump supplying the water to the starboard boiler has broken. And the iron plates of that boiler are so encrusted that the rivets no longer fit properly."

Humble sighed. "So, what are our options? I'm loathed to delay the arrival of our passengers and cargo in Dundee, when we know the boilers are prone to leaks and we've always been able to deal with them. I'm not giving the company any excuse to think that my crew is unreliable."

He paused, heard no dissent.

He continued: "We must make repairs to pick up speed and make port in Dundee as close to schedule as possible. While we're there, we'll contact the foundry and see what improvements can be made. Now, Allan, do you have everything you need?"

Peering around the downcast faces, Stewart hedged his bets. "We'll need to empty the starboard boiler, sir, replace some rivets, and fill her up again by hand. Can someone wake up Old Johnny?"

He was referring to the ship's handyman, Johnny Tulloch, a skilled carpenter, generally happy to turn his hand to any practical work, on and off the ship.

Jas Hall nodded and left the engine room, squelching through the water before disappearing through clouds of steam.

"Thank you all," Humble said. "Your efforts are much appreciated. Oh – Allan."

"Aye, sir?"

"I don't mean this facetiously, but given the lateness of the hour, please minimise the noise of the repair work, as far as you possibly can. I'd like the passengers to get a good night's rest."

Humble left the cauldron of the engine room, while Stewart motivated the crewmen to get to work on the broken engine.

Humble felt that the conference had gone as well as could be expected. His thoughts reverted to the secret presentation he planned for Annie, and in his mind's eye he savoured her delighted reaction. He had asked Jonathan Tickett, the head chef, to bake a small celebration cake.

He turned a corner, heading for the stairwell to the cabin deck, when dead ahead he saw a block of passengers marching towards him. Some were wearing coats wrapped tightly over their nightdresses.

"Ah, Captain Humble, the very man," declared the bold Irishman at the formation's apex. Still in his day clothes, with hobnailed boots.

Humble scanned their faces. He recognised a few: Alistair Bell, a factor – business agent – for Lord Kinnoull; Gordon and Hilda McCloud; and Glen Ritchie, travelling with his aunt and uncle, all returning to Scotland.

"How may I help you?" Humble asked, retaining full composure.

Just then, Johnny Tulloch came down the stairs into the corridor, followed closely by Jas Hall. Johnny looked unusually flustered, unkempt. He pushed his way through the pack, acknowledged Humble's presence – "Sir!" – and strode on to the engine room. Jas noticed the Irishman at the head of the passengers and glared at him, keeping a respectful pace behind his captain.

"I'm Daniel Donovan," said the Irishman. "I've been working as a fireman on board since Hull."

Humble stared at Jas Hall, a single raised eyebrow making his question abundantly clear.

Jas swallowed hard. His lips had mutated into hot sand, a trickle of sweat meandered down his back. He plucked up his courage and spoke with as much conviction as he could muster.

"This gentleman did board at Hull, sir. With respect, he was unable to pay for a ticket, but said he had some experience on steamships and offered to work his passage as an extra fireman. He seemed an amiable fellow and, well, we…"

"I see."

Humble nodded. He was aware that off-the-books arrangements might be made unofficially at any time, especially on larger vessels such as the *Forfarshire*. Provided his senior crew were party to the deal, he preferred not to get involved. What the eye doesn't see…, as his father used to tell him. Now, as master of the ship, he felt he should focus on the key decisions affecting the ship's journey and passengers' welfare. Fair enough?

Some of the passengers regarded Daniel Donovan with distrust, even disdain. Humble assumed that Donovan had not disclosed the full circumstances of his presence on the ship. Donovan, however, was thick-skinned, not at all embarrassed, let alone deterred.

"Captain, we feel you're not discharging your duties in a full and proper manner. In my opinion, the *Forfarshire* is unseaworthy."

If Donovan had had to steel himself to express this opinion, he hid it well. Perhaps a faint whiff of alcohol on his breath betrayed the origins of at least some of his courage, but Humble let it pass. He kept a cool head, although his cheeks had flushed.

"I take it, sir, that you are referring to our steam engine, which seems to have been a recurring topic of conversation among the passengers throughout this journey?" His eyes narrowed.

"I am, captain. Would you please put in at the nearest port until the leaking boiler can be mended or replaced? What do you say?"

"As you know, sir," Humble could not help but spit out the appellation this time, "we are equipped with not one, but three boilers and furnaces. The *Forfarshire* is a fine, modern vessel which I am proud to command. Now, it's very late and I ask you all to disperse quietly."

"Come on, dear," Hilda McCloud could be heard saying to her husband. Her wavy hair tumbled over her weary eyes. "We've been up long enough." The McClouds peeled off, made their way down the corridor.

Humble was not yet finished. "My crew is on top of the situation, as they always are. I have total confidence in their professional abilities and their knowledge of how this ship works. The boilers were checked before we left Hull. And I'll thank you, sir," he addressed Donovan directly, taking half a pace forward, "not to stir up distress without bringing your concerns to me first."

More passengers abandoned their stance and shuffled away.

"I still don't like the look of the engine." Donovan was stubborn but less aggressive now. "And the wind is strengthening, isn't it, forcing the engine to work even harder to maintain the pace. If a storm arises, captain–"

"I'll wager the *Forfarshire* has passed through more squalls than you have, sir."

Donovan realised that his mob had deserted, emitting one or two sneers at the end, and he was facing the ship's master alone. For once, he hesitated.

"Look," Humble said, seeking reconciliation. "You've made your point. Please leave it at that. If you wish to earn your keep, as a positive support to my team in the engine room, then I won't stand in your way. Let me leave you in the capable hands of Mr Hall here and bid you good night."

Humble swept past Donovan before he could utter another word. He did his best to avoid confrontations with passengers and would make a succinct note of this rare breach in his logbook. To his credit, he was not a man who bore grudges.

On the stairwell, he decided at the last moment not to return to his cabin straight away. He kept climbing until he was standing on the promenade deck. The wind was fierce, but he breathed the cold night air deeply into his lungs, letting it refresh his whole being.

He rubbed his palms together, felt a little heat on his skin, and looked up. The stars he often identified as navigation points in the night sky were invisible, shrouded in clouds.

To starboard: black infinity.

On the port side, as his eyes grudgingly adjusted to the darkness, he detected the ghostly presence of the cliffs on the North Yorkshire coast. They were progressing up to Scarborough and Whitby, not much behind schedule. A small schooner sailed by, taking a line between the *Forfarshire* and the shore.

Suddenly, in the distance to port, a huge crash made Humble freeze on the spot. He clasped his hands tightly together.

Throughout his career he had recognised the power of the tides and weather systems of the North Sea, not only to affect the passage of ships but also to bite lumps out of the crumbling coastline.

This stretch of heavily stratified coast was unstable. I believe it still is. In the gathering storm, a massive slice of rock had split from the cliff face, cascaded down and smashed ominously to pieces on the beach below. Boulders, stones and plants rampaged to the sand as an after-shock.

Just a few seconds later, the cliff was still once more. The boom of the landslip abated, leaving only the howling of the wind as it churned the waves.

— 10 —

Memories of winter and *Autumn*

Grace woke early.

She stretched, threw back her eiderdown. Thursday morning, 6 September.

As usual, yesterday had been a long day and she'd rolled into bed exhausted. After six hours' undisturbed rest, she felt refreshed and preferred to start the day rather than lie dozing. She padded over to her little window, immediately aware of the cold in the floor penetrating her bare feet.

Were Grace's motivation ever to sag, the outlook from her high bedroom window would more than replenish it. This was her complete world: the vast North Sea, extending beyond the horizon to the east; the beautiful beach at Bamburgh whose sand, fine as dust, glittered in the rising sunlight; the music of nature throughout the day; the colonies of seabirds, resident and migratory, thousands strong, that inhabited the Farnes; the significance of the local area in the history of her native land; and the everlasting importance to her of upholding the Darlings' reputation for protecting lives.

There was a squat lighthouse on Inner Farne. The largest of the chain, a haven for dive-bombing terns, this was the island nearest to the shore. Its lighthouse had been built in 1809 as a compact station less than half as tall as Longstone would later be. Grace recalled that the earliest warning light on Inner Farne dated back two centuries. The revolving light in the present squat tower shone over the islands close to shore. But it was on the outer Farnes – Brownsman and most of all here on Longstone – that the essential beacons stood.

From her upbringing and her own strength of character, Grace had derived a sharp sense of who she was and how to live her life. She knew where she belonged. On Longstone, more than anywhere else, she could be who she was.

Much as she missed her older sister, Betsy, with whom she had shared the bedroom before Betsy moved out and got married, Grace had had no difficulty in filling the vacated space, making it her own. She flipped open one of her foolscap pads – she'd kept them all from her childhood lessons and continued to add items of interest – and she scoured a list of the incidents on the Farnes during her lifetime.

They ranged from scraped hulls to catastrophic wrecks: *Hazard* (1815), *Benedicta* (1816), *Kincardine* (1818), *Juno* (1819), *Paragon* (1821), *Monkwearmouth* (1823), *Fortuna* (1824), *Thomas Jackson* (1825), *Martha* (1827), *Lord Collingwood* (1828), *Pearl Packet* (1829), *Eliza Hedley* (1830), so many others.

Alongside selected entries she'd scribbled comments or attached a newspaper clipping. When a family member rowed ashore, they would always try to pick up a newspaper. The editors recognised – and in turn stimulated – a maritime nation's interest in the fate of ships, especially in the coastal regions where shipping was multiplying.

The north-easterlies that ravaged the Northumberland coast were at their most ferocious over the protruding rocks and hidden reefs of the Farnes. On account of the devilish tides, some of the more – what shall I say? – fanciful reporters associated the islands with black magic. Knivestone, an outer rock fully visible only at low water and the site of dozens of wrecks, was dubbed in the press – a bit melodramatically for my liking – 'The Reef of Doom'.

Throughout Grace's life, the winters were harsh. In January 1823, when she was seven, a savage snowstorm blighted the north of England for six weeks, rendering travel by horse between Newcastle and Edinburgh impossible. The monochrome image of North Sunderland and Bamburgh, coated in deep snow and ice, smoke swirling from every chimney under a blanket of smog, was etched permanently in her memory.

One night three winters ago, Grace observed through the telescope a lone figure on Knivestone and a single mast protruding from the water. The wind was howling. She alerted her father, who launched the coble with three of his sons, Laddie, Robert and George, who were visiting Longstone at the time.

They were out for many arduous hours rescuing the survivor, James Cunningham, whom they eventually brought back to Longstone, but they lost an oar in their backbreaking battle with the choppy sea. William never spoke of it, but he and his sons came close to death that night.

James had been on a sloop, the *Autumn*, transporting coal from Sunderland to Peterhead, Aberdeenshire. He was one of three men on board with a fellow crew hand and the master. When the *Autumn* slashed her keel on the submerged tip of Knivestone, she sank rapidly. With only one oar, it was tremendously difficult for the Darlings to reach James as he clung for dear life to the rock.

Cruelly, the bodies of the other two men were never recovered. That did not stop James from giving a glowing account to a local journalist of the Darlings' determination and care.

The sloop's mainsail had twisted away in the gale-force wind, landing on Coquet Island near the coal-exporting village of Amble, twenty-odd miles to the south. The severed sail Grace had seen flapping by last night had fired her memories of the *Autumn* rescue, a night of mixed emotions.

Every winter, the tidal currents around the Farnes, perilous for navigators at the best of times, became even more treacherous. But when the winter storms gave way to spring, the seas and skies teemed with new life and the islands were transformed into the natural wonderland that Grace knew and loved.

In her bedroom she kept many shells, collected over the years with her mother. She was thrilled, too, that her father had developed an enduring sideline as an amateur naturalist. He corresponded with other authorities on nesting birds' eggs, mating seasons and fossils. He shared specimens with the Newcastle-born ornithologists, John and Albany Hancock, who were amassing a natural history collection of their own, and he and Grace scoured the detail of every letter they sent.

Grace decided to write to her sister, Thomasin, after getting dressed and having her porridge for breakfast. It was a couple of weeks since she'd last written, and she liked to hear how Thomasin and her twin, Mary Ann, were faring in Bamburgh, and the latest clients for whom she was making dresses.

Grace was about to go downstairs when she heard a faint clang. This was a bell she recognised – yes! It sounded again, louder, and she hurried back to her bedroom window.

Sailing by, as close to Longstone as any boat dared, was a red fishing smack, southbound for the little harbour at North Sunderland. In the stern, her dear eighteen-year-old brother William Brooks Darling was waving up at her window. Grace beamed, waved back. At least two of his friends were with him, Robbie Knox in the wheelhouse and Tommy Cuthbertson on deck minding the nets that wriggled with crabs, cod and herring.

The boat made laborious progress. Rather than moving forwards, it bobbed up and down on the furrowed expanse like a child's see-saw. A few veins of scarlet streaked the overcast sky, while the winds were quickening. Ostensibly resenting the boat's presence, the sea looked as cold and grey as in the depths of the most unforgiving winter.

— 11 —

Last attempt

The damage was blatant.

Even through the scalding steam, the rivulets of water gushing down the side of the boiler were plainly visible. So, too, the rising level of hot water on the engine room floor, which lapped farther down the corridor. So much so that the crew members had abandoned their mopping operation.

This Thursday morning, the mood of the three men meeting in the engine room was distinctly sombre.

When John Humble returned to his cabin last night, midnight had tolled. Annie was awake, her nose buried in the latest monthly instalment of *Oliver Twist* by Charles Dickens, which seemed to be making social justice, or the lack of it, a wider talking point than ever.

He recounted to Annie all that had happened since James Duncan hammered on their door, then he added a few lines to his logbook and got back into bed. He slept fitfully. First thing, he felt emotionally as well as physically drained, didn't want to get up. A mug of coffee helped to stoke his spirits and now, standing in the engine room in a pair of calf-high waterproof boots, he knew his leadership had to be persuasive.

James Duncan and Allan Stewart, his senior crewmen, waited for him to speak. The tension made them all feel more alert, more alive. Having sensed the tighter atmosphere, Humble looked them in the eye, addressing them personally.

"Gentlemen, let me summarise. Despite your hard toil overnight, we have a starboard boiler that will not stop leaking, even at low pressure, and a central boiler that appears to be losing pressure, too."

Duncan and Stewart nodded despondently.

"Incidentally, any sign of Mr Donovan up and about?"

"No, sir," said Duncan, stepping away from the boilers as the steam stung his eyes. "I believe he's still resting in the steerage quarters."

"Fair enough," Humble replied. The last thing any of them could stomach was another confrontation with the volatile Daniel Donovan.

"We do have the option of the sails, sir," Stewart prompted. "And of course, there's many a bay or river where we might put in."

"Indeed," said the captain, sounding more enthusiastic about the option than he felt. "I must detail a crew hand to check that our cargo stays evenly distributed in the hold, so that the heavy swells don't tilt us over. What speed can we manage?"

The *Forfarshire* lurched, kept upright, as a gust of wind broadsided her.

"No more than four knots, sir, and that's with no further diminution in power."

Humble stood tall, stuck to his guns. Annie would be proud.

"Allan, I'd like you to give the engine another overhaul, please. Degraded as it is, the machinery is not old, and it feels premature to give up on it. So, one more attempt."

Allan Stewart had anticipated this instruction. He may well have issued it himself were he in Humble's position, answerable to a competitive-minded, cost-conscious company. But he did not expect a different outcome this morning from last night. It would take a miracle to get this engine working sweetly while they were at sea.

At that moment, John Matson, the second mate, approached the engine room with a fellow crew hand, Alexander Murray. Standing over six feet tall, Murray had wet hair, slicked down by hand. Humble saw that his shoulders were wet, too, and his cheeks were red raw.

"Good morning!" Humble greeted them energetically. "You've been up top, Mr Murray?"

"Aye, sir." He was shivering, trying his best to conceal it.

Still a teenager, Murray was the latest addition to the *Forfarshire's* crew. His first trip had been in January, but he'd developed a maturity beyond his years and a robust sense of humour that soon put him in good stead among his more seasoned colleagues.

"Looks like a bad storm, sir," Matson said. "Sky is devilishly dark to the north and east, I've not seen anything like it. Sea is rough. Deep, deep waves."

"I'd say the gusts of wind on the surface are thirty knots, sir," Murray advised, "and getting stronger." They'd all have known that this already amounted to moderate gale force on the scale devised by the Royal Navy officer – later Admiral – Francis Beaufort, but no one questioned the lad's estimate.

"Thank you, gentlemen," Humble said simply. "Duly noted. I know you'll keep me apprised of progress. Now, I'm going to spend some time with the passengers."

"Very good, sir," muttered James Duncan before entering a private huddle with Allan Stewart.

Captain Humble strode into the dining saloon where a dozen passengers were eating breakfast from *Forfarshire*-branded platters of corn bread, cold meats, cheeses and hard-boiled eggs. He composed himself, did not let his concerns show.

"Good morning," he said breezily to no one in particular.

Mrs Allison, from York, her white hair set in tight curls, was at a table with her grandson, Harvey. The captain frowned when he heard Harvey start to whistle but said nothing. He had no truck, he told himself, with the ancient maritime superstition that whistling at sea provoked storms.

His tall boots made a drumbeat on the hard floor. Feeling momentarily uncomfortable, he stopped to sit with Sarah Dawson, who was nursing a cup of tea while watching James and Matilda demolish their breakfasts. They were sharing a table with Valentine Scott and his son, both of whom who were eating eggs.

"Hello, captain," Sarah said, not diverting her attention from her children. It seemed no time since Matilda had lost her milk teeth but here she was, wolfing down a plate of crusty bread with slabs of cheese.

"Tell me, how is everything for you, Mrs Dawson?"

"I was woken up by a dreadful sort of blasting and sputtering from the engine. We all were. There's an awful lot of hot steam about – too much – I feel so sorry for the men working down there. It's hard not to get… well, I mean, you are still confident that nothing serious…"

Valentine Scott looked up, listening in.

"I'm sorry if you were disturbed," Humble interrupted in his most velvety tone. "We're continuing to fine-tune the engine, but please don't worry. Try to take it easy. I can see you your hands full. Enjoy your breakfasts, all of you."

Humble noticed that Matilda Dawson had stopped eating, albeit briefly, and was staring at his blazer – it seemed to be the brass buttons that had dazzled her. He excused himself from the Dawsons and the Scotts and continued what he hoped was a reassuring, if admittedly brisk, stroll through the saloon.

He nodded a greeting in passing to Douglas and Robert Houston, brothers returning to their fashionable cloth trading business in Montrose. They were as deep in conversation with each other as they seemed to have been since embarkation.

At a corner table, he caught the eye of Hilda McCloud. She quickly averted her gaze, focused on her newspaper. Among the tightly packed columns of small type, a grisly headline stood out:

NEWCASTLE MURDERER SET FOR
SATURDAY GALLOWS

She licked a finger and turned the page with revulsion.

As Humble left the saloon, the *Forfarshire* creaked and rolled uncomfortably to port, battered by the strengthening north-easterly. Behind him, a plate smashed on the floor and a female voice cursed, but he did not look back.

He passed, but heard no sound from, Evelyn Martin's cabin. She had only left her cabin to find a steward to request delivery of a meal. Apart from this, she had not let her valise out of her sight. As the ship rolled and pitched, the valise slid across the floor, emitting a tell-tale jangling on every impact. She heaved it on to a mahogany table and unlocked it. Inside, on top of a few squashed clothes, were two bags bulging with gold sovereigns. Hundreds of them. A fortune.

A bit of context: The Bank of England had revived the sovereign in 1817 as part of a scheme to re-stabilise the currency after the massively costly Napoleonic wars. There were two issues of sovereign in Miss Martin's case: those minted in 1817 depicted the bull-like, laurel-clad head of George III, while those from a later pressing, in 1837, had a bareheaded likeness of William IV. They were all made from twenty-two-carat gold with a dash of reddish copper.

Evelyn had won her haul in a sweepstake at York Racecourse. To mark its centenary of hosting horse racing, the course was raising funds for a new grandstand. A prize draw was offered as an incentive to subscribe and she scooped the jackpot. Edith, her elder sister, had predicted long ago that either gambling or gin would ruin her, and she was greatly looking forward to showing Edith how wrong she was – on the first count at least.

Two hours later, ensconced in his own cabin, where Annie was reading her periodical, Captain Humble studied his nautical map, necessarily holding it close. It traced the shoreline from south of Hull to north of Dundee and indicated the water depths and known underwater reefs at specific points in the sea. A grid of squares was overlaid to help pinpoint positions.

In preparation for every journey, he would recheck the map to verify his intricate knowledge of the route. By his reckoning, based on the *Forfarshire*'s speed, bearing and journey time elapsed, they should reach the mouth of the Tyne at about two that afternoon, maybe a little after. In quick succession, they would pass the smaller coastal settlements of Shields, his birthplace, Tynemouth itself and Monkseaton.

There had long been talk of piers at Tynemouth to help protect ships from the force of the sea. None had yet been built, nor even any design approved, although there were two lighthouse towers that charged every port-bound ship a two- or fourpence fee to enter the river.

The city of Newcastle lay inland, west of Shields. Ever since he had first visited, on his ninth birthday, Newcastle had captivated him. It was a place of conspicuous contrasts. The pace and enterprise of its quayside, crowded with ships loading or unloading, was second to none. Thousands of sailors and keelmen who made a living there found refreshment and entertainment in the taverns and music halls along the quayside. Market dealers displayed their wares on the remnants of the medieval town wall, while comedians, quack doctors and orators of every persuasion took booths too.

Humble noticed that the city was endowed with glorious churches, some from as far back as the fourteenth century. One of its grandest buildings was the regional home of Trinity House, the ancient guild which promoted mariners' welfare, and which had played a decisive role in developing trade on the Tyne.

He was eager to take Annie to Newcastle's recently built shopping thoroughfares, Grey Street and Grainger Street, up the hill from the quayside, which had given the city a vibrant new centre. He had heard that these magnificent boulevards would impress any Londoner, Berliner or Parisian.

A knock on the cabin door.

Humble rolled his map and opened the door to Allan Stewart. From the wretched expression on his chief engineer's face, the news was clearly not what they'd hoped for.

Stewart was at the end of his tether. He reported that the starboard boiler was not functioning at all. It had been drained of water, but leaked more profusely when refilled, and now its furnace would not relight. The central boiler was also leaking and could only sustain low pressure – too low to drive the paddles. Finally, a pump rigged to clear the water from the engine room floor was useless; with a dash of black humour, he said you could practically swim in the place.

Annie stopped reading, watched her husband closely. She could not recollect when she'd seen him so apprehensive, so preoccupied. It was out of character – and it frightened her to her core.

— 12 —

First watch

"I don't like the look of this."

So said William Darling to Thomasina and Grace, who were chatting at the lighthouse kitchen table. "Not one bit," he added, making a mental note to check how far the barometer had fallen.

They'd polished off their teatime meal – thick bacon with a mash of potato and turnip – and William was peering out of the window. His nose was so close that the glass misted up. When he wiped it with a handkerchief, there was a loud squeak which the infant Grace would have enjoyed imitating.

That morning, using water from the well, she had washed two tubs of clothes, racking them in front of the stove. Later, she'd taken her time writing an affectionate letter to Thomasin, keeping her script small so that it fitted on to a single side of paper, which she folded and addressed. She noticed that faint blotches of ink still stained her index and middle fingers. The letter could be delivered to the mainland on the next coble trip. Or perhaps Mr Jopson, a local wainwright, would take it on his boat if he delivered the Darlings' cart, whose wheels he was due to have repaired. In the end, Mr Jopson came through the following week.

Conditions had deteriorated all day, Thursday, and the low sky was disgorging heavy rain. Visibility was exceptionally poor. The Farnes had been William's home for more than forty years, a duration matched by precious few other people, even monks and hermits. Thomasina and Grace respected absolutely his judgement and experience.

When William asked for her assistance outside, Grace gladly obliged. They wrapped up warm and stepped out. The wind was solid. They leant into it, eyes half-shut, hair and clothing flattened. Walking demanded a Herculean effort. Conversation was impossible, words were whipped away from the lips.

William pointed to the boatshed. Grace nodded, shielding her face with one hand, tightening her grip on her shawl with the other.

One summer during her childhood – she knew from her scrapbook that it was a Tuesday, 13 August, but could not recall the year off-hand – the royal yacht had sailed by the Farne Islands, carrying the King, George IV, from Greenwich to Leith. The entourage reportedly comprised three vessels, but the Darlings were unable to see any of them. A cool summer that year meant that, when relatively warm, moist air was blown across the sea, a dense fret formed, reducing visibility to a few yards.

The following spring, the same sort of fret dampened a visit by a party of servants working for the Duke of Northumberland in Alnwick. They said little, overwhelmed by the contrast between the world they knew just a few miles away and the isolated environment of the Farnes. Instinctively Grace felt that she understood their reaction but also held her tongue.

At the boatshed, William put one hand over the other in quick succession to mime a pulling action. He and Grace hauled the coble from its mooring on to the island, into the boatshed. After a moment to catch his breath, William tied it to a stanchion. The noise of the wind and rain was becoming ear-splitting and he hoped the little shed would withstand the lashing.

On their way back to the lighthouse, they gathered up anything that lay untethered – a coil of rope, a clothesline, a pair of boots whose soles needed restitching, a small stepladder, a rusty pitchfork, some nets. Suddenly, before they had reached the lighthouse, a huge wave rolled in, smashing its way on to the island, obliterating William and Grace's view. Like a giant fist, the wave clobbered them, shattering into tiny shards of spray. The pitchfork slipped from William's grasp and clanged across the rocky terrain before the wind swept it up and hoyed it into the sea.

Safely back in the lighthouse, they took a moment to recover. With Thomasina's help, they piled the loose items against the wall, away from the door. Thomasina offered Grace a linen towel to dry her hair, and she did so by the warm hearth. The three of them placed cloths and wooden blocks along the bottom edge of the door to fix a better seal against the elements. They rolled up some of their rugs and leaned them against the wall, too.

When he next spoke, William's tone was business-like.

"High tide will come at four fifteen tomorrow morning, first light of dawn an hour or so later. But the tidal streams will be very powerful, they can thrash about, switching direction unexpectedly, for a couple of hours after high tide. You take the first watch, Grace. I'll relieve you at midnight and cover the early hours."

Grace gave a comforting smile. "We'll be fine, Papa."

Thomasina's focus, meanwhile, was on the door. With the winds causing the raging sea to surge further and faster on to Longstone, their makeshift defences were already breached. A slick of foamy water was spreading from under the door, flooding the ground floor of the lighthouse.

Off Berwick Bay

The *Forfarshire* pointed to the heavens.

The three men in the engine room flattened their bodies against a wall and braced themselves for the imminent rebound, when the bow, having risen until it faced the sky, plummeted back level again. Waves of white water smothered it at the lowest point, conspiring to push the ship under. Her timbers creaked at the bruising indignity of it all.

The two firemen, Johns Nicholson and Kidd, had kept working throughout the emergency for hours after their shift would ordinarily have ended. A fellow fireman, Bill Douthy, who had just completed his shift with first-degree finger burns, had retired to the crew cabins and they were joined by a junior colleague, Martin Turnbull.

He had worked from the age of seven as a trapper at Goldthorpe Colliery in South Yorkshire. Practically the whole Turnbull family was employed down the same mine – it wasn't merely a job; it was a way of life. The trapper's task was to open and close the wooden trap doors that let fresh air in and the tubs of coal pass to and from the shaft. What he had learned about comradeship and co-operation – he'd been astonished to find that his fellow miners hailed from Nigeria, Ghana, Poland as well as Yorkshire – were valuable life lessons. But he'd had his fill of sitting hunched, hot and coal-blackened in darkness for twelve hours at a time – can you blame him? – and, when an explosion buried six of them for untold more hours, the sea was his escape.

After he ran away, he found work at the port of Grimsby. First unloading cod and haddock, and for the past ten months as a fireman shovelling coal into the boiler furnaces on the *Forfarshire*. He had always answered to 'Ginger', given his hair colour and freckles, but now the heads and faces of all three men were streaked with black. Of Daniel Donovan there was, they noted, no sign in the scalding hell of the engine room.

The cotton strips had come loose on the bandages knotted around Ginger's hands. Half an hour ago, his palms and fingertips had blistered when he grabbed hold of the nearest secure object to steady himself as the ship rolled. Unfortunately, it was a boiling hot pipe.

It had proved impossible, despite the crew's repeated best efforts, to repair the two faulty boilers. Ginger had even attempted, with help from the others, to funnel water into the starboard boiler manually, but the rivets could no longer bind the plates together. With so much hot, steaming metal, they could not even reach the boilers, let alone work on them.

The three men stayed pressed against the wall, exhausted, sore eyes watering. Surely the captain must now accept the reality of the breakdown?

Operating on a fraction of full power, the *Forfarshire* made painstaking progress north as the storm deepened. A towering wave crashed over her starboard side, pressing the port side down. The paddle casing, ten feet wide, plunged into the sea and seemed reluctant to resurface. Another wave crested and spilled a torrent of water over the ship's bow, forcing her down at the same time as she was tilted to the side. She corkscrewed on, dredging every drop of power from the deficient, ever more reluctant engine.

By six on Thursday evening, the *Forfarshire* had passed the chain of Farne Islands lying between North Sunderland harbour and the ancient fortress village – now more of a backwater – of Bamburgh. All passengers had been advised to rest in their accommodation. No one was on deck to see the young woman and the older man, in the distance off the port side, haul a coble on to Longstone Island at the base of the modern lighthouse.

Darkness fell soon after they passed Bamburgh, although visibility had been dire all day. Wind gusts exceeded fifty knots. Farther out to sea, a fully laden northbound collier passed the *Forfarshire*, apparently coping well.

Annie Humble had been as sick as the proverbial dog. She was lying on her bed, gripping the sides of the bedframe with both hands. Her husband stressed his regret, but she dismissed him, asking why he hadn't turned into the Tyne and waited out the storm in one of the local ports which he knew so well. Feeling hurt, he avoided an argument and slipped out, pausing only to take a tiny cylindrical vial from a drawer.

Captain Humble headed to the ship's forward section. He was sad to see the companionway through which the engine room could be viewed spewing out hot steam, replicating the funnel in the centre of the ship.

Reverend Robb was walking towards him, in conversation with a fellow passenger, James Kelly, a weaver by trade, returning home to Dundee. Both looked as ashen faced as his wife. When they crossed, he noticed Robb's forehead glistening with sweat.

Further along, he passed Lady Rentoul's daughter, Alice, doing her best not to spill the glass of milk she was carrying back to their cabin.

"Do you need any help?" Humble asked.

Alice turned, to ascertain that he was addressing her. "Oh, no, captain, but you're very kind. You must have a lot on your mind." Her voice was nasally.

Humble was crestfallen to see the unmistakable fear in her eyes. But it came instinctively to him to mollify her, as far as he could.

"Passengers come first," he said lightly, and offered to hold the glass of milk. She declined.

"In the North Sea, as I'm sure you know," he expanded, "storms occur frequently. Come and go. My crew and I have sailed through waves as high as these on countless occasions." She sniffled but he had her attention. "There's more maritime traffic in these waters than ever, not only along this coast but across to the European ports too – Rotterdam, Hamburg, Bremerhaven. Alas, it's the same for everyone this evening. I hope to see you and your mother soon. I'm sure the sea will be well disposed, more placid, next time."

Having blown her nose and pocketed the handkerchief, Alice replied: "I hope so, too, captain, but I fear that after this experience, my mother will stick to horse-drawn transport. British engineering may be transforming the world, but it isn't always plain sailing, so to speak, is it?"

Alice went on her way with her glass of milk. To stabilise herself, she walked like a duck, her feet splayed outwards.

Captain Humble chuckled as he watched her go, amused by her riposte. The encounter served to brighten his spirits. He always liked to keep a bigger picture in mind, however troubling the state of the *Forfarshire*'s engine had become.

It was now almost eight in the evening. They were off Berwick Bay, where the English county of Northumberland blended into the bonny Scottish Borders. Tantalisingly close to their destination of the River Tay and the *Forfarshire*'s home city of Dundee.

Humble went to the ship's pantry – actually, an extensive storage compartment for sugar, salt, spices, wines, bandages, splints, stationery and other 'dry' items. He fished out his key, unlocked the door and lit a small candle lantern immediately inside the windowless space.

Feeling their way along a high shelf, his fingers found a jar of cinnamon powder, which he had been led to believe was an effective remedy for nausea. Considerable doubt had been cast lately on the generic cure of bloodletting, for which he was grateful, although he would do anything to help Annie feel better when he presented the locket to her.

He tipped a little of the orange powder into his vial and replaced the jar just as the *Forfarshire* corkscrewed again.

As he set off back down the passageway, he heard shouting from one of the cabins. A door burst open; a man backed out. It was Glen Ritchie, one of the passengers who had confronted him last evening with Daniel Donovan. The Ritchies ran an arable farm in Ruthven, Perthshire.

"Ah, captain," Ritchie said, looking tense and not a little embarrassed. "Good evening." He steadied himself by grasping his cabin door handle as the *Forfarshire* pitched and yawed.

A rapid drumming noise overhead – had it suddenly got louder? It had to be the impact of the torrential rain on the wooden deck.

It felt as if the ship was under siege from every angle.

"Just having a discussion with my relatives. A family matter, nothing serious."

"Splendid," said the captain. He did not wish to trespass on private ground. But on the spur of the moment, Ritchie seemed eager to unburden himself.

"It's just that I've been trying to persuade my aunt and uncle to increase their investment in the farm, you see, so that we can expand, acquire the latest equipment." Ritchie wrung his hands, exasperated that his ambition had not won their backing.

"If I may make a small suggestion," Humble said, "go for a walk around the ship. Keep below decks, of course, but give your relatives some space. They may be upset in these conditions – my own wife is sadly unwell – so if you want their undivided attention, wait until morning, eh?"

Ritchie took a deep breath. "You're right, of course. I'll do as you suggest, captain, make my peace tomorrow." He inspected his shoes. "I'm far too impetuous for my own good, but I feel calmer now."

Humble thought to himself, perceptively: Whenever we are tested and put under pressure, that's when we discover more about ourselves, isn't it? See afresh who we really are.

Aloud he simply said: "Take care," and walked on.

"Thank you, captain." With that, Ritchie headed for the dining saloon, where he hoped to find something to drink, even if no food was available.

Another barrage of water pulled, pushed, squeezed the *Forfarshire*. Humble cursed and held out his arms to retain his balance. Then came a resounding bang, which many passengers must have heard, compounding their dread and despair.

Approaching his cabin, passing one of the Houston brothers, he saw Allan Stewart waiting for him outside. With a face like thunder, Stewart was breathing heavily.

"We've lost the two boilers completely, sir. That's them finished. We have one left, but it generates nowhere near enough power to drive us through these hellish seas."

Humble's body seemed to deflate, his clothes sag. Suddenly he looked extremely tired. He had to concentrate hard as his chief engineer's words sank in, and he rubbed his high forehead to help him think. This had become one of the most challenging voyages of his entire career.

Stewart fixed his gaze on the captain and rammed home his point. "Effectively, sir, the *Forfarshire* is now adrift without power."

Stewart was shocked to realise that he was trembling, hands clammy. He wiped them on his trousers.

"I've done my level best not to fall too far behind schedule," Humble said, apparently speaking to himself rather than his trusted colleague.

He paused, justifying the day's decisions in his own mind all over again. The *Forfarshire* tipped back as the sea renewed its onslaught. "But based on what you've told me, there's one course of action left open to us, and one only. We must take it immediately."

— 14 —

Mercury falling

Midnight.

When William Darling came to relieve his daughter's vigil at the lighthouse lantern, she did not hear him approach. Which was exceptional, but tonight the din of the storm hammering on the windows obliterated every other sound.

How strikingly different the chain of Farne Islands looked now from, say, on a calm day at low tide. You could be forgiven for thinking it was a different world.

Between the shore and Inner Farne was a stretch of sheltered, normally tranquil, water called the Fairway. Inner Farne, with its compact lighthouse, lay to the west of both the Wedums, inhabited by rats and rabbits, and the Noxes, the pair of islets which became one as the tide ebbed.

Further across were Gun Rock and Staple Island, one of the largest in the chain. To the north lay the Wamses, which Grace respected as a prime breeding ground of cormorants. East of them were the two Hawker rocks and Blue Caps. To the north-east, beyond Longstone, lay Knivestone, the Reef of Doom, which was normally – as now – submerged at high tide.

Grace was well acquainted with every islet in the four-mile span, having visited each of them in the coble so many times over the years. On tonight's shift, it had been difficult to make out any island beyond Longstone in any direction. She had mainly scoured the darkness to the east, following the beam of light as it revolved. Thankfully, her watch had passed without incident, which she relayed gladly to her father.

On lookout during gales in the past, they had often felt a sharpened sense of anticipation. If the dreaded wreck did not materialise and no lives were endangered or lost, the surge of relief was intense. But there were hours left in this night – they could take nothing for granted.

William had been concerned about the storm's ferocity for a while and now, as Friday 7 September began, it was still getting worse. He tapped the glass tube in the mercury barometer that was hooked to the side of a shelf. The atmospheric pressure had dropped rapidly – to a point as low as he could remember without perusing his records – and there was no force at all in the air to push the storm away. It was well set in.

He raised his voice to be heard over the clamouring rain. "I pray that every ship out there tonight is sufficiently maintained," he said. "The wind is savage, generating extremely large waves. It's still north-easterly, but that could change."

"What state is the floor in downstairs, Papa?" Grace asked. It sounded prosaic but she was thinking of Thomasina. "No serious damage?"

"Your mother blocked up the doorway more thoroughly than on our first attempt and we've soaked up a lot of the flood. It'll dry in the heat from the stove."

"Mama must be exhausted," Grace said. "Has she gone to bed?"

"Not yet."

Grace wished her father a good shift, said she hoped it would be as uneventful as hers, whatever his forebodings.

In her bedroom, she released her hair and shook it out of the bun. She lay fully clothed on her bed, trying to relax. Too many thoughts churned in her mind for her to feel remotely like sleep. She did not envy those at sea this night; it would not be pleasant for them or the loved ones awaiting their return.

The gale spat water on to her bedroom window and she sensed, not for the first time, that the lighthouse tower was swaying. Just a little, perhaps, but it was alarming. Around the tower, a whirlwind seethed.

She picked her telescope from the shelf it shared with a curvy piece of driftwood and a variety of limpets. She extended it, fine-tuned the focus.

She could see precious little, but after her shift upstairs her sight was accustomed to the darkness and the rain. She trained her eye across the thrashing waves to the segment with the rocks of Blue Caps, Clove Car, Little Hawker and – fatefully – Big Hawker. This view would typically encompass animals, in both sea and sky. It flashed through her mind that at this moment, in this storm, there was not a single one and her world looked more offbeat than ever.

First impact

St. Abb's Head.

The name of the promontory on the east coast of Scotland where the coastline turns in towards the Firth of Forth. Legend has it that the name derives from a princess of the kingdom of Northumbria, Ebba, who was shipwrecked there. She later became abbess of a nearby nunnery. There are many cultural myths like that – I seem to come across them all the time.

Formed of volcanic rock, St. Abb's Head was a nesting place for thousands of guillemots and razorbills, and it had a signal station – not yet a lighthouse – established by Trinity House in 1820. The settlement on the head – the Berwickshire village of St. Abb's – lay fifteen miles north of Berwick-upon-Tweed. Further north still were the cities of Edinburgh; St. Andrews, home of Scotland's first university; and a dozen more miles up the coast, Dundee.

It was off St. Abb's Head, shortly after midnight on Friday morning, 7 September, that the *Forfarshire*'s sails were raised on both masts. Captain Humble issued the instruction after his last conversation with Allan Stewart, of which he had entered a verbatim note in his logbook. It had been some months since the sails were used, but the crewmen managed the task adeptly, despite the rain flogging their heads and backs.

Perhaps they were comforted by the knowledge that an official lifeboat station had opened in Berwick a couple of years ago, should they need its assistance. In any event, her engine powerless, the *Forfarshire* was surfing at the mercy of the waves.

As her bow was buried under an intimidating deluge, a young crew hand, Nathan Ephgrave, became convinced that the ship was about to cartwheel. He rushed to the portside railings and vomited, then returned to help his drenched colleagues, whose thin clothes had turned to rags, as hand over hand they hauled and knotted the sails in position. An excellent sportsman, Nat was a well organised team player, popular among the crew.

James Duncan joined Captain Humble for a brief foray on deck. Each man wore an overcoat and carried a lantern which cast barely any light through the darkness and downpour.

The trapezium-shaped white sails had been raised correctly from the horizontal spars or yards on which they rested. The yards were mounted perpendicular to the two masts, to allow the sails the maximum free movement in the prevailing wind. This format of rigging had endured for many years on the ocean-going sailing ships now being superseded by steamers.

Even while signing his approbation to the crewmen, Humble doubted that any of them could see it. When he returned below deck, he was struck by how much water had accumulated inside the *Forfarshire*, making the stairwells, passageways and many rooms slippery, if not flooded. He could not recall, in his entire career, a more vicious storm.

No one slept. The fearsome noise, deepening for hours, was more than enough to prevent rest. By far the worst aspect, though, was the now constant corkscrewing. Many steerage passengers, feeling disorientated, seasick, were huddled together on the benches in the low-ceilinged bow section, drawing as much warmth and comfort from each other as they could.

Sarah Dawson was in the group with one child under each arm, near to Reverend Robb and James Kelly, the Dundee-bound weaver. On his own initiative, he had found a woollen blanket, which was now draped around Matilda's shivering shoulders.

Sarah regretted her uncharacteristic impetuosity in boarding the *Forfarshire* despite her husband being delayed. But the captain's words on the quayside had reassured her and she had wanted to get the children home to Dundee as planned and not have to fork out for another night in Hull.

Further aft, the twenty passengers with cabin tickets were all in their beds, many of them, Annie Humble included, gripping the bedframes as something stable in their quaking, nightmarish world.

In the engine room, Captain Humble checked on the coal trimmers and firemen, who were practically zombies, dead on their feet, strapping up their scalded hands. He thanked them for their valiant efforts and promised to commend their work to the company when the *Forfarshire* docked in Dundee. Swirls of hot steam lingered, and he had to clear his throat twice, but at least the clanking and hissing of the engine had ceased.

"We won't be docking in Dundee any time soon, sir," said an accented voice behind him, at the entrance to the engine room.

Humble recognised the lilting brogue. He turned, clapped eyes on Daniel Donovan.

"Mr Donovan, I–"

"Captain," said Donovan, raising both hands in surrender, "I'm speaking more in sorrow than in anger. All that matters is finding a solution to the awful predicament in which we find ourselves."

"Mr Donovan, I–"

"Captain, what I mean to say is that we're making no headway with the sails up. None. The wind is too strong. The ship's rudder hasn't any purchase in these waters."

"Mr Donovan, thank you," Humble said, trying to sound patient not patronising. He still did not want an argument with this charismatic maverick of a man in front of his crew – especially when what he was saying was palpably, and so regrettably, true.

Donovan bowed his head in a conciliatory manner. "Well, thank you too, sir, and good luck."

With that, he left the engine room. What a relief! John Nicholson, one of the firemen, uttered something inaudible which he did not repeat.

The *Forfarshire* lurched wildly as another giant wave broadsided her. She levelled off, then pitched steeply forwards as the next incoming wall of water cascaded on to the bow. From somewhere above, a woman's scream pierced the ears of everyone in the engine room.

Allan Stewart entered, white hair plastered to his head, blue eyes sunken in their sockets.

"Sorry to say that the ship is drifting south, sir."

"What!" gasped one of the crew as the gravity of this news registered.

"We are literally being forced back to where we've come from. She's not responding to the guidance of the helm."

Humble led Stewart up to the bridge, where his helmsman, David Grant, was wrestling with the eight-spoked wooden wheel that steered the rudder. They saw first-hand that the *Forfarshire*, with no engine to drive the paddles and despite having both sets of sails up, was facing south and ignoring every turn of the wheel. The storm had full control of her direction, her destiny.

Humble marched on to the promenade deck. Welcome streaks of moonlight had, at least temporarily, tempered the black night to a dark grey. He held a hand into the wind, and checked the alignment of the sails, both of which flapped as if possessed by murderous spirits.

"I fear the wind direction has changed," he said to Stewart when they'd returned to the bridge. "It has shifted further to the north. However unmanageable the ship, we must prevent her from being blown aground."

His voice was calm yet underpinned by desperation. He could feel his heart thumping.

"Aye, sir. Surely we must seek shelter?"

"Our location is close to Berwick, but as you said, we're being driven south at a rate of knots. We must…"

Humble was thinking quickly. Besides Annie and him, there were sixty-one people on board and the responsibility he bore for their safety sharpened his mind. The risk he was contemplating was appalling, he was loathed to carry it out, but he was in charge, he was out of options, and he could not do nothing.

"We must make it to the lee of the Farne Islands." Humble spoke decisively. "There's a basin of sheltered water between the shore and Inner Farne." He recalled the small details of his sea chart. "It's named the Fairway. We'll drop anchor there and stay safe for as long as needed."

Allan Stewart admired the master's clarity and resilience, despite the pressure on his shoulders. They had worked closely together for almost a year, built a strong relationship. He was not a man given to impetuosity. But now Stewart detected a queasy vulnerability that he had not witnessed before. Racing through the geography of the area in his own frazzled mind, he was certain they had no better option, while accepting that the outcome of the impending manoeuvre was horribly uncertain.

"Very good, sir. I'll relieve the helmsman with fresher hands, and post two men on lookout."

"Splendid," Humble managed. "Keep me posted, whatever the hour."

Most of his words were swallowed in a dry cough. But with his decision made and shared, he felt much relieved. Neither man asked aloud what they would do if this emergency plan failed.

When his chief engineer departed, Humble returned to his cabin. He kissed Annie, who looked no better, and gently rubbed her back. Then he lay down on his bed and closed his eyes, but now the unpredictable motion of the ship made his head spin.

He must have dozed off because the next thing he knew was a knock on the door. He tried to answer it quickly so that Annie was not disturbed. In swinging himself off the bed, one of his brass buttons snagged on the frame and rolled like a farthing across the floor.

At the door was James Duncan, bringing news that the lookouts thought they had sighted a beam from the Inner Farne lighthouse.

"I'll be at the helm in a moment, thank you, James." A beat. "The lookouts have done their job, that's excellent. They can be redeployed, I know they'll be useful elsewhere."

Urgently, he straightened his clothes and checked on dear Annie, whose eyes were closed. He still hoped to find a moment to give her the locket, even if it would not be at all as he had planned.

David Grant was struggling with the wheel when Captain Humble walked on to the bridge a few minutes later. It was almost three o'clock on Friday morning. James Duncan and John Matson were there, running on pure adrenaline. Matson was assisting Grant to steer while the *Forfarshire* was blown southwards. No adjustment to the sails had made a difference; the crew still had virtually no control over her heading.

"I reckon this storm has further intensified," Humble ruminated incredulously, kneading his forehead.

Duncan produced a chart of the Farne Islands, which he offered to Humble as they fast approached the notorious chain. Humble was irritated that the small type-set text swam before his eyes and he was thankful that Annie was not there to notice his myopia. He waved the chart away, advising Duncan that he had already checked his own and did not need another.

"Do we have a man at the windlass?" Humble asked quickly. Just in case you're unsure – the windlass is a large winch, whose handle was installed in the forward area of the promenade deck. Via its crank mechanism, the ship's anchor chain was raised and lowered.

"Aye, sir," Duncan confirmed.

"As far as possible, maintain our present course towards the light beam. We'll drop anchor as soon as we're in the Fairway, with Inner Farne on our port side."

Notwithstanding the strength of the pelting rain, the *Forfarshire* continued her wind-blown passage south, as the captain had anticipated. The revolving light was getting ever closer.

Suddenly a shard of doubt stabbed Captain Humble. He recoiled physically from the impact.

"Sir?" John Matson was shocked to see the panic contort Humble's face.

The light towards which they were speeding looked considerably higher in the sky than the beam cast by the Inner Farne station which he had been expecting. It appeared brighter, too. Strangely, unforgivably, he had not questioned the lookouts' assertion regarding the light they had identified, or their degree of certainty.

Now it was too late – they had gone, assigned to other tasks.

Had he assumed too much of them, that they were as familiar with the islands as he was? Was it just too dark and foggy to see anything clearly? Had he been distracted by the plans for his anniversary? Was his apparently fading eyesight troubling him more than he'd admitted, even to himself? Had his fatigue and the stress of their situation got the better of him – and the lookouts – after all? His desolate thoughts went round in circles.

"My God–"

Staring ahead, Humble now knew for sure that what the lookouts had sighted was the taller light shining from Longstone. He could see what was going to happen, he could do nothing to prevent it.

The realisation sickened him; his blood ran cold. He had accepted the call that the light was on Inner Farne, which lay three-plus miles nearer to the coast. Although they could hardly have known their exact position, it was the most catastrophic error. The *Forfarshire* was being blown, powerless, on to the treacherous Outer Farnes, a renowned graveyard for ships. Devastation.

Without warning, a hideous *crunch* filled the air, obliterating even the shrieks of the storm. It went on for an eternity. The *Forfarshire* jolted to a stop, shaking from side to side.

Everything, everyone was hurled forwards. On the bridge, only Captain Humble managed to stay on his feet. The groans and cries from the others were mostly chopped away by the storm. A huge wave battered the stricken steamer from behind, a torrent of spray shot skywards. Her timbers creaked again as the forward mast toppled over, smashing through the side railings down to the black rock against which the ship had been dashed.

"My God," Humble murmured. "We are all doomed."

— 16 —

Spotting the stricken ship

The witching hour, 3 a.m., when the darkness was at its deepest.

Grace stood very still. Her racing pulse seemed to intensify her senses, her powers of concentration. She polished the telescope lens and tried again to refine the focus, but her existing view through the foul night was as good as it was going to get.

She took another long, hard look. Suddenly a hint of moonlight penetrated the darkness, creating vague shadows where earlier none had lived. Black shapes were moving. She strained her eyes. Could it be…? Or in this storm, perhaps…? No, she was certain.

Replacing the telescope on its shelf, in her haste she knocked a small shell to the floor. She ran upstairs to the lantern, where the frenzied reverberations of the wind and rain persisted.

Her mother had joined her father on his east-facing vigil. As was their wont, they were sitting alongside each other in the wicker chairs, holding hands. Grace thought for a split-second whether she should leave them undisturbed but knew that she could not do so.

"Papa," she said from behind them. Neither had heard Grace's footsteps and they twisted round in unison.

"Can't you sleep, angel?" Thomasina asked, her mop hat sitting low on her forehead. She stifled a yawn but would not catch up on lost sleep any time soon.

"I've been watching the area to the south-west," Grace told them in such a rush that it made her breathless. "It's just a few hundred yards across open water to Big Hawker. I swear, there's a huge black – I'm sure it's black – shape that's just appeared. It's not a rock – I know them all so well – and it's far too big to be storm debris. It's a ship, a stricken ship, I know it is."

"All right, angel," Thomasina soothed.

William stood, rubbed his cheeks, checked the last entry in his logbook and skirted the lantern until he faced south-west. "Show me."

Grace and Thomasina finished a brief conversation about the state of the flood. Thomasina had wiped the floor with a solution of salt and lemon, mopping up with stale bread as well as absorbent cloths. What she did not know was that, while they had been at the lantern, some of their rolled-up rugs had fallen over into the saltwater and would be stained forever.

At this point, I imagine William's telescope trained steadily on the two Hawker rocks.

"My God," he said, almost a whisper. "I believe you're right. There is a ship. Yes, one ship, a large paddle steamer. The funnel, the wheel casing, the bridge, all quite prominent."

What must be happening on that rock, Thomasina thought with a shudder. Was it the storm, a collision, a navigation blunder, mechanical failure, what could have caused this? The poor people caught up in it, they'll be terrified out of their wits.

Grace's response was immediate. "How can I help? We must take the coble–"

"Absolutely not," William cut her off. Away from them, the relief spread like sunshine on Thomasina's face. "Out of the question. It would be suicidal to row out in these conditions."

He peered out. "A mist is rolling in on top of everything else, so visibility will be worse than ever."

"Then what can we do? We–"

"Wait until first light." William held up his palms to quell further protest. "It's only a few hours. Then we'll have a better view and we can make a proper assessment. At the moment, no rescue attempt could possibly be launched from North Sunderland. Or Bamburgh, either. In these conditions, there's no prospect of getting to the rock and it would mean even more lives put at risk."

Grace accepted her father's judgement. She had always relied on his counsel, he was her guiding light, he had never let her down.

"Well done for sighting the ship, though," William added. "I don't know whether I'd have seen it without you. I'll start a new entry in the log. Now, please, try to get some rest. We'll re-group at dawn."

Grace said goodnight for a second time. Her heart was still pounding as she returned to her bedroom.

Up at the lantern, Thomasina had listened to their conversation. She knew that Grace would press William to take the coble out in a few hours – and that she could be highly persuasive.

When Thomasina was born, in 1774, she had a twin sister for a matter of minutes before she died at birth. Her mother, whose name was Grace, was going to call this twin Grace, and Thomasina had longed to use the name for a daughter of her own. Of course, all her children – she had borne two sets of twins herself – and the wider family knew that her own twin, Grace, had not survived childbirth, but it was seldom mentioned.

Grace Darling was very precious to Thomasina and William, who loved her deeply. Now, as William kept his eye trained on the unfolding calamity on Big Hawker, Thomasina's stomach felt like an ice block and her brow was riven with worry. Oh, please be careful, my angel.

A loud boom cut through the storm. It seemed to echo in the heavy air until a second detonation followed sixty seconds later. Thomasina realised what it was – and she knew the ground around the gun would be shaking enough to spill a drink. The coastguard system at Bamburgh Castle was still working as planned for ships in distress. This was the nine-pounder being discharged from the timeworn ramparts.

17

Second impact

Chaos reigned.

But the night's horrors were not played out yet, not by a long chalk. A white fog enveloped the shattered *Forfarshire*, lending the scene a ghostly pallor.

The impact of the crash had caused the troublesome starboard boiler to rupture and one of its thick metal plates had slipped to forty-five degrees. Water gushed out, still warm despite the boilers being off for hours.

At the same time, seawater cascaded into the hull through a gaping hole left where one of the paddle axels had snapped.

In the dining saloon, a steward swept fragments of smashed crockery into the corner, not suspecting what was about to happen to the ship. To be fair to him, I don't believe anyone did.

The twenty stunned cabin passengers were regaining their bearings. On her knees, Evelyn Martin scurried to pick up the gold sovereigns spilled from her upended valise. She stashed handfuls in her pockets so that the case was not so heavy.

Glen Ritchie, who had found an open bottle of Rémy Martin before retiring to bed, was wiping blood from his forehead where it had collided with the corner of a table. He gathered up his clothes – there didn't seem to be any blood stains on his shirt, that was something. Now, for goodness' sake, where had he left his trousers?

Alice Rentoul was holding her mother's hand, trying to reassure the old lady that they would be fine. Help would soon arrive. A pool of milk, speckled with broken glass, flowed close to her feet, but she kicked the glass under the bed and ignored it.

Similarly, Arthur Ellison was at his son's side, stroking his hair, vowing that they would never be separated. That was all young Albert wanted to hear.

On the covered benches in the forward section, Sarah Dawson hugged James and Matilda so tightly that they both complained and wriggled free. Matilda used her towel as a pillow on her mother's knee.

Having chanted a short prayer, Reverend Robb tended to those closest to him. Notwithstanding the extreme cold, his brow was drenched in sweat. As Captain Humble had observed, he'd been feverish even when he embarked in Hull.

On the bridge, James Duncan was holding his map of the Farnes, now torn almost in half. He let it fall from his fingers.

"We'd been blown miles off your presumed course, sir." His voice was sour. "That light is beaming from the outer, not the inner, Farnes." The most terrible miscalculation. "I think it's Big Hawker that we've struck. Do you want to weigh anchor, or…?"

He did not complete his question. Cap missing, hair dishevelled, John Humble was fleeing from the bridge, desperate to be with his wife.

"Ring the ship's bell!" he screamed as he departed. "Everyone on deck!"

On his way, Humble paused at the storage compartment, unlocked the door. The pungent swill of wines and other substances on the floor revolted him. He grabbed handfuls of dry bandages and left them outside in the passageway for those in need to help themselves. Every few paces he yelled until he was hoarse: "Emergency! Everyone on deck! Pass it on – everybody out!"

As Humble approached his cabin, he heard a scream followed by a heavy splash as a plunging body hit the freezing sea. My God, he thought. The initial shock of entering water like this would trigger extremely rapid breathing, after which a person would survive for minutes only before the body started to shut down.

He burst through the cabin door. It was dark. In bed, Annie was weeping, head in her hands, a shattered glass jug and two ripped paintings strewn across the floor. One of the wardrobe doors hung loosely by a single hinge. Saying nothing, he hugged her tight, and she let him rock her from side to side.

Matilda Dawson, having dropped her pillow, wandered among the steerage passengers, sucking her thumb. She was curious. Many people were in a daze or crying. What had happened to the ship? At least now, after that big, scary jolt, it was at a standstill. There was less engine noise, but a bell had started to clang – repeatedly. What did it mean? Ignoring her mother's pleas for her to come back, Matilda headed for the corridor where she saw a man walking about, wearing a white tunic with shiny brass buttons.

The man was Jonathan Tickett, chief cook on the *Forfarshire*. Raised in Hull, he had worked in kitchens for most of his life, latterly as the head cook at Darnley Hall, home of the gregarious Lord and Lady Darnley. He enjoyed planning menus and took pride in the flavours and presentation of his dishes. His speciality was fish.

Although no food was served last night, he remained in the kitchen to fulfil requests from passengers or his crew colleagues. He mixed the ingredients of a small cake for which the captain had put in a special request. He shuddered to think how much of the ship's bespoke crockery had been smashed in the storm.

Late evening, two passengers, a man and a woman, with spotless fingernails had come to him with a proposition. There must be a good deal more food left unused at the end of this journey than usual, they suggested. When he concurred, they offered to take the unused stock off his hands at the quayside in Dundee, selling it on their local market stall and cutting him in on the proceeds.

He had said he would think about it and was searching for the couple when the ship struck Big Hawker. He'd banged the back of his skull on a door leading to the crew berths and felt dizzy. He was walking gingerly back to the galley when he heard tiny footsteps behind him.

From overhead came a babble of voices, shouting urgently on top of each other. As soon as John Humble had left the bridge, leaving few immediate instructions, James Duncan assumed control – not of the ship, but of his own and his crewmates' predicament, which he deemed at that moment to be the more important consideration.

He and John Matson rounded up half a dozen colleagues and together, four on each side, they unfastened the front starboard quarter-boat and lowered it from its davits. One of the group, Alex Murray, was shivering uncontrollably and in the pale light of a lantern strung up lopsidedly on the rigging, his lips had turned blue.

"Come on, lad!" Allan Stewart roared, sounding his most ferocious.

Alex smiled thinly in gratitude for the encouragement but could not prevent the chattering of his teeth.

The quarter-boat splashed down on shallow water at the starboard side of the *Forfarshire*, hard rock below it. Despite their concentration, the men hardly heard the splash as the wind howled. By now it must have been gusting around sixty knots – violent storm force plus.

Every one of them doubted that they would be safer in a small wooden boat than staying on board the stricken *Forfarshire*. But James Duncan's insistence that they act as a team and set an example had been galvanising, and in the moment their adrenaline vanquished their scepticism and fatigue.

Ginger Turnbull ran past, clutching his right forearm, moaning in agony. Stewart knew that the young fireman had broken his ulna or radius, perhaps both. A stub of bone appeared to protrude through his skin. He called out for Ginger to join them, but he seemed not to hear and darted off. I'm afraid Stewart would never see him again.

The bell clanged, a death knell as much as a warning. Was someone ringing it or was it the wind?

"Nat!" John Matson barked as he saw young Nathan Ephgrave. He'd always liked the kid, plenty of potential.

"Release one of the other quarter-boats – get as many people in as you can – follow us!"

Nat tried gallantly to inspire a new group of crew and passengers. There were three other quarter-boats on their davits. But his organisational skills seemed to desert him as he struggled to persuade anyone in the panic. A ghastly shame.

James Duncan's group of eight – John Matson, Allan Stewart, Alex Murray, Jas Hall, Rob Fox, David Grant, James Hill – clambered into their quarter-boat while he held its rope as tight as he could. They sat on the three bench-seats, three apiece in the bow and stern, two in the centre. Those two men reached for the oars to attach them at the oarlocks.

Duncan himself was the last man in. Through the murk, he looked up at the black flank of the *Forfarshire*, vanishing into the sky. A row of scared faces peered down from the promenade deck. They were waiting to be told what to do.

"We've space for one more!" he bellowed. "One of you come down, quickly!"

Thomas Woodrow, the Yorkshire tea merchant, grabbed his case and made for the stairwell.

"Come on, hurry!"

Woodrow got as close as he could to the water level and eased one leg over the railing. With one hand he reached for James Duncan, whose right arm inched towards him.

As their fingertips were about to lock, a figure leapt high from the edge of the *Forfarshire*, having taken a running jump and knocked Thomas Woodrow's case into the sea. After what seemed an eternity in mid-air, he landed in the centre of the quarter-boat and rolled sideways. Rob Fox and David Grant lost their balance and fell over inside the boat, which rocked frantically and felt on the verge of capsizing when Allan Stewart steadied her with the oars.

The jumper pushed himself up in the floor of the quarter-boat. His shirt was unbuttoned and his trousers hung loose, unbelted, below the waist. He tried to fasten them; his fingers were numb.

He thanked the crewmen for the place but studiously avoided eye contact with the hapless Thomas Woodrow, now stranded on deck having never gripped James Duncan's hand.

Without any of them having to pull an oar, the quarter-boat was captured by a forceful tidal current. In seconds, it had vanished from sight of the *Forfarshire*. As if possessed by an invisible power, it was whisked northwards through the channel of water called Piper Gut, away from the Hawker and Wamses rocks. Before the nine men knew it, they were miraculously floating in the North Sea.

Far too late, another man swept past Thomas Woodrow with a blood-curdling scream. He jumped, arms flailing, aiming for the departing quarter-boat. But the gap between it and the side of the ship was already far too wide and, in his haste, he misjudged the space. With a large splash, he landed on his back in the sea and sank below the surface. The undercurrents muscled in. His clenched fists were the last parts of him ever seen.

Woodrow peered into the water – was his case within reach? – but he soon concluded that it had been swallowed up. He retreated, cursing, vowing to secure a place on the next quarter-boat. Nat Ephgrave, however, was nowhere to be found.

In the captain's cabin at the rear, John Humble was shaking. He would return to the bridge, of course he would, his job was in his blood. He had not abandoned his post but, at that moment, he could not bear to reflect on what had happened on his watch. After the crash, his over-riding concern was for his family and, above all, his sick wife. While staring disaster in the face, he knew he wanted – needed – most of all to declare his undying love to Annie. He had taken the locket out of the blue velvet box and straightened the ribbon.

He was sitting on her bed, holding her hand, when the *Forfarshire* shuddered to her core. Her timbers creaked louder than he would have thought possible.

"What on Earth–?"

Annie sat up, pale, groggy. It was the inner pain, reflected in her eyes, that most devastated him.

Less than five minutes after the crash, the *Forfarshire* was afloat again, free from the Hawker rock. A massive incoming wave was enough to lift her clear, even though she was letting in water and losing her buoyancy. With one mast down, the remaining sails flapped desperately in the gale as they took the full strain of the vessel. But no one was at the helm and another towering wave, more forceful than the last, rolled in, hurling white foam in every direction.

James Kelly's hand came down on Matilda Dawson's shoulder. He had followed her out of the steerage area and tracked her down the corridor, where she was walking alongside Jonathan Tickett.

"Come on, Matilda, quickly, please!" he called. "I'm James. Let's get back to your mother. She's waiting for you with your brother. His name is James, too, isn't it?"

The five-year-old looked up at this man – she recognised his kind face from the benches, where he had brought her a towel – and she accepted his hand. It felt coarse and calloused, like her own father's hands. She said farewell to the man with the brass buttons, who ruffled her blond curls and walked off. He seemed to be searching for someone or something.

She was walking hand in hand with James Kelly to rejoin her mother and brother when a second huge crash knocked them clean off their feet. Kelly held out his right hand to break his fall. A breath later, he was sprawled on the floor, nursing his wrist. He had lost sight of the child.

Everyone on board absorbed the tremendous blow. All at once: more crying, more shouting, more trepidation, more terrified screams.

No sooner was the *Forfarshire* free of Big Hawker than she was dashed, bow first, on the rock again.

Within seconds of this latest, much harder, impact, the *Forfarshire* began to split in two. The fore section remained, stuck fast, on Big Hawker. But the ship's back was broken.

The entire aft section, including the engine, funnel and paddles, was ripped away as though it were made of cardboard.

It slipped backwards into the convulsing sea, becoming for a moment a separate vessel. But instead of floating, it continued to slide backwards, descending below the surface.

The water had not swallowed the whole of the section before the wind bit into it and spat pieces across the sea and the rock. The surface of the water boiled. Jets of steam hissed upwards, debris began to litter the waves. The destruction of the ship, which took less than a minute, seemed to happen without sound as the gale devoured all noises but its own.

The few passengers on deck, clinging, frozen, to the bow-end railings, were stunned by what they had seen. Some screamed, others wept. I can't imagine anyone who lived ever forgetting the disaster and loss of life they witnessed. A handful of people emerged and tried to swim but they were quickly sucked back under.

Shockingly, from the aft section came not a single survivor.

The lost section included every one of the ship's cabins. John Humble was embracing his wife when his beloved *Forfarshire* cracked apart like two pieces of a giant egg. He heard the awful splintering but, even then, could hardly comprehend that his whole ship being torn asunder. The second pounding against Big Hawker was too much for her to bear. He closed his eyes.

With her new locket placed in her palm just moments earlier, Annie gazed at him, the red ribbon still draped around her fingers. His face was fixed in a strange, lifeless mask. Even more than the wrecking of the *Forfarshire*, it was this final image of her loyal, well-meaning husband that jabbed terror into her heart.

Then a wall of seawater invaded their cabin, seemingly crashing in from above and below at the same time. Annie was swept away, an arm outstretched to no avail. Her husband's tall boots, overflowing with water, weighed his legs down as if they were concrete. He was not moving as the sea filled the disintegrating cabin and claimed his life.

In the long passageway through which James Kelly led Matilda Dawson, what sounded like an explosion followed by the tearing of fabric and a blast of cold air drove everyone to bury their heads in their hands for protection. Having lost her footing, Matilda began to slide face down along the sloping passageway towards oblivion.

Within seconds, her legs were flailing over the torn edge of the ship's fore section, her torso and arms still inside. Her body was almost at tipping point. Another inch or two and she'd be gone.

Ignoring his throbbing wrist, James Kelly reached hard, caught Matilda's arm. Digging in with his fingers, he dragged her, inch by inch, desperation disfiguring his face. She squealed. And then her legs were back inside the wreck. She squealed again but he never let go. When he picked her up, she was bruised, shocked, soaked to the skin. Her left shoe was missing.

He carried her back to the steerage area, chanting: "It's all right, she made it! She's all right!"

Sarah sprang to her feet, pulled Matilda into her arms, rubbed her with the towel. They both burst into tears. Kelly stood in silence, breathing deeply with relief. Reverend Robb, looking increasingly frail, shook his hand and emitted a rasping cough.

The gold sovereigns that filled Evelyn Martin's pockets appeared to slow down her reactions. When the ceiling of her cabin cracked and split from the walls, she could not get to the door in time. When the entire ceiling caved in, her body was weighed down under the rampaging wall of water. Sadly, it never surfaced.

The stairwells on the *Forfarshire* had been crowded with crewmen and passengers, dozens of them, heeding the captain's last-minute call to go out on deck. As the stairwells buckled, they were all swept away.

Sarah Dawson wiped her eyes on her sleeve and thanked Kelly for bringing Matilda back to her. As vigorously as she and James rubbed Matilda, still she shook.

Reverend Robb had gasped out a prayer of petition for Matilda to be returned safely and he was intoning another prayer now, one of thanks. His voice got ever quieter: he had precious little energy left.

Daniel Donovan appeared at the entrance to the steerage area. There was Reverend Robb, Sarah Dawson and her children, James Kelly, Thomas Buchanan, and Douglas and Robert Houston, the cloth traders from Montrose. Johns Kidd and Nicholson had fortuitously dived for cover on those benches, too, just as the ship struck the rock for the second time.

Donovan looked around the group's discoloured, frightened faces. He had an open wound by his left eye, from which blood masked the side of his face, and both his lips were cut.

"Listen, everyone," he said thickly. "The aft section of the ship has gone. All of it, the engine, the cargo hold, everything. The captain's gone, too. There's only this bow section left standing."

Johnny Tulloch shuffled up, leaned against a wall alongside Donovan. Tulloch had been clinging to the windlass – the most secure fixture he could find – and saw first-hand the *Forfarshire*'s aft section shear off and sink. A crew member since her maiden voyage, the sight would haunt him forever.

"He's right," Tulloch said, supporting Donovan. "We're wedged on a rock, stuck hard and fast. I think it's the Hawker, the big'un, in the Farne Islands. In which case, it has a definite slope to the south, so it should offer a bit of shelter."

"We should all get down on to the rock, as fast as we can," Donovan continued. "There may be very little time. The next big wave that comes along might… well, it could…"

A sudden violent movement in the position of the wreck was all the convincing the group needed to scramble off the benches. They wrapped coats, blankets, whatever they could find, around their bodies and went up on deck. It was still raining heavily, and huge waves broke over them with unrelenting ferocity. The sheets of water felt as hard as they were cold.

Jonathan Tickett was already on deck, clinging to the railings above the bow. His white tunic was ripped, several buttons missing. He had never found the two passengers who put their proposition to him last evening. He was petrified of the same fate as must have befallen them, and at that moment he was not capable of moving.

Further along, two other passengers, one of whom he knew to be named David Churchill, were also gripping the railings, awaiting their fate, their knuckles and faces as white as bones.

Douglas Houston stopped abruptly on the stairwell and signalled to his brother, three steps behind, to turn around. Douglas felt sure he had heard a cry for help. Yes, there it was again. Out of the two of them, born just over a year apart but with such different personalities, he was always the one to lend a hand, go the extra mile.

Back in the passageway, Douglas and Robert groped their way towards the source of the cries. They each kept a hand on the wall to steady themselves as they made for the gaping end of the passageway.

Robert tapped his brother's back, pointed ahead. It was then that Douglas saw the two sets of fingers, bone-white and shaky, grasping the shattered edge.

The brothers leaned over what seemed like a precipice with the wild sea below – and saw the top of a man's head. He was hanging on for dear life, but his strength was deserting him. They recognised him as Alistair Bell, one of the staff on Lord Kinnoull's estate – they had chatted to him on the quayside at Hull while his luggage was loaded. His left eye was blood-shot. As he looked up, the brothers knew that he was in a lot of pain.

"We've got you!" Douglas called out, dropping to his knees and extending an arm. Robert stood behind him and locked his hands around Douglas's chest, trying to support his centre of gravity.

"My right knee is busted," Bell yelped in agony.

At that moment, the wreck jerked backwards on the rock. It was a small movement – the remains were pinned to the island's surface. Yet it was forceful enough to unbalance the brothers. Both men toppled as one, head over heels, into the abyss, Robert involuntarily giving a glancing blow to Alistair Bell on his way down. Bell screamed as his fingers lost their purchase on the torn floorboards and he too plummeted into the sea.

Within seconds, their lungs flooded and their airways seized up. All three had a sense of their bodies getting heavier before they lost consciousness completely.

Johnny Tulloch and Daniel Donovan were down on Big Hawker. The wet rock was as slippery as ice but, as Johnny had told the passengers, it did slope to the south and would offer some refuge during the rest of this dreadful night.

"Get some rope!" Johnny yelled up to the deck. "Tie it to the railings, it'll help you get down here."

John Kidd went to find a length of rope, which did not take long.

Sarah Dawson was still rubbing some life into Matilda, who had not stopped shaking and could not talk. James Kelly was flexing his sore wrist.

"Can you help, please?"

The speaker was Sean Macqueen, one of the coal trimmers, who had appeared on deck. He had his arm around the distressingly rag-and-bones form of Reverend Robb. Thomas Buchanan, who was nearest, rushed over and helped to prop the reverend upright.

"The good clergyman needed a bit of support on the stairs, that's all," wheezed Macqueen. "I was checking below deck – we don't want anyone left behind."

Buchanan realised that Macqueen needed attention himself. Both of his hands were swathed in bandages and he had another knotted around his forehead. All of them were soaked in seawater and blood. He had a few days' stubble below his bleeding nose and his eyes were dark and puffy.

"I've got him," Buchanan promised. "You can let go, you've done more than your share."

Gratefully, Macqueen part-sat, part-collapsed on deck and tried to inhale some strength back into his aching limbs.

Acting as a crutch, Buchanan manoeuvred the reverend to the railings. Robb did his best not to wince, but Buchanan realised that every step was causing him more pain. "Are you able to use the rope to climb down?" he asked. "If you can make a start, there are people on the rock who'll help you with the last part. How about it?"

One by one, as a few yellow-billed kittiwakes circled inquiringly overhead, the survivors picked their way off the smashed remains of the *Forfarshire* and on to the glossy black terrain of the Big Hawker rock.

18

The vicious sea

Daybreak.

"Are you quite sure about this?"

Thomasina did not wait for an answer. Her husband had pulled off many rescues, some of the most audacious, reputedly, when he had been assisting his own father years ago. He had never suffered a serious injury as long as she'd known him, while saving scores – no, make that hundreds – of lives.

But he was a man who lived in the moment. He did not dwell on the past and was determinedly unassuming about his track record as keeper. One failed rescue and his copy book was blotted, he would tell himself. Yet he assessed risks shrewdly, from a position of formidable experience. He'd already have computed a flurry of 'what if…?' scenarios. She would trust him with her life.

But now, Thomasina knew, she was going to trust him with her daughter's life. Grace's life. Grace was determined to accompany William on the rescue attempt and there was no point even trying to dissuade her, especially when the matter was as urgent as this.

As Thomasina looked admiringly yet nervously at the strong, capable, twenty-two-year-old woman standing before her, pulling a large cap belonging to one of her brothers over her hair, she saw her all over again as the red-faced newborn she'd cradled in her arms at her father Job's cottage in Bamburgh, a thickness of reddish-brown hair already making her scalp resemble a brush. Whenever Grace the toddler had stumbled, walking on the uneven rocks of Brownsman and cut or bruised her knees, she had needed not a jot of encouragement to stand up. All her life, her resilience had shone through.

And yet…

There was something about this rescue outing that petrified Thomasina. Grace knew the islands and the tides practically as well as her father, and there was plenty of daylight oozing into the livid sky. Thank heavens that dreadful night was over, but the on-going storm was so vicious that Thomasina could not shake off the sickening feeling that it carried a sting in its tail.

While she busied herself at the stove, brewing coffee, William fastened on his warmest overcoat and wrapped a woollen scarf around his neck as many times as it would go.

"We'll take the safest possible option," he promised when Thomasina handed him his sweetened coffee. "Thank you, that's perfect. We won't go by the most direct route – I don't think we'd make it – and I'm still sure that no boats can get through from Bamburgh or North Sunderland, they'd be heading straight into the wind."

He swallowed some coffee, as hot as he could bear, feeling it gouge a channel deep into his body. "We'll go the long way round and approach from the south, so that Clove Car and the Hawkers shield us from the brunt of the storm. It's the worst we've had for years, isn't it?" he levelled with her. "But it's our duty, pure and simple. Grace is adamant that she can cope, and I would feel wretched if we stayed here without trying."

Thomasina came close. "I know you would, my love, and I'd never want that." She hugged him. "But bring her back to me, please."

He stood back, looked her in the eyes. "I shall," he said, thumbing a tear from her cheek, but keeping to himself just how dangerous he knew their impending attempt to be.

A lump in her throat, Thomasina hugged Grace, who had put on her thickest cardigan and a shawl. She had also taken a green-and-white blanket from her bed and tied it around her waist.

Grace swallowed the last of her coffee and grabbed the coil of rope they had brought in the previous evening.

"Come on, Papa!" she urged.

"I'm with you," he said, and sure enough, there he was at her side. His heart was warmed by a flare of pride: she represented the third generation of his family to protect lives at sea. He said a silent prayer.

As Grace opened the door, a blast of wind slammed it back on its hinges. Her cap flew off. William picked it up, dusted it down, handed it back.

"We must get to them," Grace said. She blew her teary mother a farewell kiss and stepped out of the lighthouse, followed by her father.

Neither of them had been able to tear themselves away from their telescopes at the lighthouse windows since their 3 a.m. conference in the lantern room.

By 6 a.m., Grace was sure there were three or four people walking about on the rock by the wreck, which had somehow changed shape since it first ran on to Big Hawker. It was smaller now – had parts of the ship broken up? Or had her eyes deceived her in the darkness earlier?

William was unsure, due to its distance of several hundred yards from Longstone, how many people were there. He thought it might be more than four – and earnestly hoped so, given the apparent size and likely capacity of the wrecked vessel. What on Earth had happened to them all?

Leaning into the wind, he and Grace marched as if through treacle to the boatshed and untethered the coble. Both were physically weary after the tense, sleepless night but, pumped full of adrenaline, they dragged the coble to the water's edge. Grace laid the rope inside, looping it around a pike.

At the lighthouse door, Thomasina watched them clamber into the little wooden boat, Grace first, and push off from the island. They sat amidships, Grace nearer the stern, William behind her, his back nearer the bow. Thomasina, the pit of her stomach still ice cold, watched him bellow instructions.

"Off you go, angel," Thomasina said to herself, lips quivering, "and God will go with you."

A loud boom travelled from Bamburgh Castle as the nine-pounder fired, scattering a flock of gulls. It was the starting gun for William and Grace's perilous journey.

Thomasina closed the big door. She went up to the lantern room to view their early progress but kept losing sight of them, due more to a succession of monstrous swells than the mist.

After a few upsetting minutes, she returned to the ground floor. She had seldom been in the lighthouse alone since it was built. She swept the ashes out of the oven, then scoured both the oven and the stove with her blacking brush. As well as cleaning the surfaces, this stopped them from going rusty. Ten minutes later, sitting at the oak table with scrubbed hands, she began to chop vegetables. She did not find these distractions dispelled the tangible sense of fear in the air.

At first, as William had instructed, they did not row at all. Rather, they let the coble drift southwards with the tide through Crawford's Gut. They used the oars to steer and warded the coble off the rocks with a pike when she was blown too close.

On the back of the tide, they ploughed through a churned-up slick of jellyfish, bobbing passively on the surface. Up close, William recognised them as the lion's mane variety. They pulled in their prey with underwater tentacles coated in minute stingers that could stick to human skin and inject venom on contact. Though seldom fatal, he knew from personal experience how painful those stings were.

"Keep your hands in!" he bawled to the back of Grace's head.

She nodded, but never let her concentration falter. Thankfully, neither of her parents had ever let slip that they wished one or more of her brothers had been present on Longstone that morning – no hint of it. What would Papa have told her? 'Comparisons with your brothers will ruin your happiness. You are you', or such like? They had accompanied William on many more rescues than Grace, but she was determined to make a virtue of necessity, reward his faith, prove herself to be every bit their equal.

Stay vigilant, Grace. The sea is unpredictable. Respect it, never let your guard down.

After turbulent minutes that seemed like hours, the coble was forced all the way through Crawford's Gut to the tiny islet of Blue Caps – the turning point on their mission. William tapped Grace's shoulder and they angled the oars against the sea to swing the coble to the right.

Now heading due west, with Blue Caps and Clove Car on their right, they started, one oar each, to row. They kept as close to the islands as they dared – and as the vicious sea would permit. A long way ahead – it was still hundreds of yards – lay the Hawker rocks. William was far from certain that they could make it.

A flight of migrating redwings, orange flanks adding highlights to their brown plumage, swooped and soared, seemingly pointing the way forward. Grace felt the strain of pulling the oar in her back and her shoulders. Almost as soon as they started rowing, the wind snatched away her cap, which this time could not be retrieved.

She thought she heard her father's voice ask whether she was all right, so she yelled "Yes!" and hoped that, if it carried, its meaning was clear.

The sea that she knew so well in all its moods and hues had become a monster, hostile to her. It grew angry heads in the form of tall waves which imploded, folding in on themselves, ejecting showers of spray into the driving rain, then giving rise to new heads, each more belligerent than the last. The spray darted into Grace's eyes. The more she tried to blink away the pain, the more tears rolled down her cheeks. She was pleased that Papa could not see her streaked face and red eyes.

"Pull!" William roared, "pull!"

He tried to focus Grace's mind on the regularity of her strokes and away from the heaving, pulling, shoving, sucking, twisting sea, which was doing its utmost to prevent them from reaching their destination, let alone returning from it.

Although it was a stretch of water with which the Darlings were extremely familiar, navigation in this storm was as difficult as William had ever known. Every minute they spent on this water prolonged the risk to life – their own included.

Their journey was far from a straight line through the water. The coble was buffeted from side to side and subjected to mountainous waves, even in the lee of the islands. Heads down, keep rowing, think of the survivors.

On one – mercifully, only one – occasion, as the coble tipped over the crest of a wave and down the other side, it all but capsized. Grace slipped from her seat and was rolling to her left when William grabbed her, pulled her upright. They were soaked, hair plastered to their scalps. Their fingers were so numb that it was an exacting task even to hold the oars, let alone drag them through the recalcitrant water.

As one wave broke over them, William got a mouthful of brine. He had swallowed some before he even knew it, but spat the rest out, choking and gasping to refill his screaming lungs. Grace heard him and held her oar in the water to slow the coble down until he had recovered.

"Thank you for taking control," he cried. She gave a quick thumbs-up.

Grace ignored her burning muscles and shut her eyes against further smacks of spray. She tried to keep her bottom still on her seat and to heave the oar in time to her father's chants. Her thoughts were with the shipwrecked souls they had seen through the telescopes. Had they survived the night? What injuries had they sustained? How many of them were there?

William turned his head to face their direction of travel. They were closer now – he was so impressed with the all-round strength that Grace had shown, matching him stroke for stroke – although the remaining distance was still enough to hollow them both out. They must have rowed the greater part of a mile. At least the tide was more favourable at this point, seemingly pulling with them as they neared Piper Gut.

There was what looked like debris from the wreck all around them – broken wood tossed about like matchsticks by the waves and wind. It was pitching up and down but not moving through the water, William observed. In a moment he saw the reason why. The debris was entangled in a field of floating seaweed and the coble was now mired in it, too. When William and Grace lifted the oars, ready for the next urgent stroke, they emerged draped in claggy green algae.

19

On Big Hawker rock

They were so bitterly cold that they could not envisage any other state.

Rather than three or four survivors, as Grace had estimated, twelve people had managed to climb off the wreckage of the *Forfarshire*. As best they could, they were taking refuge on Big Hawker.

Deluges of water crashed over them as wave after wave slammed into the rock and ricocheted off the stranded bow. They shivered, yawned, stamped their feet and mulled over disturbing thoughts of the dozens who had disappeared into the sea with the aft section of the ship. How many had perished? All of them? Could anyone who surfaced be recovered? What had become of the quarter-boat full of men, swept away by the tide?

Sarah Dawson sat with her back to the wreck, cradling her two children, who now seemed to be sleeping. Matilda was wrapped in her blanket, which over-reached her shoeless left foot.

Reverend Robb sat by the Dawsons, his weepy eyes shut. He took shallow breaths and inhaled a pinch of snuff. Two others, Thomas Buchanan and James Kelly, were hunched together, blowing into their cupped hands.

Four crewmen formed a circle – Tickett, Macqueen, Nicholson, Kidd – each nursing a wound of his own. The group was overseen by Johnny Tulloch and Daniel Donovan, who stood like mismatched shepherds watching newborn lambs.

Through the otherwise impenetrable rain, Tulloch and Donovan watched the revolving beams cast from the Longstone and, much further away, the Inner Farne lighthouses. They also heard periodically the boom of the nine-pounder at Bamburgh Castle. The next time it blasted, splitting the wind and the rain, Tulloch cried: "There's the Bamburgh gun – you heard it, everyone? It's the signal that our plight is known – they'll be on the lookout and will send help as soon as they can."

"Stay strong!" added Donovan, which I doubt helped much. None of them could envisage a rescue attempt amidst such a storm, and there was no sign of it blowing out.

"Can you hear me down there?"

Donovan was the first to react to the faint cry. He stared up at the wreck, saw nothing. When the cry was repeated, he homed in. Not a soul was on the promenade deck. But lower down, near the keel, at the jagged edge where the ship had been ripped apart, a man was waving both arms.

"I see you!" Donovan shouted through cupped hands. He looked first to the quartet of crewmen; no assistance was forthcoming. I'd have thought Donovan might feel slighted, humiliated – presumably this was the intention – but not a bit of it. Years ago, a favourite *aintín* – auntie – had warned that if he held on to the toxicity of a grudge, he would only harm himself, and he'd never forgotten her advice. In fact, his thick skin had served him lavishly. He knew full well that he was a chancer, he enjoyed the *craic*, and you needed a thick skin for that.

James Kelly stepped up, ever watchful, and grateful perhaps for the distraction and the call to exercise his frozen limbs. He picked a path over the slippery, debris-strewn rock to the open end of the wreck.

Donovan joined him. Together, with one hand under each of the newcomer's arms, they underpinned his faltering steps off the carcass. But the moment they let go, he slipped and lost his footing.

Kelly and Donovan lunged for him but succeeded only in tugging his sleeves. The man fell and landed hard on a pile of wooden blades which had formed sections of the starboard paddle, now shattered. He heaved himself up and inspected a fresh cut oozing blood from the full width of his palm.

"You all right?" Kelly asked, his arm around the man's shoulders. "Who are you?"

"I'm in one piece, yes, thank you for your help. My name's Wilfrid Baxter. I am – was – a passenger–"

"Is anyone else in there?" Donovan interrupted, abrasive. "Did you see anyone alive?"

Baxter shook his head. "I was down by the engine room. You see, I run a small foundry and enjoyed the opportunity at dinner – it seems ages ago – to discuss steam power with the captain…" His words tailed off as the likely fate of the captain struck him.

"And the wreck is deserted?"

"I – I think so. At least, I didn't see anyone moving."

The ruins of the *Forfarshire* creaked in the gale but held fast.

"Come and rest," urged James Kelly, leading Baxter to a smooth, knee-high ledge near to Reverend Robb.

"A boilerplate had come loose. It was right there in front of me. I used it as a shield when the ship broke up," Baxter explained, patting dust from his lapels. I'd say he had a bit of luck there: the plates for the furnace flues were nearly half an inch thick – heavy to lift but effective protection.

Kelly helped Baxter to sit on the ledge. He was jittery, wobbly.

Then, a towering wave walloped the side of Big Hawker. A wall of water surged forward, engulfed James Kelly, Wilfrid Baxter and Reverend Robb, and swept them off the rock into the sea. All three men disappeared. There were gasps from the others who, before their very eyes, saw them tugged away like puppets on strings.

Five seconds ticked by, seemed like five hours.

Kelly surfaced. He was screaming – at first, the others thought because he was injured, perhaps having smashed into a submerged rock. They soon realised that he was holding Reverend Robb. Kicking frantically, Kelly's left hand was across Robb's chest, his right was cupped under his chin, and he was battling to keep Robb's mouth closed and his head above water. His legs wouldn't support them both for long.

This time, the quartet of crewmen rushed to the water's edge. Macqueen fetched the rope they had used to descend from the ship and flung one end out to Kelly. His throw was accurate and Kelly plucked the rope out of thin air with one hand, emitting a roar of triumph and gratitude. The crewmen heaved them both on to the rock and helped them to their feet.

"I'm going to go back in, see if I can find what's his name, Baxter," Kelly gasped, scraping the water from his eyes.

It was then that Reverend Robb collapsed. He sank quietly to the ground, toppled to one side, lay still. Kelly scrambled to him, drops of water plopping from his nose and chin on to Robb's cheeks.

Robb half-opened his eyes and focused on Kelly.

"Thank you for saving me," he gasped. "You're a good man, a generous man. But I haven't been well for weeks, you see. I've been travelling around the country, in case the air suits me any better. But, well… I don't have much fight left."

Robb's complexion was ghostly pale, his entire body trembled. More like rattled, Kelly thought.

"Don't blame yourself if we don't all make it through this mortal danger," the reverend muttered, his voice faltering. "If any one of us survives, that's good, an important outcome. Now, please, look after the others. I'm in firm hands."

Robb's voice gave out completely. His breathing became very laboured and only guttural rasping escaped his throat. Kelly held his hand, freezing to the touch. He watched the eyelids flutter, then come to rest.

"God be with you, reverend," he said, relieved at least that Robb had died having accepted his fate.

Suddenly Kelly remembered Wilfrid Baxter. He looked urgently out to sea but there was no sign of him. Part of the ship's rigging floated by, with more slats from the paddlewheels, snarled in seaweed. High tide had apparently passed, but the sea still looked extremely full and disturbed.

"He's gone," said an Irish voice at his shoulder. Donovan was standing there, shivering, watching the heaving, toppling waves. "You did everything that could be done for the poor soul."

Donovan rubbed his hands, stamped his feet. "Besides, if I may say so, it's the lady over there who needs a big shoulder to cry on."

Kelly turned to Sarah Dawson, nearby, who was still cradling James and Matilda. Their faces were resting against her chest, their bodies motionless, although she stroked their backs and their hair and sang a bedtime verse under her breath.

"May I?" Kelly asked, sitting on the rock next to Matilda. A sickening feeling spread in his belly. Sarah said nothing but repeated her little song over and over.

Very slowly, Kelly reached across and put an arm around Matilda's body. As he had feared, she did not stir.

"Let me take her for a moment?"

As gently as he could, he prised Matilda away from her mother.

"That's it, come on, little one."

There was no life inside the body. None. It was too white, too stiff, grotesquely doll-like. He shut the eyes and brushed a lock of curly hair off the face.

Kelly had known someone die of exposure to the elements once before. A casual labourer, merely a teenager, who occasionally helped him repair a loom or deliver goods. He had been working on a nearby farm. Dicken, his name was. One March night, Dicken had slept outdoors, perhaps having worked late or with nowhere else to go, and they had found his body in the same spot at sunrise. The temperature in the depths of the night had plummeted lower than expected, well below zero, and he had no warm clothing.

A doctor had kindly explained that, while the versatile human body could withstand a lot of punishment and pain, it could not bear extreme cold for hours without something to keep its own body-heat in. Dicken had been buried where he died. Some neighbours dismissed him socially as the lowest of the low, but Kelly eschewed the strictest hierarchies of the day. Where was their compassion, their fellowship, their duty? The incident had troubled him for a long time.

He leaned over to the boy, James Dawson, and turned the cold face upwards, towards him. Again, it was too late.

"Sarah," he said quietly. Sarah Dawson did not move. Had his words been whacked away by the gale? Or could she not bear to hear?

"Sarah."

He'd raised his voice and she faced him with tear-stained cheeks. Her eyes screamed defiance, a disconsolate plea for him to save her babies.

"I am so, so sorry. James and Matilda are gone, both of them." Kelly swallowed, composed himself. "They've passed away in your arms, knowing that you loved them and cared for them. They are together at peace now."

Sarah Dawson stared at him in disbelief. She hugged the two bodies more tightly. Then, suddenly, she let out the most anguished howl that Kelly and, I expect, all the men on the rock that dreadful morning had heard or would ever hear.

— 20 —

The woman with the wind-blown hair

Soaked to her skin, cold to her bones.

Grace's fingers, nose and ears felt so raw, the flesh must have been ripped off them. Her hair, often salty and tangled, now wringing-wet, whirled in all directions.

She and William had part-rowed, part-manhandled the flat-bottomed coble through the field of seaweed and stripped the sickly green muck from the oars. While it had slowed their progress, to their immense frustration, it had at least afforded them a brief respite. Now they were rowing again, and Grace's back was aching, but she was determined that her father would have no grounds to doubt her willpower or ability.

William glanced skywards as they rode the crest of a huge wave. The storm's evil tantrum was unremitting. The rain and spray stung his eyes. He knew that the survivors on the rock would be having the most torrid time, despite the slight shelter, and he hoped to God that they were warmly dressed.

Grace folded her shawl in half and draped its double thickness around her shoulders to no avail. Heaving her oar, she remained bitterly cold.

They were rounding the south-west tip of Big Hawker through Piper Gut, the Wamses islets to their right. It was approaching 8 a.m. on Friday 7 September when they sighted the wreck. Yes, there she was. Grace would never forget her first glimpse of that huge hulk, stranded on the rock and torn in half from top to bottom so that, as they rowed around her, they could see inside the smashed cabins and eerie corridors.

She was called the *Forfarshire* – there was her nameplate, mounted proudly on the glossy black panels. The figurehead protruding from the bow was a capped bust of a young soldier in the Forfarshire or Angus Artillery, a volunteer unit of the British Army in Scotland.

A group of men, six or seven or more, gathered by the cadaver of the ship and waved unsteadily in their direction. William realised that not one, but two trips in the coble would be needed to get all these people to Longstone. After their shocking ordeal, would any of them have the strength to row?

Johnny Tulloch saw the water sloshing in the bottom of the little boat. He read the exhaustion in the faces of the young woman with the wind-blown hair and the older man with dark eyebrows who had rowed through well-nigh impossible conditions to reach them. Who were they? Where had they come from? Much as he admired, and was oh so thankful for, their dedication, could they physically make a return journey, seemingly against the tide this time? He gravely doubted it, but who on the rock could stand in?

A mountainous wave grew out of the foaming sea, the little boat perched on its crest. As the wave broke, it flung the boat forwards, almost dashing it against the side of the *Forfarshire*. The man inside leaned forward and shouted into the young woman's ear. She took hold of his oar as well as her own.

This woman was now rowing single-handedly in the worst storm any of them could remember. Surely these conditions would sap the greatest strength, the most indomitable spirit. Who *was* she? It was incongruous: the tousled figure with the oars, come to save the motley bunch on the rock, looked barely more than a child. One false move and her coble would be dashed to pieces.

This was the moment when William, too, was most afraid. Not for himself and what he was about to attempt, but for his daughter, whom he was necessarily leaving to handle the coble alone. For the rest of his days, he never forgot that icy blast of paternal fear.

Mark Batey

William shuffled to the side of the coble while all of Grace's energies went into keeping her as steady as possible. Freezing though Grace was, she could taste her own salty sweat in her dry mouth, sense it blocking her nostrils. William waited, hunched, for the next monster wave that would lift them high.

In it barrelled, building, towering, the coble rising inexorably on top. He pulled the coil of rope tight around his waist and prepared to pounce. Split-second timing was essential.

The wave cresting, William fixed the gap between coble and rock in his mind, stretched out his arms for balance, and – *go!* – he leapt.

He judged the jump well but landed awkwardly on the wet, uneven rock. His left ankle turned over. There was no sharp crack of pain. He knew the joint would be twisted and bruised, not broken. But he winced and cursed as he stumbled, and limped for a few paces while he straightened his clothing.

He looked back at the coble, which Grace was rowing backwards and forwards, backwards again, straining to hold a position on the heaving water. He rubbed his aching biceps, wondered how much strength Grace had left.

The coble was so low, Grace felt attached to the water itself, and when she glanced up, the biggest waves swamped her field of vision.

Hold her steady, Grace…

She spat out a mouthful of her hair. The tingling in her exposed ears was sharper now, and she saw through half-closed eyes that the level of frothy water in the coble was rising. Squeezing the panic from her mind, she wiggled her fingers around the oars to force some feeling back into the rubbery numbness.

As silent signals of encouragement, William beamed and nodded, but Grace was concentrating too hard, shaking too violently, to respond. Her entire focus was on controlling the coble, to let the rescue proceed. In a way, she thought as the sinews of her arms burned and her heart thumped, this moment was a validation of her life, everything she had learned, everything she believed.

Hold the line, Grace…

William wasted no time – every second mattered. The men had gathered around the instant he landed on the rock – although, as a group, they seemed more subdued than he'd expected. Their jubilation at the arrival of a rescuer was tempered by shock, fatigue – and something else, a raw sadness too. Now, in the teeth of the gale, some of them struggled even to stand.

"This is all the survivors?" William asked urgently. He could barely speak, his mouth like stone. He ran his tongue around his lips.

"There are nine of us," Johnny Tulloch said. "And we have three dead bodies – the Reverend there, and two wee bairns."

Now William was shocked. Dear God, two small children! Could they have set off from Longstone even a few minutes earlier? Would it have made any difference, all the difference?

Hold your nerve, Grace…

"They had no defence against the elements." This was James Kelly, his jaw set. "They just didn't wake up…" A lump in his throat choked him as he welled up.

William in charge. "My name is William Darling. I am keeper of the Longstone light. My priority is you, the survivors. We must get you to safety. We'll leave the bodies and recover them later."

Jonathan Tickett could not help wondering how much of the corpses would be pecked away by the flocks of ever-hungry seabirds. Wisely, he said nothing.

Deep breath, Grace. Don't even *think* about the coble over-turning…

Sarah Dawson, still nursing the bodies of her son and daughter, looked up, her face a distressing sight. "I can't leave my babies, I won't," she wailed.

William glanced out to the coble. The agony, the alarm he felt were excruciating.

Hold on, Grace…

Thomas Buchanan went to sit with Sarah and, very gently, rolled a consoling arm around her shoulders. He was relieved when she leaned in, perhaps drawing warmth from him.

"We need to do this in two shifts," William was saying quickly. "I'd like to take two of the strongest men with me now, immediately, so they can help me row back for the second trip."

Every one of the crewmen volunteered, Daniel Donovan included.

"Thank you, gentlemen. Would you two come forward, please?"

William pointed to those nearest to him: Sean Macqueen, whose bandaged hands were lodged behind his back, and John Kidd.

"I'll take the bereaved mother, rather than have her stay here any longer than need be."

Buchanan encouraged Sarah to stand. Kelly helped her to lay the bodies on the rock and wrap them in the blanket that he had found on the ship for Matilda.

William looked out again at Grace. Thank God, she continued to row back and forth, keeping the coble near, but not too near, to Big Hawker. She fended off more than once when it came perilously close to being dashed on the rock. She held her head down when the largest waves crashed in, smacking her face and tipping more water at her feet.

All the while, she was tiring visibly. William knew he must hurry, perhaps there were only seconds to spare, he must keep his promise to Thomasina. Grace would be high on adrenaline. It would boost her heart rate, rush blood to her muscles, give her power, help her to survive her greatest trial.

Hold firm, Grace, *please*, just a little longer...

William handed the rope to John Kidd, told him to get into the coble and throw one end back, to form a makeshift mooring while the rest of the first group stepped aboard.

"Come on!" William urged. All their lives were at stake.

Sarah Dawson approached, painfully slowly, holding on to both Kelly and Buchanan.

William expressed his profound sorrow for her loss, which had evidently affected them all. "I just don't know what else I can say. But I'll do my utmost to keep you safe. Please, come now."

John Kidd had leapt into the coble, managing to coincide his jump with the boat being low in the water. Excellent timing! He mouthed brief words of congratulation and encouragement to Grace, noticing between the strands of wet hair that her eyes were dilated.

Kidd hurled an end of the rope, which was caught by brave Sean Macqueen. Then he took one of the oars from Grace's clawed fingers. Her grip was tight.

"All three of you, get in," William cried. "The wreck might break up or work loose – one big wave could do it! And the coble…"

Macqueen pulled the rope, steadying the coble against the rock. He grimaced as the pain shot from his hands up his arms. Grace kept her oar down in the water like a low-slung anchor.

The coble trembled and pitched as Dawson, Kelly and Buchanan stepped into the centre, but it stayed balanced and did not drift away. Macqueen boarded next, followed swiftly by William, who flinched when his sore ankle hit the bottom of the boat. He palmed out some of the seawater and sat beside John Kidd.

Four men were left alive on Big Hawker – Tickett, Tulloch, Nicholson, Donovan. William hollered that he would return as soon as possible. He took the oar from Grace, congratulating her on holding the coble off the rocks for longer than he'd thought possible. He began to pull strokes with Kidd – he could not remember the coble ever being heavier than it was now. Please, let them all make it back.

In the bow, Grace unknotted the sodden green and white blanket from her waist. She offered it to the wretched Sarah Dawson, who was shaking all over, staring ahead out of dark, empty eyes that looked as though they comprehended nothing in this world at all.

— 21 —

In the quarter-boat

Guilt.

The man who had leapt from the deck of the *Forfarshire* after the first impact with Big Hawker, defying death and landing in the only quarter-boat to escape the scene, was now wracked with guilt.

The nine men in the boat, eight crew members and him, the sole passenger, were huddled together, facing inwards. None was adequately clothed to be exposed to the gale. All were exhausted, feeling weaker than they would ever care to admit.

Mercifully, one of them, with a shock of white hair and fang-teeth, had a half-bottle of gin. They shared it round, passing the fuel from man to man, then back. It became clear in the conversation that this was Allan Stewart, chief engineer, blue overalls streaked with grime.

The powerful currents in Piper Gut had propelled them into the North Sea. They had no choice but to let the tide and wind control their course. Stewart and James Duncan, first mate, argued that they should stay afloat and rest awhile, conserving their vestiges of energy until the worst of the storm had passed. Heads inclined against the rain, they were blown through a field of floating debris – wooden fragments, strips of clothing, linen, cases, personal belongings.

The passenger who had jumped, and was now wiping blood from the cut on his forehead, identified himself as Glen Ritchie.

Amid the debris, the quarter-boat thudded into a dead body, which rolled over as they hit it. Ritchie looked with horror into the chalk-white face of Arthur Ellison. As the body was lifted and tossed by a wave, he saw that Arthur's waist was tied with thin string to another body: that of his young son, Albert. He noticed that Allan Stewart registered Albert's chalk face with revulsion, too, and drained his gin bottle.

The guilt that plagued Ritchie's mind sprang from several sources, all clobbering him at once. He tried to disentangle the strands, but the experience of doing so made him feel sick and he swallowed hard to keep it down. He was thankful that his mouth was coated with the floral taste of the gin.

What was the fate of the *Forfarshire*? When their quarter-boat had left, she'd already smashed into Big Hawker, but was she still there, marooned? The bodies of the poor Ellisons proved that there had been fatalities, but how many? There were dozens on board, a full complement. Above all, what had happened to his aunt and uncle? Oh Lord, were they still in their cabin? Had it been damaged in the crash? Had they made it to another quarter-boat? What if…?

Ritchie shuddered. In his mind, the ship's bell tolled. While he craved answers to questions presently unanswerable, he couldn't stop them forming.

The destroyed ship had quickly waned into darkness and the noises and shouting from the deck faded soon afterwards. Through the wind, he'd heard a distant gun blasting two or three times but that too had receded. When they lost sight of the lighthouse beam, they were blind.

He looked at the drained faces of the eight crewmen. Were they, too, consumed by thoughts of those left behind? Should they have stayed? Had they done wrong? How would their captain manage with such a depleted crew?

Ritchie could not work out how far they had come, or even whether they'd travelled in a constant direction. He suspected that the boat had twisted and turned, changing heading more than once. But the sky was filthy grey, shedding rain, and the early light of dawn suggested there was nothing around them but vast, stormy sea.

For too long, he had acted first and thought later. His family and the few locals he regarded as true friends knew him to be impetuous, headstrong, make that reckless. Why was he so slow to learn? Or was his dangerous leap simply influenced by the cognac he had knocked back after the argument? He knew his instinct for survival was strong – was that selfish?

Well, if he survived this ordeal, he resolved there and then to make sure it counted. For something. He would put his fitness and strength to good use. If the farm needed investment, he'd work all hours, put in extra work, if need be, to raise the funds and secure its future himself.

The vow for greater responsibility made Ritchie feel better. His spirits were dashed when another mighty wave almost deposited another body inside the boat as it broke over them, churning their stomachs, soaking them all yet again and adding to the water swilling under their benches. It was another passenger, Nicholas Paston. The crewmen did not recognise him; Ritchie did. Paston had occupied the cabin opposite his and they'd exchanged pleasantries when they paid for their tickets. When he eventually fastened his trousers, Ritchie had found in a pocket the change he had been given with his own ticket.

Two crewmen, John Matson and Rob Fox, were bailing out the quarter-boat, each using one of their shoes. The level of water inside, from the waves and the pelting rain, was alarming. Ritchie removed one of his own shoes and mucked in.

"Look – there!"

The unique growl could only have come from Allan Stewart, whose bedraggled moustache had overgrown his lips. He heaved himself up, forcing life into his muscles, and ran a hand through his white mane. He nudged the turquoise-lipped Alex Murray sitting next to him, and they all stared hard into the night.

There, dim but unmistakable, was a mast, a tall one. After an agonising moment, more emerged into sight. The mast stood about a third of the way along a vessel, which had a headsail fore and a mainsail aft.

The vessel was thirty feet long, maybe more, and would have a deep hold for merchant cargo. It was a sloop, fast and agile, with a bowsprit that projected a long way forward.

I gather that by the end of the Napoleonic wars, specially designed sloops-of-war had been among the most plentiful vessels in the Royal Navy. Today, many sloops travelled up and down between trading towns. Heaven bless this one for sailing by in their hour of distress.

The nine men waved, yelled, maniacally. As the sloop adjusted its sails, diverted its course, they saw that it was named the *Corvette*. A rope came flying towards them, which John Matson caught at the second attempt and made fast. With a minimal crew of seven, the *Corvette* was sailing from Montrose to Shields. Yes, there was just space for nine more on board. What in God's name were they doing drifting in a quarter-boat in this savage storm?

Before going below to join the inevitable discussion about their predicament, Glen Ritchie gave the last man, Jas Hall, a helping hand on to the sloop. Just as well – Hall slipped and might have fallen in had Ritchie not clasped his wrist. Hall was wearing Stewart's tartan scarf as a stopgap bandage around a bleeding shin. Very quietly, their heads bowed, both men wept with overwhelming relief.

— 22 —

Off Big Hawker rock

"There you go, my dear, you can rest now."

The first time Grace let go of Sarah Dawson's hand was when she helped Sarah to lie on her bed on the third floor of the lighthouse, resting her quivering head on the pillow.

Many times, Grace had met shipwreck survivors who were suffering sudden bereavement or reacting to traumatic experiences. She felt so sorry for Sarah's unimaginable loss and recognised many of the symptoms that she had come to expect.

Sarah's cold lips had a greenish-blue tinge, but she was also sweating, dizzy, nauseous. Her breathing was rapid. Her eyes continued to spill tears, her hands shook. Grace pulled a dry woollen blanket over her and fetched a glass of water.

Grace mopped Sarah's brow as she sobbed. "That's fine, let it all out. Your mind and body have been through so much, you'll feel better if you manage to sleep."

"Thank you, thank you for your kindness," Sarah whispered. She was looking off into a hazy middle distance, not at Grace. "You must be exhausted yourself after your heroics in the coble."

"Heroics?" Grace was puzzled. "It's what we're here for, what we do." There was the link already, note, the suggestion that Grace was a hero.

Sarah shrugged, laid her head on the pillow, shut her eyes. She opened them again immediately. The darkness swarmed with terrors, but she lay still.

"I'll come back in a few minutes," Grace promised and returned to the ground floor.

They had been welcomed to Longstone by a party of playful grey seals that had danced under and around the coble in all directions. It was nearly 9 a.m. when she accompanied Sarah up the lighthouse steps. James Kelly had shared the rowing on one oar with John Kidd, while her father had kept sole charge of the other. Having introduced the group to Thomasina, William returned to the coble, not stopping even to change his coat and scarf, sopping wet as they were, or to inspect his ankle. He took Kidd and Macqueen with him. The three of them turned the coble around and set off for Crawford's Gut on a second mission to Big Hawker in as many hours.

At the stove, Thomasina served bowls of piping hot vegetable soup to James Kelly and Thomas Buchanan. A baker by trade, Buchanan offered to cut some stottie cake and he left a plateful of crusty slices ready for when the coble came back. Thomasina had put out a pile of blankets and both men gratefully wrapped themselves up while wolfing down their soup by the fire.

As their bodies thawed, and blessed warmth permeated their bones, they began to chat, opening up to Thomasina about the *Forfarshire* crashing not once but twice on to the rock, breaking apart on the second impact, with the aft section and everyone in it vanishing into the sea. They relived the clanking, creaking, tearing, hissing – the terrible sounds, as well as the sights, of the disaster that were all too raw in their minds – yet the very act of recounting them was cathartic.

Thomasina knew the fate of the *Forfarshire* from the shattered wreck that Grace and William had briefly described. Still, the first-hand accounts of the tragedy made horribly compelling listening.

Grace checked on Sarah Dawson every quarter-hour, taking fresh water, occasionally a clean towel. Sometimes she was dozing, at other times sitting up with her head in her hands, weeping inconsolably.

"Why, oh why? What have I done?"

On one occasion, Grace heard Sarah cry out. A severe headache had punched her like a thunderclap. The throbbing peaked within a minute or two, but she had never known a headache like it.

While Grace supported and soothed her, Sarah began to mumble. Grace asked her to repeat the words slowly. Shortly before their departure from Hull, Sarah had heard the Irish gentleman who was among the survivors on the big rock discussing a leak in the ship's boilers. How bitterly she regretted going ahead on the journey when Jesse, her husband, was delayed. How completely she blamed herself for the loss of their beloved James and Matilda, and how she dreaded the prospect of facing Jesse, having to explain how both the children had perished.

At 10 a.m., William came through the door with Macqueen, Kidd and the four remaining survivors. They looked petrified by the cold and their brush with death. The crewmen embraced each other, reuniting. Macqueen's hands were bloody, and it was only now, in the lighthouse, that he was aware how painful they had become. His fingers were swelling.

The newcomers relished their soup, holding the bowls with both palms before eating, and the chance to warm up after the hard hours in their thin clothes in the storm. Buchanan handed round the chunks of stottie, trying but failing to keep some back for later.

William folded himself into an armchair and shut his eyes, utterly spent. He needed kip but his left ankle was excruciating. The second trip had been as daunting as the first; the storm unrelenting. The relief he felt at completing the two journeys, rescuing the nine survivors and seeing his wife and daughter at home was overwhelming, yet he suddenly felt – and looked, no doubt – like a man in his seventies rather than his fifties.

Thomasina excused herself from the survivors and crossed the room to give her husband a hug. She said nothing but William appreciated everything that her gesture conveyed.

It was an hour later when Grace came down the stairs, having nursed Sarah back to sporadic sleep. She was feeling weary herself – no doubt the long day's events were catching up with her. As she re-entered the room, there was a loud, impatient rap on the lighthouse door. She kept walking through the room to answer it before either of her parents rose. She was astonished to find standing outside in the downpour, the wind whipping their clothes, a group of seven weary men at the end of their tether.

At the front, his dripping fringe scraped back from his forehead, was the slim figure of her nineteen-year-old brother, William Brooks Darling.

— 23 —

The Castle Agent

The Darlings were not the only observers of the wreck of the *Forfarshire*.

In the east turret of Bamburgh Castle, a twenty-eight-year-old lookout, Peter Collingwood, had spent the night on duty, flayed by the storm. It had bellowed at him persistently, but Peter had found throughout his life that the best way to see off bullies was to stand up to them, so he stood his ground against the onslaught.

It was between 4 and 5 a.m. that he spotted the wreck, a great black hulk on Big Hawker, and a smattering of survivors doing their best to stay sheltered. When the nine-pounder gun was detonated, it felt for a moment like the whole castle was exploding. Soon after five, Peter left the turret, dried himself off and marched the length of two dark corridors to a wooden door sign-boarded:

CASTLE AGENT'S APARTMENT

He knocked three times and stood back as soon as he heard motion inside.

A short, thick-set man opened the door and peered out through bleary eyes. He had a small mole on his right cheek and long brown sideburns on an otherwise clean-shaven face. His prematurely grey temples belied his relative youth: Peter knew he was still in his thirties.

"Good morning. It's Peter, isn't it? I trust the night watch wasn't too grim. What news?"

Collingwood described what he had seen in as much detail as possible. The agent was a stickler for detail, and though Collingwood himself had never seen it, he'd heard reliably that the agent had an explosive temper.

"I doubt that a rescue attempt can be launched from the Farnes until the storm subsides," he concluded. "So, the North Sunderland crew may be the best, or the only, hope for the survivors."

"Thank you, Peter." The agent spoke quickly but clearly. This sounded like a major maritime disaster, not merely an accident, and if anyone were to take command of the situation, it should be him. Many cogs whirred in his brain. "Please relay my instructions that the castle's flag should be hoisted at half-mast and the heaviest possible shells deployed in the signal gun. And let the hostler know that I shall be coming for Inferno, if you'd be so kind."

Collingwood gave a small bow and hurried away with his messages. He knew the agent would expect them to be passed on promptly and precisely.

Barely twenty minutes later, the agent emerged from his apartment in riding attire and a full-length black overcoat. He strode as briskly as the coat would allow to the livery stables at the rear of the castle.

The sun was coming up through the menacing sky. Graham Fairburn, the hostler, was holding Inferno's reins with one hand whilst giving the saddle a final polish with the other. The storm had brought down many branches, and a gate on one of the other stables had disintegrated.

Thanking Fairburn, the agent mounted Inferno, sat square in the saddle, squeezed with his lower legs and pushed his bottom forwards. Obediently, the reddish-tan colt set off at once, avoiding the storm debris. When they reached the coastal path, heading south, the agent lowered his head, kept looking forwards, and urged Inferno into a trot, then a gallop.

The agent's name was Robert Smeddle. A competent rider, he was in full control. Since childhood, his abilities and intelligence had shone through. He excelled at literacy and numeracy – to the extent that he was regarded as odd, an outsider, even within his own family. He developed small, neat handwriting and, as Peter Collingwood appreciated, an eagle-eye for detail.

When, in 1828, due to ill-health, Reverend Michael Maughan terminated his three-year stint as Bamburgh Castle agent, William Hamilton succeeded him, for one year only, 1828–29. Robert Smeddle was already working for the Lord Crewe trustees, who were charged with appointing the agent, and his meticulous clerical work had not gone unnoticed.

Smeddle became the castle agent in 1829, assuming day-to-day responsibility for the welfare hub that the castle had been since the heady days of Dr John Sharp. Effectively Smeddle ran the infirmary and the dispensary and the granary and the school. And he had charge of the castle's innovative maritime support, including the accommodation reserved for shipwrecked sailors.

He so impressed the board of trustees that, after three years, they made him their land agent, while simultaneously renewing his duties as castle agent. In recent years, the roles had been separate, but in Smeddle the trustees believed they had a man who could manage both jobs. As a sign of their faith, they paid a generous salary of £500 per annum. Now Smeddle also had responsibility for the tenancies on the trustees' land, in Bamburgh and extensively across Northumberland, collecting rents and supervising the development of farms and their use of labourers.

He resided in the agent's spacious apartment in Bamburgh Castle, where part of his working week was spent at his desk book-keeping. He filled the remainder dealing with local people – Bamburgh itself had a population of 500 – negotiating agreements and solving problems. Inevitably, the advice of the trustees' agent was widely sought on many matters, and Smeddle revelled in the influence and social status that the combined role conferred on him.

There was more to it than that. Somehow, just seeing his advice enacted made him feel gratified. Always. The bigger the incident, the more inflated he felt. Nothing of any significance happened in or around Bamburgh in which Robert Smeddle did not have a say.

He was shrewd enough, however, not to get too big for his size nines. He answered to the trustees who had selected him and would in due course appoint his successor, too.

Since Nathaniel, Lord Crewe, died more than a century ago, in 1721, the Lord Crewe charity that he established in his will had been an exemplar of administration. Minute books were kept detailing every decision affecting the distribution of the income derived from the charity's estates, to benefit which local citizens, restorations, new developments. These books formed part of the castle's magnificent library and Smeddle's ego salivated at the prospect of *his* records being part of the collection.

He was determined that his paperwork should be more accurate, more comprehensive even than that of his illustrious predecessors. As far as he knew, the six years since he was awarded the combined role had served to reassure the trustees that they had made a sound decision. They must not be dissuaded from that judgement.

It was still early morning when Smeddle arrived at North Sunderland harbour. Inferno's twin streams of exhaled breath were swatted away in the wind as if they had never existed, but he had not broken a sweat during the three-and-a-half-mile gallop from Bamburgh. High on its rock, far in the distance across countless meadows, the castle dominated the landscape.

Smeddle tied the reins to a post on the verge of the coastal path and walked down the slope to the wharf where the colourful fleet of little boats was moored, bow to stern. His nose wrinkled: even winds as fierce as these could not dissipate the odours that tainted the harbour area. Many villagers were braving the gale to inspect the havoc wreaked upon their rooves, fences, paths, crops, animals. A huddle of workers examined one of the lime kilns.

Smeddle headed into the wind towards a red fishing smack, his coat adopting a frenzied life of its own, flailing about his body. He had seen a tall young man with a floppy fringe unspooling a tangle of wet rope.

"No damage, I hope?" Smeddle called to William Brooks Darling, who only just heard him. Smeddle stood straight, legs apart, eyes fixed ahead.

Before William Brooks could answer, his friend Michael Robson appeared with a couple of empty lobster pots. The Robson family had fished in North Sunderland for generations. From the records I've seen, they paid a fee of thirty shillings a year to use the harbour plus an acknowledgement of five herrings and two lobsters for the harbour master. Importantly, they doubled up as the harbour's most reliable lifeboat service, too.

William Brooks recalled his father meeting this visitor occasionally, but Robson seemed to know him well.

"What brings you here so early?" Michael asked. "It must be something urgent to have come in this storm!"

"Yes, it's urgent," said Smeddle. "There may be a fee in it for you, if it all works out."

Tommy Cuthbertson, another fisherman, had joined his friends. The visitor had piqued their interest, and they were waiting for him to put his request.

"There has been a shipwreck overnight – a large paddle-steamer. The survivors are on Big Hawker and there may be bounty to salvage."

"Has the coble gone out from Longstone?" This, as you'd expect, from William Brooks.

"My lookout isn't certain as he wasn't sighted, but he thinks not in these hideous conditions."

William Brooks was unconvinced. His father would make the best-informed assessment, of course, and Grace was on hand to help. While William Brooks had no knowledge of what had happened in the Outer Farnes, he felt instinctively that they would not be deterred and would probably have launched their rescue bid already.

"From here it'll be five miles each way," said Tommy Cuthbertson. "In this fishing smack, it would be brutal–"

"If you gentlemen aren't up to the task," Smeddle goaded them, "I'll need to consider other arrangements." He hoped his face had not shown too much of a sneer.

"We'll go," declared Robson. "You know you can rely on us." Without looking at Cuthbertson, he briefly explained that Robert Smeddle was, sort of, the Lord Crewe trustees' estate manager.

Smeddle looked pleased – and perhaps a little relieved. He asked: "How many of your crew are available this morning?"

"Including William Brooks here, we're seven," replied Robson. "There's James and Will," he counted two other members of the Robson family, "plus Robbie Knox, Bill Swan and the three of us."

"I'd recommend taking a large coble," said William Brooks. "Tommy is right, the storm does not favour the fishing smack. And the coble is more manoeuvrable – it'll be much better when we need to get close in. With a crew of seven, we'll be six oarsmen plus one on the tiller. That's probably our best option, giving us most control."

"Very well," Robson agreed readily. "But it should be you steering the tiller," he pointed at William Brooks. "You know the waters around these islands even better than we do."

Smeddle felt self-satisfied, superior. In a matter of minutes, these men had accepted his challenge and outlined a plan of action. "The castle will, of course, be pleased to tend to the survivors," he called out. "Thank you, gentlemen, and God speed."

He raised his collar against the sheets of rain and trudged back up the slope. Two of the workers at the lime kilns observed the short fellow with greying hair walking with a swagger from the fishing boats. One was sure he recognised the Bamburgh Castle agent, representing the Lord Crewe trustees, no less; the other grunted and continued to sweep up.

Smeddle reached Inferno, who gave a knowing shake, and he patted the horse's fetlock and shoulder. Behind him, the Robsons' crew had put their heads together, preparing for their audacious sortie on the North Sea. What on Earth would they find on Big Hawker when – if – they landed there?

— 24 —

A crowded home

Every drop of mischief had drained from his eyes.

Grace handed a bowl of soup to William Brooks, then unfurled one of the dry rugs on the ground floor of the lighthouse. They sat cross-legged, leaning back against the curved wall.

"We set off at about half seven," her brother imparted between spoonfuls of broth. "It must have taken two hours or more to reach Big Hawker. The sea was fighting us, chucking us back, the whole way."

Needless to say, Grace understood exactly what he meant by that remark.

"A steamship passed close by," William Brooks resumed, "the *Liverpool*, I think it was. We signalled but it didn't or couldn't stop. You didn't see it?"

Grace shook her head.

William Brooks exhaled deeply. "All we found on the rock were three dead bodies, two of them young children." He stirred his soup round and round, shell-shocked by what he had witnessed. "We moved them up to the highest mound and draped a net over them. It's not much protection, but it's something."

He paused. Grace gave him time to marshal his thoughts.

"There may still be more bodies – we didn't search the wreck. When it became clear that the survivors had already been taken off, the Robsons were furious. All that effort, all that risk, to no avail, and probably no reward either. Really, I've never seen James and Michael so livid."

"Well, at least you're safe." Grace snuggled up to him.

"We were so shattered, we couldn't face the five miles back to the harbour – the swell would have overpowered us. But we thought there'd be a warm welcome here." He managed a thin smile. "And even if it was you who beat us to it, we were right."

"Always," said Grace firmly. "You know that."

"We're moored on the lee side of the island. But there were seven of us. How did you and Papa cope – just the two of you – at the height of the storm? When one of you got on to the rock, the other must have been in the coble alone! Was that you, Grace? It beggars belief what you've done, what you've achieved. How many people did you end up saving?"

As the questions tumbled out of him, she stroked his arm.

"Nine," she answered. "Most of them are here. Papa made two trips, with the ship's crew supporting him."

"He looks even more knackered than I feel."

William Brooks glanced at their father, who was still recuperating in an armchair. His left ankle was up on a stool, his sodden scarf on the floor beside it.

"We must have reached the wreck within minutes of him leaving it for the second time. But visibility was so poor, I was never sure where to steer."

"Well, you made it. Sarah Dawson, the mother of the two children who died, is resting upstairs."

"Oh, that poor woman," he said compassionately. "God bless her. How will she ever be able to put this behind her?"

"Her husband doesn't know what's happened yet," Grace told him. "As far as she knows, he's still in Hull, where he works."

William Brooks finished his soup, licked his lips. He closed his eyes from the blood, sweat and tears of the morning. Within a minute, Grace thought, he was asleep where he sat.

With further assistance from Thomas Buchanan, who seemed happy to be kept busy, Thomasina rustled up lunch for everyone – nineteen people – although Sarah Dawson did not feel like eating anything and Thomasina herself held back. Grace continued to check on Sarah regularly, taking up water and hugging her to assuage her crippling demons of grief and guilt and loneliness. On more than one occasion when Grace looked around the door, Sarah was lying in a foetal position, hellishly tormented, eyelids flickering, lips twitching.

Grace changed Sean Macqueen's bandages, taking extra care with his chafed fingers, and tended to the cuts, bruises and blisters that every one of the survivors had sustained. Donovan asked her not to bother with his split lips, but to pass on his deepest condolences next time she was with Sarah. Grace also carried out the day's tasks expected by Trinity House and cleaned the lantern room thoroughly. Outside the storm raged on.

As evening approached, her father limped out to the old barracks, built thirteen years ago in 1825 as accommodation for the masons, carpenters and labourers who built the place. He took a small lantern and cast its beam into the stone corners, up at the rafters, back down again. The building was dilapidated, wet and draughty. Two cormorants flapped out of a hole in the roof.

A last look around, then William returned to the lighthouse. He called Thomasina, Grace and William Brooks over, and the family gathered by the well.

"The barracks are unsuitable to host our North Sunderland friends," William reported to no one's surprise. "They can shelter there if they must, but really, they're not fit for use, and it would take quite some time to restore them. The tide is even more likely to break in there than it is here."

Massaging his ankle, William went on: "All our beds and bunks are promised to the survivors of the *Forfarshire*, and the spare clothes too, there's none left. But do we have enough blankets for the lads to spend the night in here?"

Thomasina did not hesitate. "Of course, we'll make do," she said. After all, a crowded home was nothing new to this family! "If we move some of the furniture and spread the rugs around, there's ample floor space, don't worry." For once, the Darlings' hospitality standards would have to be compromised.

William Brooks shrugged, thanked his parents. Having decided not to take their coble back to the mainland, what alternative did they have? His friends enjoyed unpredictable adventures, and at least on the lighthouse floor they should be safe and warm. Provided it didn't flood again.

"Tell me," William said to him, "what made you take your coble out in the first place? How did you learn of the wreck? Did you see anything?"

"The Lord Crewe agent came to us this morning, first light. Robert Smeddle – you've met him, haven't you? He was keen that we went to the survivors as he didn't think anyone else would attempt it."

"I see," said William. "I may well meet Mr Smeddle again tomorrow. I'll join everyone when they return to the mainland. I want to be sure there's enough support for the survivors, especially Mrs Dawson. We need to take the bodies off the rock, too."

"Yes, thank you, Papa," Grace murmured.

"I'll relay that to the others," said William Brooks. "Let's hope the storm passes over tonight."

Grace tried to recall the occasions on which she'd encountered the name Robert Smeddle in her father's logbooks. She could not have known it then, but this character was to loom large during the remainder of her life.

— 25 —

The Half Moon

Saturday morning, 8 September. Somewhere in the street outside, a clock chimed six.

Allan Stewart felt recharged after a night's rest, although his mouth was rancid. Despite the horrors knotted in his mind – what more could he have done to prevent the loss of the *Forfarshire* and heaven knows how many lives? – he had been so exhausted by Friday nightfall that his body was screaming for sleep.

When the *Corvette* arrived in Shields, Glen Ritchie had bid farewell to the eight crew members. He had some money in his pocket and a burning desire to discover the fate of his aunt and uncle, whom he had last seen in their cabin. He went off in search of a hackney coach to take him up to Bamburgh, while the crewmen hired one to take them ten miles inland to the city of Newcastle. The eight of them sat tight on seats designed for six.

"Are you going to the hanging?" the stagecoach driver asked them at the outset, four reins dangling from his fingers as the horses champed at their bits. He introduced himself merely as 'Tremain'. He seemed excited at the prospect of a public execution and picked his nose as he awaited a response.

"Who is being hanged?" asked James Duncan. "We've been distracted – we work at sea."

"Aye, and she's been a cruel mistress by the look of you," Tremain said, leering at his dishevelled passengers. "The convict is Jasper Tyrrell." A glob of saliva formed at the corner of his mouth, stuck there. "He killed his neighbour and the neighbour's good lady with a carving knife, so I hear. Two strokes, ear to ear." He mimed the bloody deed, then licked away his saliva.

"I don't think I'll be going," Duncan said with an air of finality. He had never seen a public hanging, and while he knew that a fear of the noose had perpetuated for generations, he felt no desire to experience one now.

Tremain looked down on him from his perch at the front of the coach, utter disdain on his face. He wiped his mouth on his sleeve, leaned forward and flicked the reins. The four horses responded as one and the wooden wheels bumped along the black cinder path. The wind was bracing, but there was no trace of the storm that ravaged the coast forty miles to the north.

As the passengers had no luggage, Tremain had hastily struck a deal with a Shields merchant, for a heart-warming fee, to carry four barrels of molasses to the St. Nicholas Poor House in Newcastle, officially home to thirty-six inmates but at times, in practice, rather more. Unfortunately, one barrel slipped off the roof when a back wheel jolted through a pothole, leaving a sticky trail of brown treacle for stray dogs to follow. He was also carrying a sack of unfranked letters from traders and lawyers in Shields to their Newcastle clients, bypassing the next official mail-coach.

The city's belching smokestacks and squalid tenement blocks soon hove into view. Tremain's route took them past St. James's hospital and its adjacent chapel into Leazes Terrace, where a few teenagers were kicking a ball about. He had intended to continue into Gallowgate but was prevented by a brace of carts delivering newly blown glass bottles to a substantial, brick building. I struck lucky here – early photographs reveal that it was a nunnery, whose inhabitants fermented their own strawberry wine.

Tremain steered to the side of the road through the traffic of stagecoaches and pedestrians and lifted the reins. By the time his coach came to a halt, he had already jumped down.

"Will this do, gentlemen?" he asked, scratching his stubbly chin with black, bitten fingernails.

To encourage an affirmative answer, he talked up the location: "The new monument to Earl Grey, the local guy who was recently prime minister, is that way. A road leads from there down to the River Tyne, which might be of interest, you lot being seafarers. The Town Moor where the hanging's taking place is this way, at the far end of Gallowgate." He chuckled to himself as he pointed along the temporarily blocked road.

"Yes, this will do fine, thank you."

James Duncan, relieved to be out of Tremain's crammed coach seats, spoke for them all. He rubbed the small of his back.

Allan Stewart and John Matson looked about, getting their bearings, as the coach cantered off to deliver the letters and molasses before picking up new passengers.

"What about this one?" Stewart suggested, indicating an inn with a public bar and rooms above, just a few yards ahead on their right. Neither he nor any of the others felt inclined to walk farther than necessary. The smoky, grimy, stinking city, whose population was fast approaching 75,000, was a world apart from the North Sea.

They trudged into the inn, The Half Moon, past a ragged beggar and a sandwich-boarded vendor displaying the latest newspapers. Luckily, they negotiated the rent of two rooms on the second floor, each with four beds but precious little floor space, for one night with the option of more.

Stewart's heart stopped the moment he clapped eyes on the landlord. He was the image of Captain John Humble, from the trim of his sideburns to the cut of his blue blazer. Stewart looked away.

At the uncluttered bar, the landlord's wife was pouring gin for a man, mid-thirties, wearing a grey frock coat with black lapels.

They ordered a meal and local ale, which was hand-pumped and had a full-bodied, caramel flavour. It was only when the food was served – bread smeared with dripping and a thin mutton broth – that they realised how ravenous they were.

After a second round of ale, they tramped upstairs to their utilitarian, low-ceilinged rooms, which smelled stale, unaired.

The thin curtains were caked in fingerprints. One bed in Stewart's room had a torn pillow bearing clumps of brown hair. Inside the pillow was an infestation of ants: when the pillow was thrown into a corner, they spilled on to the floor like black pins.

Each man laid down on a bed, unavoidably replaying images of last night's disaster and their fortunate escape via a helpful tide and a passing sloop. They were plagued by intrusions of "What if…?" and "How…?" and "Why…?" but eventually sleep overcame them and the rooms fell quiet.

By six on Saturday morning, all eight men were awake. Street noise and daylight streaming through the windows spurred them to rise. They were careful where they put their feet to avoid any lingering ants.

Down at the servery in the public bar, the landlord was dragging a wooden spoon through a cauldron of porridge, adding salt. A queue of locals had formed outside, some carrying their own metal bowls. Jas Hall, John Matson and some of the others took a table near the door and waited for service to begin.

Allan Stewart, James Duncan and David Grant approached a corner table with three vacant chairs. The only one occupied was taken by the man Stewart had observed drinking gin in the bar last night. He was attired in a grey suit with a fawn waistcoat and a stiff white shirt. His frock coat was hanging from a peg with a black fedora. He was reading a newspaper, one of the regional weeklies that usually published on Fridays.

"These seats are free?" Stewart growled, daring anything but an affirmative reply.

"Be my guest."

No sooner had Stewart, Duncan and Grant taken their places than the suited man was instantly curious. He folded up his paper.

"Good morning, gentlemen. What brings you to Newcastle? From the accent, you're down from Scotland?"

"Aye, we are," said Stewart.

"We're not here for the hanging, if that's what you're thinking!" said Duncan.

"Strange, isn't it? The government claims we're a booming, modern, industrial nation, yet we persist with this centuries-old form of barbarism." The man knitted his fingers together on the table.

As it happened, the infamous gallows would be phased out within a few years. But it wasn't only used for murderers. Consider this – capital offences included forging banknotes and stealing horses.

"You don't like these hangings, sir, but you're following this one very closely?" Grant posed his observation as a question.

"Well, it's been months since the last one. Thousands of people tend to turn out to watch. In court, the trial of Jasper Tyrrell lasted just a couple of hours. The jury found him guilty in all of fifteen minutes. He's twenty years old. Sometimes, after the hanging, there's not even a record of what happens to the body."

For a moment, the three shipwreck survivors stayed silent.

"Let me address your perceptive observation more directly," the man said to Grant. "My name is Vincent Atkins. I'm a newspaper reporter. I assure you, my interest in today's gibbeting is purely professional."

Atkins sat back as the landlord's wife brought their bowls of porridge. Stewart and Duncan exchanged glances; after a beat, both men gave a slight nod to each other.

"Mr Atkins, we have some information, some dreadful news, that we want to share," Stewart began. "We came to Newcastle, the nearest city, because it seemed the most likely place to…"

"Run into a newspaper reporter?" Atkins suggested.

"Well, yes."

"You've picked a good day. On a day like today, with the first public hanging in ages, plenty of newspapers will be represented."

Atkins saw that the faces of the three men had dropped as they recalled whatever the ordeal was that they had lived through.

He gave them a prompt. "From the emblems I can make out on your clothing, you appear to work for the Dundee &

Hull Steam Packet Company. Is this connected to your news? Is your steamer berthed on the Tyne?"

James Duncan looked momentarily startled. He was so accustomed to donning the company's uniform that he'd forgotten the name was on show. How long had he – all of them – been wearing the same outfits?

"We do work for the Dundee & Hull company, that's right," Duncan said. "But it's probable that no one at the company knows our news yet. And no one who was expecting passengers to arrive in Dundee will know, either. They really ought to be told."

Atkins leaned forward, said nothing. This was the time for these men to tell the story they wanted to tell, and he sensed it was an important one. From the look in their eyes, they had recently had the shock of their lives.

"I am first mate on the SS *Forfarshire*, one of the grandest steamers to come out of Scotland," Duncan explained. "We were travelling from Hull to Dundee – we departed on Wednesday evening – but we ran into a colossal storm."

"We were unable to complete the journey," Stewart added, rubbing his temples. "The conditions were so atrocious that we were dashed on to a big rock in the Farne Islands. This was in the wee hours of yesterday morning."

"Is your ship lost?"

"Aye, we believe so. We launched a quarter-boat and hoped that others would follow." Stewart paused, averted his blue eyes. "We didn't see any."

"How many were on board? Was the ship full?"

"We normally carry – sorry, carried – a full load of cargo and passengers. Including the crew, there must have been at least sixty." Stewart swallowed hard. "Ye may find there's a more complete record of the cargo than of the passengers."

Atkins did not raise an eyebrow. "Gentlemen, you must give me as many facts as possible – times, names, who did what, all the details you can recall. If I may, I'll write down what you tell me?" From an inside pocket he extracted a leather-bound notebook and a pencil. "I am delighted to have met you. Can we start with your names and your roles on the ship?"

Between them, Duncan, Stewart and Grant gave a thorough account of the death of the *Forfarshire*. They did not dwell on the leaking boilers but covered everything from their perspectives up to and including their sighting of the *Corvette* and disembarkation in Shields.

Don't forget, as yet, they had no knowledge of the rescue missions by the Darlings and the North Sunderland crew.

Atkins probed them about the navigation error that triggered the shipwreck. The closer you sail to the coast, of course, the greater the danger. What other causes could there be, he wondered aloud. To what extent were the storm and the faulty boilers contributory factors?

All three crewmen emphasised the storm – without doubt the most tempestuous they had faced in all their combined years on the North Sea.

Atkins thanked them for the information, grabbed his hat and coat and hurried out of The Half Moon. In his head, he was already composing the opening lines of his exclusive article. He sensed the editor would be delighted to receive the scoop – and he could still contribute first-hand to coverage of Jasper Tyrrell's execution.

"Right place, right time, sir," he would be sure to say to the editor, leaving him in no doubt that Vincent Atkins was indispensable.

When the *Forfarshire* crewmen stepped outside later that morning, crowds were building along either side of Gallowgate. Wrapped in chains, the condemned man would soon be transported by cart, sitting on his own coffin – or he was told as much – from gaol to gallows. At noon, he would be hanged from the crosspiece between the two uprights and left there suspended for hours; such display apparently being intended to deter other offences.

The very thought of it made James Duncan shiver. The only gallows he had seen in use were at Scarborough, where the wooden frame supported scales for weighing sacks of grain.

That afternoon, Saturday's *Gateshead Observer* broke the news of the *Forfarshire* catastrophe. The story was given more space and a bolder headline than the hanging of Jasper Tyrrell. As usual, express riders distributed copies around the region, well beyond Gateshead.

By the time Robert Smeddle read the story – still on the day after the wreck occurred – Vincent Atkins had polished a longer version and a second edition was rolling off the presses.

— 26 —

The first inquest

"Big steamship wrecked with heavy death toll."

After the headline, Robert Smeddle recited the whole article. He savoured his latest moment as the centre of attention, despite the meagre audience.

He was seated in the warm living area of the Longstone lighthouse. Five others were present: William, Thomasina, Grace and William Brooks Darling, and Mr Jordan Evans, a customs officer from Bamburgh. That morning, Monday 10 September, Smeddle had brought him across from the mainland to visit the wreck site.

It was only yesterday, Sunday, when the Great Storm had abated sufficiently for everyone staying in the lighthouse to feel confident, physically and emotionally, to go out to sea again.

The swell was still boisterous, but with none of the angry violence of the previous days, as William Brooks brought the coble out of the boatshed. She had dried out and seemed undamaged. William Brooks held her at the water's edge while the group said their goodbyes to Thomasina and Grace at the lighthouse door.

Sarah Dawson gave them long, tearful embraces that came from deep within her. Grace, she said, had helped her immeasurably through the immediate devastation of losing her children, and they vowed to exchange letters once Sarah was reunited with Jesse.

"You've nursed a little life back into me. Words can't express my gratitude."

Minus William Brooks, the Robsons' crew numbered six. They took with them in their large coble three men from the *Forfarshire* – Tulloch, Tickett, Macqueen – and William Darling. The others, including a very fragile Sarah Dawson, stepped into the Darlings' coble with William Brooks.

Directed by William, the Robsons rowed first to Big Hawker, to recover the dead bodies. They carefully loaded the cold Dawson children first, then John Robb. The onset of *rigor mortis* had begun to stiffen the reverend's corpse. Exploring the wreck, they located a fourth body, that of the passenger, James Gallagher. They placed it on the coble floor alongside the others. When they arrived in Bamburgh, a parish undertaker was awaiting them in St. Aidan's churchyard.

One of the Robsons accompanied William and William Brooks into Bamburgh Castle. They were taken to Robert Smeddle, at work in his office. Meanwhile, the other members of the Robsons' crew remained with the nine survivors on the village green. They shared a stottie, then helped the locals to pick up far-flung storm debris of branches, twigs and leaves. Two shop signs that had been wrenched from their fascias lay in tatters on the green, beyond repair.

Smeddle had made good on his promise to accommodate the survivors, which was greatly appreciated. He also committed to free access for any who needed it to the infirmary and to support them when they were ready to return home.

Today, 10 September, Robert Smeddle and Jordan Evans were the second in a string of visitors to Longstone.

Early morning brought the regular boat delivering provisions. Thomasina was still putting items away when Smeddle arrived. The first thing he did – discreetly – was to hand payment to William, as Trinity House had requested, for sighting the wreck, putting out the first boat and saving lives. He said he'd pay a minority share to the North Sunderland crew for making it to Big Hawker and recovering the bodies.

Even while Smeddle was reading reports of the wreck from the newspapers he'd brought from Bamburgh, and drinking cups of Thomasina's finest tea, the day's next visitor landed. William Brooks went to help him drag his boat into the shed.

Entering the lighthouse, the newcomer couldn't stop emphasising what a great pleasure it was to meet the Darlings in person. No sooner had he introduced himself as James Sinclair from Berwick than he apologised sincerely for the absence, due to illness, of Bartholomew Younghusband.

Younghusband was the well-regarded Lloyd's agent for the area, and Sinclair was deputising for him.

For more than a century, since London became an important centre for trade, the demand for specialist shipping and cargo insurance had gone up and up. More recently – in 1811, to be precise – a global network of Lloyd's agents was assembled. It did its job, boosting the flow of accurate intelligence, enabling Lloyd's to enhance its reputation for settling valid claims promptly.

In representing Younghusband, the less experienced Sinclair was most eager to inspect the wreck at the earliest opportunity.

"Excellent!" exclaimed Smeddle. "I'll be happy to take you and Mr Evans over to the wreck site – he needs to see it too. Follow me, let's get started without more ado. Mr and Mrs Darling, thank you for your hospitality, I'm sure I'll see you again soon."

In fact, Smeddle returned to Longstone later that day.

While he rowed Sinclair and Evans to Big Hawker, where they were each affected by the sight of the hulk smashed on the rock, the Darlings cleaned. William Brooks and Thomasina finished clearing up after the horde of visitors over Friday and Saturday nights. Upstairs, Grace and her father waxed the windows and the reflectors, and William took the opportunity to update his logbook as succinctly as ever.

Mid-afternoon, Grace noticed through her bedroom window a small, white rowing boat approaching Longstone. Her bow was low in the water due to the two passengers both seated at that end.

When she opened the lighthouse door, they already had notebooks in their hands. One, representing the *Tyne Mercury*, had a gap between his front teeth; the other, from the *Berwick & Kelso Warder*, a stubby nose that looked as though it was broken. They were quick to say that their hired oarsman had already rowed around Big Hawker, enabling them to sketch the remains.

William joined Grace by the fire to answer the pair's questions, which focused on the storm conditions, the destruction of the *Forfarshire* and the names and whereabouts of the survivors. One of them claimed to have been in contact already with Johnny Tulloch, the carpenter, who had left Longstone the previous day.

During this interview, Smeddle arrived back on the island. He had deposited James Sinclair and Jordan Evans in Bamburgh, where Sinclair's wife was awaiting his return, having placed an order with a local dressmaker. Sinclair had retrieved a small section of cracked, rivetless boilerplate, which he was sure had come from the ship's engine room.

As Smeddle re-entered Bamburgh Castle, Peter Collingwood advised him that two reporters had just embarked for Longstone via Big Hawker. He did not want to miss out on discussions of local news that he felt in his bones would soon attain a national eminence.

Taking his coat for the second time that day, Grace asked Smeddle whether by any chance a caring lady, Bess Wansbeck, whom she remembered from a childhood visit to the castle, still worked there.

"I know the name," Smeddle replied thoughtfully. "Bess worked for one of my predecessors, didn't she? She retired before I started. I don't think I've met her, but I can assure you, she is fondly remembered by those who knew her."

"That's good to hear."

"If I may say so, Grace," Smeddle said, suddenly conspiratorial, "you yourself may be fondly remembered for your part in Friday's rescue. Your solo handling of the coble was extraordinary, extremely brave. Your father told me all about it yesterday. Do you know, if things work out as I believe they might, there'll be a silk gown in it for you, as befits a heroine. You mark my words!"

Grace blushed, lost for words. It had never occurred to her that the rescue might spawn lasting effects – why would it? The Darlings had done their job to their best of their ability, as they had for generations.

Grace and, she was certain, her Papa too had regarded it as all in a day's work, that was all there was to it. But first Sarah Dawson and now this aloof man Smeddle, the Lord Crewe agent, had suggested she had acted heroically.

Unless they were simply exaggerating, what were they really saying? She had taken his reference to a silk gown figuratively – why would she need a silk gown anyway? She was a lighthouse keeper's daughter. If she were ever able to buy expensive garments, she would want to discuss her selection with her sister Thomasin first.

Quite so. But still sad to record that, as events were to transpire, Grace never got a silk gown.

Smeddle patronised her with a smile. She could not help but feel that his comment had been a little test, which she had failed by not rising to the challenge and giving a quick-witted answer. Had he meant to destabilise her? Surely not. Avoiding eye contact, she escorted him to her father and the reporters. Smeddle introduced himself and took a seat.

"We were just saying," the *Tyne Mercury* man recapped helpfully, "that the national press may pick up the news of the ill-starred *Forfarshire* from the reports we print locally. The nationals often reproduce stories from local papers, especially if they don't have a correspondent of their own on hand. And of course, maritime disasters are always a popular read in coastal parts."

"Is there any word on how many people lost their lives?" Grace asked. "Drowning must be such a horrible way to go."

"We're saying at least forty lives lost, including the captain, a fellow named John Humble. Someone has said that his wife was on board too, we're trying to check that."

There was silence until Smeddle jumped in. "I myself have written to the *Dundee Courier*," he revealed. "Dundee was not just the intended destination of the *Forfarshire*, it is of course where the company that owns her is based."

"And where she was built," added the man from the *Berwick & Kelso Warder*, flicking through his notes.

"It's also the place," William cut in, "where the *Forfarshire* should have docked several days ago and where dozens of families must be desperate, increasingly so by the minute, for word of their loved-ones, friends, colleagues."

I can picture Grace nodding vigorously at this.

"Just so. Now I have another headline for you – for all of you," Smeddle announced. He paused until certain that all eyes were on him. "An inquest to consider the cause of death of the bodies on the island is to take place tomorrow, Tuesday the eleventh."

"Tomorrow!" William gasped. Just two days after the bodies were recovered.

"I was able to secure the services of a coroner, Mr Stephen Reed, at short notice, and I've commandeered the upstairs room at Hugh Ross's place in Bamburgh."

The Darlings had met Hugh Ross, a forty-seven-year-old, Scots-born innkeeper, whose large family now helped to organise the annual St. Aidan's Feast. Inquests were commonly held in inns where there were private rooms with tables large enough to fit all the jurors, witnesses and reporters, and to display a body.

Changes to the law introduced the previous year, 1837, required coroners – now paid one pound six shillings and eight pence per 'duly held' inquest – to file reports and certify the cause of death. Still, more detailed accounts of proceedings often appeared in the newspapers. As you'd expect, demand for inquests continued to rise, but only a few hundred coroners operated in the country while several hundred thousand deaths occurred each year.

Coroners could act only when formally notified by a member of the public. In practice, local parish officers tended to serve as middlemen between coroners and the public, and Robert Smeddle had taken it upon himself to ensure that in this case a coroner was duly notified.

"Besides," Smeddle appended, "you know how voracious is the public's appetite for gossip and scandal." Presumably, at this moment, the two reporters found something in their notebooks to study intently. "Half the time, people simply believe what they want to believe. But with so many lives lost in this disaster, it must be better to actuate a proper process than to give free rein to the inevitable rumour mill."

As so often, Smeddle phrased his remarks with such precision that no one could disagree with him. Grace admired his ready eloquence, even though she somehow felt wary of him.

In the event, the inquest convened the following afternoon was a biased, botched affair.

It began promisingly enough with a preamble by Stephen Reed, which I believe went along these lines:

"Our nation has known two or three thousand years of seafaring, for the purposes of exploration and trade. Inevitably, part of the legacy of that seafaring is some loss and disaster – always has been. We must strive today to uncover the truth of what happened on 7 September, because it is only by doing so that we may learn from any mistakes made and move forward better informed."

Well said, sir. But – and it's a big but – the inquest went downhill rapidly from there.

The Darlings were not present; nor were the North Sunderland boatmen. The two directors of the Dundee & Hull Steam Packet Company, Messrs. Just and Boyd, who travelled from Dundee to Bamburgh at their earliest opportunity on the Monday, and visited the wreck on the Tuesday morning, were not even admitted to offer any evidence of their own.

Those who did speak seemingly had little knowledge of the Farne Islands or of the prevailing conditions. The hapless James Sinclair, representing Lloyd's, gave poor testimony, drawing unproven conclusions from the fragment of boilerplate he had taken from Big Hawker. When it was pointed out that it may have come from the cargo in the ship's hold rather than from the engine room, he had no answer.

Nevertheless, as the accounts of the night in question unfolded, a sense of outrage infected the jurors. How could the captain have knowingly set sail in a death-trap? Why did the company not have proper procedures to prevent this?

Despite an impromptu appearance in the room by Hugh Ross's youngest daughter, eight-year-old Jane, when he was summing up, as coroner he affirmed the jury's knee-jerk conclusion that the deaths occurred because of the malfunctioning boilers and the captain's abject failure to return to port. A fine of £100 was imposed on the company, and Reed wrote to the Home Office asking for safety obligations on steamship operators to be tightened in law.

I learned that the case was passed from the Home Office to the Board of Trade, which established its own inquiry.

The inquest had another significant outcome. For the reporters in the room, this was the moment when the story of the *Forfarshire* changed tack. It was no longer a dry matter of mechanical failure and corporate and/or personal culpability.

Now, amidst the scandalous loss of life, a new heroine was born. An apparently ordinary girl, twenty-two years of age, thrust into an extraordinary situation. With no expectation of reward, she had put her own life on the line to help others when her own prospects of returning safely through the storm were far from certain.

It's easy to see that here was a living, breathing, human interest angle – a gift to the media.

For Grace Darling, life saver, it was the moment when her life changed. Irrevocably and forever.

— 27 —

Circus Royal

Come one, come all, roll up!

For fifty years, the city of Newcastle had a Theatre Royal on Drury Lane, an alley off Mosley Street. When it opened in 1788, it fast established itself as one of the region's – no, let's say the country's – most prestigious stages. In February last year, 1837, it relocated to a splendid new site on Grey Street as part of the city centre regeneration.

Approaching the theatre through the bustle of people and horses, the bearded man with long, thinning, fair hair looked up at its sandstone façade. It was one of the grandest he had ever seen, welcoming, but with an undeniable hint of asperity. The façade was dominated by a high portico with six columns overshadowing the wide steps to the ornate entrance.

Inside, he bounded up to the second floor, where he was using an unexpectedly spacious, high-ceilinged office reserved for the impresarios or producers of shows playing there. On the whitewashed wall behind his desk was a framed playbill of his current touring show:

WILLIAM BATTY'S CIRCUS ROYAL

He had come a long way as a showman, he liked to reflect, since his first equestrian performances ten years ago. Whenever he was asked, I believe he generously acknowledged Philip Astley as his inspiration.

Back in 1768, Astley, a former cavalry Sergeant Major, had opened a riding school in Lambeth, south-east London. Having taught all morning, he performed feats of horsemanship in the afternoon. The performance space he constructed, forty-two feet in diameter and coated in sawdust, is considered the first modern circus ring. Endowed with a foghorn voice, Astley built up a world-class company of acrobats, jugglers and clowns, which continued to be popular after his death in 1814.

Though he rarely expressed it, William Batty's dream was to run an amphitheatre like Astley's. I might as well let you know that his dream came true in 1842, when he took over Astley's Amphitheatre itself.

Since he launched his provincial touring circus in 1836, Batty had earned a reputation as one of the smartest, most successful proprietors of the age. He fanned the careers of various artistes, including Pablo Fanque – there he was on the multi-coloured playbill – a versatile rope dancer, tumbler and, above all, horse rider.

Born in Norwich as William Darby, Pablo had been apprenticed to Batty since the 1820s. At first, they billed him prosaically as 'Young Darby', but the change of stage name had done the trick and Pablo Fanque became famous. He had recently shared his ambition to become, in the fullness of time, a circus proprietor in his own right.

Happily, Batty's own nephew, Thomas, barely six years old, was showing that he had a temperament to perform, as well as a passion for the big cats. The lad had a bright future in the ring.

No one who worked for Batty, or tried to analyse his success, ever doubted his entrepreneurial spirit and commercial acumen, in addition to his equestrian brilliance. He was an implacable believer in the power of publicity. He insisted on his circus cast conducting street parades at every host city on the tour.

He had honed a crystal-clear sense of the public audiences he was targeting, with tickets priced between sixpence and three shillings. Whether to the crowds of new working-class employees in factories, mines and workshops toiling long hours for low pay, or to the expanding middle-class shopkeepers, bank managers and factory owners, Batty understood that the circus offered escapism. They all craved big dreams. It opened a window on to an unseen yet exotic world of derring-do, stunts and oddities. Alongside his beloved stallions and mares, he presented wild acts featuring as many elephants, zebras, lions, tigers and leopards as he could source from the colonial world.

During a seven-thirty evening show at the previous venue in York, a leopard had escaped from the cage and sunk its teeth into the sleeve of a female spectator in the front row. Mercifully, the coat she was wearing was a thick one, well padded. Despite her screams, many in the audience believed this turn of events was all part of the act. The leopard, as graceful as it was powerful, behaved instinctively, just as it would in its native Rajasthan. It dragged the quaking woman to a pillar, substituting for a tree, where its kills would naturally be devoured.

On this occasion, at the sharp crack of a whip, it had loosened its grip. The lacerations on the woman's arm were cleansed and patched up and she seemed placated with a bottle of Veuve Clicquot. You can hear the reassurances, can't you: no real harm done, my dear, thank you for your commendable forbearance. We'll most certainly change the lock on the cage as soon as we can.

Besides, there had been minor abrasions before, to over-reaching spectators viewing the wild animal menagerie between circus shows. Nothing too serious and, to be honest, Batty was contented whenever the word-of-mouth authenticated his advertised promise of danger.

Still, it was just as well that that sort of accident did not occur too often, he told himself as he turned to the pile of newspapers before him and separated the back issues from the current editions.

He had taken to inviting well-known sportspeople, actors and public figures to his circus, for the publicity value and kudos they brought. It helped to elevate his production from the pack. After two months – August and September 1838 – in Newcastle, the next tour venue in October and November was to be an arena on the Earthen Mound, which stood between the old and new towns in Edinburgh.

Whilst wondering who to ask gainfully to a show there, he had been struck by the recent newspaper coverage of the twenty-two-year-old woman from the Farne Islands, who had not simply shown remarkable – unprecedented, it seemed – fortitude but, more broadly, embodied the very values that contemporary society held most dear. She could hardly be more perfect, could she?

Batty had thought hard about the nature of 'heroism', an epithet he applied wilfully on every playbill and advertisement, relating to one or more of his sensational acts. Heroes, he believed, were brave, noble, altruistic. They were inspirational, too – their actions uplifted everyone else emotionally, psychologically. Their feats necessarily involved sacrifice – putting others first, even when doing so endangered themselves. Therefore, heroes were not born – anybody could become one – rather, they were made, both by what they overcame to make their mark, and by the wider recognition of their peers.

Surely, he reasoned, by this or any similar yardstick, this woman was a hero. A hero with a deliciously 'marketable' name to boot: Grace Darling. How well it would sit on his playbill!

And yet, as far as Batty could tell, there was another layer on top of Grace Darling's heroism that made her, well, *everyone's* darling. The press was portraying her as self-effacing, honest and polite, a young woman entirely capable within her own sphere – the lighthouse and surrounding islands – yet not apparently courting fame.

There seemed to be no letters from her, nor any face-to-face interviews, in any newspaper – which, of course, made readers all the hungrier for fresh information about her.

Nothing, either, from her father, whatever his name was. His role in the valiant rescue was conveniently downgraded or even omitted.

Although Grace's rise from obscurity had been rapid, her star was showing no sign of fizzling out. Quite the reverse. Yes, Batty was on to something special here. No, he couldn't think of anyone better to approach. Leafing through the pages gave him a chance to check which other entertainments were advertised in which publications, so it was time doubly well spent.

He noticed that a report on the shipwreck in the *Tyne Mercury* on Tuesday 11 September had been reproduced in *The Scotsman* the following day and in *The Times* the day after. Also on 11 September, the *Dundee Courier* printed letters about the disaster from three correspondents, Robert Smeddle, Glen Ritchie and James Duncan. I can confirm that the latter, the *Forfarshire*'s first mate, had just made it home to Dundee from Newcastle, completing the last leg on a steamer from Leith.

Ritchie, meanwhile, his forehead bandaged, had reached Bamburgh, where he bought himself new – or second-hand, it didn't matter – trousers and shoes. Unable to find any information about those lost in the wreck, he feared the worst for his aunt and uncle, about whom no one had seen or heard anything. While he fretted, he felt compelled to give a statement to the inquest, which declared that the accursed boilers had leaked from the moment they left Hull, which he believed to be true.

Following the inquest, news of Grace Darling's heroic rescue appeared in the *Newcastle Courant* on Friday 14 September, a week after the wreck, and on Saturday 15 September in the *Newcastle Chronicle* and the *Berwick & Kelso Warder*. News and opinion spread in fits and starts, not only in the north-east but UK-wide.

Numerous reporters had raised the prospect of a reward for Grace, befitting her tremendous act. On Wednesday 19 September, *The Times* ran a lengthy article, much of which reiterated testimony from the inquest. It also deliberately raised the tempo of the discussion about safety at sea, and elevated Grace Darling to the status of national heroine.

William Batty, stroking his beard, made up his mind there and then. He filed a mental note to discuss the next steps with Thomas Sylvester, the manager of his touring company. Batty's pulse never failed to quicken when he thought of the company preparing for its next performance. They put on a breathtaking, beautiful show, rippling with skill and wit, and he was proud of them. He himself would soon need to change into his top hat and tails.

First, he had time to compose a pithy, but careful, letter. He took out a single sheet of thick, silver-edged, cream notepaper and dipped his fountain pen into the inkwell. As he wrote, a phrase in that pivotal *Times* article whirled incessantly in his head:

Is there in the whole field of history, or of fiction even, one instance of female heroism to compare for one moment with this?

— 28 —

National treasure

Just a light offshore breeze.

On Thursday afternoon, 20 September, Grace and William rowed to the mainland. The contrast with the violence they'd experienced during what was already known locally as 'The Great Storm' of 6–9 September could not have been starker. It was a beautiful, cloudless, autumn day, more like summer. Conditions around the Farne Islands were flat calm.

Grace handled the coble with familiar ease, which was a relief. She'd been troubled by nightmares involving the Dawson children, locked in eternal sleep from which their parents could never rouse them, and dozens of other men, women and children in freezing water, desperate to breathe and yet drowning. Grace wondered how Sarah Dawson was coping with life... poor soul, it doesn't bear thinking about, does it?

Two fishing boats came close to them, each with a cloud of gulls scavenging overhead. William altered course to avoid their wash and they ended up rowing near to Staple Island at the centre of the chain.

Rising vertically out of the sea off this island were four stacks of black rock, the tops of which had long been stained white by bird droppings. Grace knew that the Pinnacles, as the stacks were named, were home to a multitude of birds, and she was as delighted as ever to see many pairs of puffins, serene and still, bobbing on the ripples.

They beached at Bamburgh and made use of the castle's large boatshed in the dunes. As William had last done eleven days ago, they walked up the steep path into the castle compound and were escorted to the agent's apartment.

"Do come in," Robert Smeddle said, holding the heavy door wide open. "A pleasure to see you both again."

Despite his welcome, Grace felt that he radiated no warmth. They sat down by a window.

"Thank you for making the trip over, I know you're busy."

William Brooks had willingly stayed on Longstone to carry out the routine tasks set by Trinity House. Thomasina wanted to spin yarn, from which she would weave a fine cloth, some of which was already promised to her near-namesake dress-making daughter.

"Do you know," Smeddle asked, "how many items the GPO delivers each year? In the country overall, I mean, not just here."

Grace and William said nothing – well, what an opening gambit that was! They can't have expected it but, regardless, they felt sure they were about to be enlightened.

Smeddle held court. "In excess of a hundred million!" he exclaimed, clearly admiring the scale of such an operation. "Amazing, isn't it? Most of them are letters, of course, but about thirty million newspapers are included, too. Many literate folk such as your good selves correspond regularly. For commercial traders, lawyers, universities, monasteries and many more, a reliable postal service has become a necessity."

Smeddle took a sip of water and offered some to the Darlings, who politely declined.

The General Post Office was established way back in 1660. For the first time, it mandated a postal service for the whole country, superseding local arrangements. Some of those had originated when Britain was part of the Roman Empire, which needed deliveries of tablets and parcels to connect its widespread territories.

Mail coaches, whose drivers and guards wore distinctive scarlet uniforms, kept to the main roads, covering a hundred miles a day, or fewer when inclement weather led to the roads being churned up. Horses travelling at speed were changed every ten miles at coaching inns, where two minutes were permitted to switch over a team of four and their driver.

Mail coming north from London would take three days to reach Edinburgh, via Doncaster, Durham, Newcastle, Alnwick, Belford, Berwick, and all points in between. Local letter-carriers would take the mail to its stated address, usually collecting payment on a per-sheet basis on delivery. Having to wait for the cash and give change made every stop slow-going.

Smeddle sensed that big changes were in the air. He'd know that last year, 1837, a series of Post Office Acts passed by parliament had repealed a ton of old laws, clearing the path for a more fully integrated postal service in future. From this year, mail was being carried on the railways, which were not only speedier, they also enabled letters to be sorted en route.

"The last week has seen more mail delivered here to the castle than any previous week on record," Smeddle proclaimed, filling his glass from the pitcher of water. "And most of it isn't even for us, it's for you!" He brandished an arm at Grace, who blushed and looked away.

"I'd say the same regarding the lighthouse," William told him, which rather burst his bubble. "Every day brings more mail than the day before – the trickle is turning into a flood. Letters of appreciation, poems that people have written, bids galore for an autograph."

"And requests for a snip of my hair," Grace protested. "If I replied yes to each one, I'd have no hair left!"

"Oh, you must reply, my dear," Smeddle said icily, eyes brooding. "It's not every day that a native of Bamburgh becomes such a national treasure."

"Hardly that..."

"Very much so, my dear, you're well on your way. Working in the lighthouse, as you do, you may have little opportunity to perceive the wider picture, as I try to do myself." There may have been some truth in this, but it sounded unnecessarily patronising. William shifted awkwardly on his chair.

Smeddle indicated the separate bundles of newspaper cuttings and unsealed letters on his desk. He scratched the mole on his cheek, gathering his thoughts.

"You see, what's happening is, I think, something rare. Exceptionally so. News of the rescue of the nine survivors is spreading far and wide. People are astounded at first, but soon they're thrilled, that a woman, a young woman, played such a pivotal role. And not just any young woman, if I may say so, but one who is reserved, selfless, modest. Can you see how that makes you an ideal, a form of perfection, in the eyes of the press and the public?"

"Grace has no wish for publicity," William asserted, seeing his daughter squirm. He was a subtle man and he knew the castle agent wasn't. "Nor, for that matter, do I." Well said. For one thing, he wouldn't want Trinity House suspecting that he and the family were distracted from their duties.

"Which is all part of the attraction, isn't it?" cried Smeddle. "By preserving the scarcity of something – in our case, access to Grace – you make it more valuable, don't you? Everyone knows that! But it's already clear that the public will not be satisfied with merely reading about the rescue. They want trinkets, souvenirs, something tangible."

Smeddle pulled forward the letters.

"Displaying on a mantlepiece an article connected to a paragon of virtue is simply the custom, my dears. It's a status symbol. I've received dozens of requests for strips of Grace's clothing, locks of hair as you say, even proposals of marriage. From all over the country."

He looked at Grace, who was staring at her feet, too uncomfortable to look either man in the eye. She could not bring herself to ask who or where the marriage proposals had come from.

"A fortnight tonight," Smeddle was speaking again, consulting the top letter in the pile, "a sumptuous dinner will take place after the Northumberland Agricultural Society's annual show. It's in Wooler this year, in a plain by the Cheviot hills. They wish to raise a toast to you."

"I don't know anyone in that society," Grace objected. "I've never met–"

"Precisely!" said Smeddle. Was that a flicker of anger colouring his cheeks, threatening to crack the veneer of patience? "But they are seeking to be friendly, inclusive. Lord Ossulston will propose the toast. People are eager to celebrate your achievement, Grace, that's all. These requests come from kind hearts, you must see that."

Smeddle's right hand had coiled into a fist, his fingernails digging into the flesh of his palm.

"One of the letters we opened at the lighthouse this morning," William said, "was from the recorder at a dinner held by the Mayor of Newcastle. He informed us that a toast to the health of 'Grace Darling, the heroine' had been drunk to immense applause." Those were his very words.

"Well, there you are," Smeddle exhaled, calm restored. He spoke slowly, as if proving to himself that he had regained full control. "There will be many more such toasts, I fancy, in the coming weeks. Some formal and planned, others quite spontaneous."

"May I ask your advice?" William asked. Grace stared at him.

"Only too pleased to help, sir." A sigh.

"A printer in Durham has written to enquire about adding Grace's name to a calendar he is producing for 1839. It would just require a signature–"

"Say yes!" Smeddle urged. "Why on Earth not? Now, I have some additional correspondence from newspaper reporters. Some are requesting interviews, others rather more bluntly stating their intentions to travel to Longstone. Please welcome them into your home as warmly as you do everyone. Even me."

Smeddle smiled thinly. William simply said: "Of course."

"May I use a WC please?" Grace asked. Smeddle directed her along the corridor. He had noticed that her left eye had developed a twitch that he had not observed before.

Once Grace was out, Smeddle and William both began to speak at the same moment. William apologised, gave way.

"Please try to get her to go along with all this," Smeddle pleaded, rustling the letters. "As I said, a lot more of these will come, and you can't turn back time. For better or worse, that rescue is going to change Grace's life."

"Alas," was all William muttered. He thought of asking: How exactly will my daughter's life change? What will become of her? But he refrained.

"I also want to let you know," Smeddle continued after another glug of water, "that a second inquest is to be held. Monday week, 1 October, in Hugh Ross's rooms in the village."

"Oh?"

"As you know, the remains of the *Forfarshire* have been pored over, fine tooth combs deployed, and many interesting pieces have come to light. I gather the ship's bell has been recovered, the anchor, the nameplate from the bow. There is to be a public sale of these items on 2 October. Sadly, the wreck also yielded one more body, a man named..." Smeddle checked among his papers "...yes, Bill Douthy. He was a crew member, one of the firemen, I am told. He was not included in the first inquest, so we are obliged to convene another."

William had heard about the partial evidence admitted at the first inquest, and he thought Smeddle must be relieved to have this heaven-sent opportunity to put matters right. Partly in response to that poorly informed session, William had sent an unusually long – 270 words – letter to Trinity House, setting out what had transpired hour by hour on the night of the rescue.

Four doors along, Grace was admiring what was an unfamiliar, very modern WC room. It was really a bathroom: along one wall was a rolltop bathtub with lion's claw feet. On a long shelf: a row of clean, white chamber pots, just like the ones she and her family used at Longstone. Below it, a wrought-iron washstand. On the floor, small square tiles laid in a black and white check pattern – which is fashionable again two hundred years later, isn't it?

Facing the bathtub was a WC that Grace thought was brand new. It had a high-level cistern with a chain pull. She wondered where the waste went when the chain was pulled. She had heard of places where it dropped into a cesspool, where at night it was covered in soil and sold to farmers as fertilizer.

Grace sat on the WC and put her head in her hands. She was as keen as mustard to do her best by her family, and the rescue on 7 September, as she had already told Mr Smeddle and others, was simply an example of the Darlings fulfilling their duty. Suddenly it seemed to have been blown out of all proportion. She did not recognise this 'national heroine', it wasn't her.

She had shaken off the awkward shyness of her childhood. She was part of a large family, after all, and visitors came and went frequently on Longstone. This was all part of the everyday life she loved as the lighthouse keeper's daughter. She had implacable faith in her father, a shrewd, measured man, a wise judge – and the lack of acclaim for his leadership of the rescue seemed perfunctory, hurtful, wrong.

She was not fazed by risk, either. Jeopardy in many forms was present throughout her life. For goodness' sake, any of her beloved seabirds took risks when they left their nests unattended: the gulls she had watched following the fishing boats on today's journey were the most aggressive predators she'd ever seen. With their five-foot wingspan and yellow beaks, they'd swoop on other birds' eggs and drive them out of their nests. In the world she knew well, risk was built into everyday life for all creatures.

What had distressed her most was the idea that – purely because she had rowed her heart out a couple of weeks ago – she was becoming public property. The thought of being forced to *perform*, to compete for applause, to play the part of this other person, this idealised Grace Darling that wasn't her, mortified her. She knew herself and her purpose very well, and detested the thought of being paraded in front of unknown spectators who would see through her, judge her, mock her.

She was sure Smeddle had seen the tell-tale twitch in her eye. But she was more concerned that he was pushing her into an intrusive, fake new world, rather than protecting her from it. Well, more than ever, she hoped, that would be her father's role. And yet, was she loading difficulties unfairly on to her family's shoulders? Should she keep her worries from them? She only wanted to do her best by them...

When Grace returned to Smeddle's apartment, she had splashed water on her cheeks and combed her hair with her fingers, and she felt less agitated by her inner conflicts.

Smeddle brought a new letter to the fore, ran a finger along its silver edge.

"This one arrived this morning," he said, holding the single cream sheet. "Please take your time to consider it, there's no need for an instant reaction. It's from a Mr William Batty, esteemed proprietor of the Circus Royal – you may have heard of it?"

"I think there was a notice advertising his show in one of the newspapers we've been looking at," said William. "Was it on in Newcastle?"

"Exactly so," Smeddle said, delighted. "The next venue on Mr Batty's tour is Edinburgh and he would like you, Grace, to make an appearance. I'm sure that, if you so wish, your father may accompany you. Batty is suggesting a visit, to put his case and settle any qualms or questions. Now," Smeddle continued without a beat to preclude any objections, "I have a second letter sent from that fine city. The Edinburgh Ladies, a dining society of impeccable repute, has been impressed by your – let me see – yes, 'your generous devotion to the good of your fellow creatures' – I couldn't have put it better myself. They are proposing a tribute dinner and are enquiring as to your potential availability. Have you ever been to Edinburgh?"

Grace frowned. "No, I haven't."

"Or perhaps that should be no, not yet," said Smeddle, eyes wide with encouragement. "Let me leave both of these letters, indeed all of these letters, with you." He squared off the pile, handed it to William.

"We'll consider every request and send a reply," William promised.

Grace's heart sank further. If Smeddle knew how long she took writing each page, he would realise how many weeks of work lay ahead for her in answering that lot. And what about the stack, growing daily, sent directly to the lighthouse? How was she meant to deal with all of them too?

Smeddle opened a drawer in his desk. "This came for you," he said. "It's a bible from an admirer in Hull."

"An admirer?"

"An ordinary member of the public, so moved by your actions and by your character as he appreciates it, that he's sent a gift. There's an inscription on the flyleaf. It's rather lovely, isn't it?"

William thanked him and placed the leather-bound book under the letters he was holding. Grace nodded and stood up. Perhaps it was from someone connected to the *Forfarshire* or to one of the survivors?

"Ah, one more thing." Smeddle withdrew from his drawer a bundle of plain white cards. "Grace, my dear, would you sign your autograph on these, please? They're useful and it'll save you the bother later… that's excellent, thank you so much."

Grace accepted his blue ink pen, her face like stone. Deep inside, she had reached the hopeless, repellent conclusion that her life was no longer her own.

29

The artist and the smugglers

"Come in!"

The room was flooded with light from two picture windows. The shadows of the easels, which had crept across the floor, were now inching up the wall, looking like barricades.

As the door swung open, the forty-three-year-old artist rose from his desk, setting aside the pencil sketch of the Bengal tiger whose hind legs he had been shading.

This room, at the top of the apartment in Pilgrim Street, central Newcastle, had been his studio since he and his wife, Amy, moved in years ago and it had served him well. It was appreciably more salubrious than their first home in the city and he would do anything to avoid telling Amy, especially now when she was lying pregnant and sick in bed in the next room, that they might need to relocate to live within their means.

His name was Henry Perlee Parker, the middle name which had so helped to distinguish him being thanks to his paternal grandmother, who was French. He himself was born in Devon in 1795, the same year that Robert Darling moved his young family from Belford to Brownsman Island to start his new life as lighthouse keeper.

Henry's Methodist father taught marine and mechanical drawing for the Royal Navy. He had trained young Henry, too, until he could competently produce drawings for his father's students to copy. Soon Henry felt constrained and yearned to give his artistic abilities full expression. Well, that's only natural, isn't it?

He was twenty when he married Amy and ventured for the first time to the north-east to stay with Walter, Amy's land-owner brother. Henry felt at home there, as, thankfully, did Amy too. He set himself up in a little shop, where he drew portraits for subjects willing to cough up a guinea each, and he taught art classes for the extra income which had allowed them to move to Pilgrim Street.

Leveraging the initial sponsorship of his brother-in-law, he cultivated others. Charles Brandling, who owned coal mines and was elected MP for Newcastle in 1820, admired Henry's paintings and became a client. So, Henry had his entrée into Newcastle society just as the city was expanding with engineering and shipbuilding, as well as coal mining and glass blowing.

Co-operating with other local artists, Henry founded the northern Academy of the Arts and Fine Arts Exhibition. He chose his subjects shrewdly, painting large civic events as well as personal portraits, and he exhibited works for sale in London.

The 1820s were a marvellous decade: he felt, justifiably, that he had made a good name for himself. In the 1830s, inevitably perhaps with the passage of time, he found new patrons and commissions harder to come by, but by then he had a growing family to feed.

Mary, who had just entered his studio, was his first child. He always thought she had been a lucky charm in his career and his life. He would remind her of the family holiday they'd taken up in Northumberland when she was five. They had found a secluded beach between the villages of Amble and Boulmer.

One afternoon, ever confident, ever inquisitive, Mary had gone exploring. In a tiny cove, barely five minutes from where her parents were relaxing on the pristine sand, she stumbled across six men, talking secretively around a stash of ten-gallon barrels and wooden crates. The cove was bigger than it looked. At the back was the mouth of a narrow tunnel whose tall sides, lined with ships' timbers, were stacked high with bales of tobacco.

When Henry found her, she was chatting to one of the men as if they'd been pals for years. He must have been relieved and terrified at the same time – I know I would have been!

Two of the six were from Holland. They were frequent, stealthy visitors to these shores, importing goods to order, under the cloak of darkness, for local distribution, avoiding cripplingly inflated taxes.

The other four were labourers, their faces concealed beneath wide-brimmed hats. They were supplementing their meagre incomes by delivering the contraband to grateful – and discreet – clients in shops, inns and farmhouses. In these parts, smugglers tended to have more sympathisers than adversaries.

The following morning, Henry sighted a black cutter close to the shore. Her crew must have numbered two dozen men and boys, and she was armed with at least three six-pounder cannons. He did not tell Mary that it was a revenue boat, searching for smugglers. But he had been inspired to make smugglers the subject of a new painting. When it was snapped up for a handsome price, he produced another, and the smuggler series became successful for him in the 1820s. Indeed, an early one was acquired for Bamburgh Castle.

Now, Mary handed over a slice of cake with dried fruits.

"Father, you must eat something," she said and watched as he spilled crumbs in his bushy beard. Curiously, it made her happy. With her mother expecting again, she had returned to help mind her younger siblings. The sheep's head she'd picked up yesterday for thruppence should feed them all for a few days. However, she was spending as much time looking after Henry as the rest of the family.

Three weeks ago, he had confided in Mary that he was concerned about repaying some debts – unspecified, and she didn't ask. But he made her promise not to tell her mother. She'd known from the look in his eyes that he was serious. The implications were unbearable.

"I've had an idea," she said now, walking to one of the large windows. Over the rooftops across the street was the peak of Grey's Monument, standing proudly against the azure sky. She sat down next to him and gave the back of his painting hand a comforting rub.

Henry grinned.

"This extraordinary woman on the Farne Islands," Mary said. "Grace Darling, her name is. She and her father saved nine people off a stricken steamer in a storm, and she's become a sensation, hasn't she? Well, why don't you go and paint her? And, I'm not finished yet, there must be an opportunity for you to do mezzotint engravings, too. With Christmas on its way, what better than souvenirs of an heroic sea rescue?"

She sat back and let the suggestion percolate in his mind. Seconds later: "That's wonderful!"

Then: "I could invite John to join me – his credentials would be particularly compelling, wouldn't they? If we worked on a piece together, it could be very – well, commercial. Oh, thank you, my dear."

Henry beamed at his lucky charm.

Mary knew that the 'John' was John Wilson Carmichael, one of the circle of Newcastle artists whom he had befriended. John's father was a ship's carpenter and he himself had been apprenticed to a firm of shipbuilders. But he soon devoted all his energies to artworks. When the plans for the city centre regeneration were being developed, he was hired to produce drawings of a new central railway station and a covered market in Grainger Street. He was paid a hundred guineas by the City of Newcastle Corporation for a commissioned painting, *A View of Newcastle upon Tyne*. But it was in his paintings of seascapes that John found the greatest fulfilment.

Surely a combination of Henry Parker and John Carmichael would find approval on Longstone? Unbeatable! At the risk of gilding the lily, who else did he know in Newcastle society who might make an impressive introduction on his behalf?

"You should act fast," Mary warned. "Other artists will no doubt have had the same idea."

"But no other artists' daughters," he countered, a glint in his eye. She was thrilled to see the weight lift off his shoulders.

It was then that Henry realised Mary was the same age as Grace Darling – give or take a few months. Perhaps Mary was slightly younger – recently he'd read so many facts and figures about the Darlings and the debates about maritime safety. Yes, Grace would be an interesting subject to commit to canvas, but there was a wider story unfolding, too, with her at its centre. Henry's mind conjured up images of shipwrecks, tempests, brave young rescuers.

"I'll go and see if mum wants–"

Suddenly the door burst open. In raced another of his children, nine-year-old Henry Raphael, who had inherited his love of design and could not stop communicating his passion to everyone in and out of the apartment.

"Is it true?" A high-pitched squeak.

Mary, who was his eldest sister, picked him up at the waist and sat him on her lap. "Is what true, young sir?"

"Are we really going to the circus?"

William Batty's Circus Royal was in the final week of its residency in the city, and it would soon be Henry Raphael's birthday.

Mary and Henry said nothing. They looked on as, agonisingly slowly, Henry picked up the pencil sketch from his desk. When he saw the prowling tiger, Henry Raphael made claws of his outstretched fingers, bared his teeth and whooped with delight.

30

In the eye of a storm

Encroachment.

Every day that autumn brought new visitors, more intrusions, to Grace's door.

It was on a Tuesday morning in mid-October that the circus proprietor, William Batty, and his grandly titled Theatrical & Equestrian Manager, Thomas Sylvester, arrived on Longstone. Both accomplished riders, they rode their own well fed, finely groomed horses south from Edinburgh.

They took lodgings in Bamburgh, shelling out a premium for private rooms at Hugh Ross's inn. He kept a pair of hedgehogs indoors to help reduce the population of beetles and earwigs. Lonely occupants of the adjacent rooms included a discharged soldier and a retired funeral director, both of whom appeared to be long-term tenants and made no noise. There were also two sisters, middle-aged, in multi-layered skirts whom Batty thought in passing would make excellent programme sellers at the circus, but Sylvester was not inclined to follow it up.

They secured the trip to Longstone on the day's provisions boat. Sylvester helped to carry a crate of water bottles and a bulging sack of mail to the lighthouse steps.

Inside, they felt warm and comfortable and enjoyed the cups of tea served with currant biscuits that had a moreish almond flavour. They flattered Thomasina by showing interest in her spinning wheel and the material she used. When they sat down for a discussion with William and Grace, Batty's first impression was that William was thoughtful but quiet. A shield had gone up which may be tough to break down.

Grace looked attractive – her long, glossy hair was down over her shoulders, and she was wearing a light blue shawl with a crescent-shaped silver pin brooch. But, Batty surmised, her eyes revealed the inner turmoil – dark rings encircled them, and they darted nervously about the room, even in her own home, as if she were a deer being stalked on the moors.

"It's several weeks now since the steamship was wrecked. How do you feel about everything that's happened?" Batty asked. "Your profile, to my eyes at least, has swept the country."

"More than forty lives were lost in that disaster." It was William who answered. "Some of them were infants. The shock of that, for those families at least, will never entirely go away." No one spoke, so he went on: "From our viewpoint, it was a hard night but a successful one, in so far as I think we saved everyone we could have saved. And of course, we try to stay prepared for the next time, whenever it may come."

"Let's hope it's a long time until another storm like that one batters these shores," said Sylvester. "People think our wild animals don't frighten easily, but they can get extremely disturbed in violent weather."

"And you, Grace, how are you? After all, you're the one at the centre of the storm, if I may put it that way?"

"Thank you for asking," Grace said to Batty. Beyond her parents and Thomasin in her latest letter, no one she had met in recent weeks had enquired how she was dealing with the extraordinary aftermath of the rescue. "Fame is not a state I covet," she said simply, adding: "I agree with my father's views. Whole-heartedly."

"I'm sure we all do. But I detect a conflict," Batty said, lifting imaginary weights in alternate hands. "This is why I was so keen to come and meet you in person, to see for myself. The newspaper reports focus on what might be called your masculine qualities – bear with me – your strength, courage, determination, yes? But what I'm seeing before me are female attributes – humility, radiance, concern for others."

Grace protested mildly. "Surely each of us possesses a mix of such qualities? In differing proportions, according to our different personalities. And I'm afraid that the personality portrayed in the newspapers is not me in real life."

Batty and Sylvester would later discuss how breathless Grace sounded when she unbottled her feelings about her public persona.

"In what way?" Batty asked. "Tell me more."

Grace shrugged. "I'm diffident… I'm not a hero."

Batty said: "Don't be too hard on yourself, Grace. Heroism is valued in many cultures. Heroes serve those in need, while making us all feel better about ourselves." He sipped his tea, smacked his lips and glanced at Sylvester.

"Anyway," he continued, "I believe I can offer a solution to your dilemma. You know from my letter a little about my travelling circus. Equestrian skills are our speciality, but audiences adore the wild animals, the lions and elephants in particular."

Sylvester nodded vigorously as William said: "I salute the educational merits of your production, Mr Batty, and I know you've worked hard to cater for all tastes."

Batty acknowledged the compliment. "My proposal, that you kindly attend one or more of my shows, will give you the opportunity to set the record straight, to reveal what really happened on the morning of 7 September, and to correct for good any misconceptions, as you wish."

Her brow furrowed, Grace studied her Papa's face for guidance.

Before William could react, Thomas Sylvester spoke up in support of his boss. "If I may, Grace, I think I see another conflict raging inside you. On the one hand, you're fearless. We know that from the breathtaking bravery of the rescue. Yes, really. On the other hand, you seem apprehensive of the public and how they might behave were you to appear in the ring. Well, please, let me reassure you. The public wants to like you. They know when something special happens, something skilful, daring, true. Performers and artists are communicators, aren't they, and yet out of the ring, lots of them are jarringly bashful – you'd be astonished. In our show, you can slay your demons, Grace, set your mind at rest. Tell the truth so that the record of your exploits is accurate and correct, for the present and the future."

Pin-drop silence.

Sylvester recognised that Grace had precious little experience of what he considered the 'dog eat dog' world outside the Farne Islands, and, shrewd fellow, he was not surprised that she was struggling to come to terms with the unrelenting attention.

The accelerating progress of science and technology had far outpaced the regulated protections for professional sailors and passengers. Public opinion had swung behind the Board of Trade and the newspaper campaigns which pressed for licenses to carry passengers, more frequent inspections, checks on engineers' qualifications and such like. The groundswell of support was by now, I suspect, well-nigh unstoppable.

At a Trinity House meeting in Newcastle, further demands for new legislation had been raised. Grace found the reform of shipping laws an obviously important yet rather tedious topic. But just as the wreck of the *Forfarshire* was a national talking point and a catalyst for change, so too had Grace herself become the totem of every new initiative to safeguard life at sea, every new measure proposed for steamships, where serious accidents, often due to boilers bursting, were all too common. At every turn, her name, her image, her achievements on 7 September were repeated.

"Thank you so much for coming to see us," William said at last to Batty and Sylvester. "We appreciate you going out of your way to visit."

"Grace, your name is on everybody's lips, with the most positive associations," Batty chipped in his parting shot. "You would appeal to every section of our audience. You'd be well protected – as are all the acts in the show – whether you opted to make a single appearance in Edinburgh or perhaps something longer-term. Your call. The door is always open."

"We shall consider the opportunity very carefully," William promised.

"Life is short, Grace," Sylvester whispered. "Enjoy it, won't you? And the very best of luck to you."

That afternoon, William recounted the meeting to Robert Smeddle in his apartment at Bamburgh Castle, while Grace leafed through the latest sheaf of correspondence sent to her care of the castle authorities.

Predictably, Smeddle urged them to attend the circus and to enter detailed negotiations with Mr Batty, who, Smeddle suggested, would be flexible and accommodating if he got what he wanted. I wonder whether William thought Smeddle was going to offer to negotiate on their behalf because he was mightily relieved when, instead of doing so, Smeddle moved on.

"I have been rereading the coroner's report from the second inquest," Smeddle confided. "There's a meeting of the Lord Crewe trustees later in the week, and I want the facts at my fingertips. The findings of the second inquest were much less—"

"Hasty?"

"Less controversial, I'd say." He gave William the eye. "The management of the Dundee & Hull Steam Packet Company was adequately represented, for one thing. The verdict of accidental death in the case of the poor fireman, Mr Bill Douthy, seemed fair, a more balanced conclusion."

"I read that the auction of the wreckage raised £500," William said as Grace continued skimming through her letters.

"Yes, quite an occasion," Smeddle recalled. "The person who purchased most lots was none other than Thomas Adamson from Dundee, whose yard built the *Forfarshire*. He paid £70 for the carcass of the ship. I gather its rather splendid bell has gone to Belford Hall." That was correct; I hope it brought better luck to the new owners.

"I was sent a slab of marble chimney breast from one of the cabins or lounges," William said, "which was very generous of the donor. I am minded to make something practical, hopefully long-lasting, out of it."

"Good for you," Smeddle warmed to the idea. "Oh, I should let you know that I've written to the Duke of Northumberland, enclosing a detailed report on the wreck and the discussion of safety on steamships that it has magnified. You know he takes a keen interest in seafarers' conditions?"

Yes, they did know. William might have mentioned that the duke had witnessed the construction of the Longstone lighthouse, but I don't think he had any desire to prolong the meeting.

Smeddle opened a drawer. "Grace, my dear." His tone bordering on the obsequious, she wondered what was coming next. "What do you make of all that correspondence?"

"People are so kind."

The letters, like so many already received, requested a ringlet of hair or an autograph. Some contained verses extolling her virtues – grossly exaggerated in her view, and she said so.

"Poetic license!" Smeddle scoffed, inhaling deeply. "Now, look, I have some other gifts for you."

He lifted a wooden box on to his desk and removed its loosely fitting lid.

"One of the passengers lost on the *Forfarshire* was a Mr David Churchill. His friends banded together and bought a fine set of silverware in his memory. This cream jug is engraved 'to the mother of Grace Darling'. This cup is for the father–" Smeddle handed both items to William "–and these are for you, Grace. Six silver teaspoons, and they've sent an illustrated bible, too. If you'll permit me, there's an inscription, which reads: 'To Grace Horsley Darling, the brave-hearted girl who, on the morning of 7 September 1838, thought not of her own life while assisting to save the lives of others, this book is presented by some of her admirers residing in Sneinton near Nottingham'."

"That's lovely, so thoughtful of them when they are grieving," said Grace, privately dreading writing the thank you letter to Mr Churchill's friends.

"That's not all," Smeddle said, extracting from his drawer a silver goblet. It was embossed with a coat of arms that included a prancing horse and two lions. "Last weekend, Lord Frederick Fitzclarence stayed here with his wife during a break in Lord Frederick's army activities. He was delighted, truly, to leave this for you, with a note testifying to his admiration of your deed. You'll know, of course, that Lord Frederick is a son of our recent king, William IV."

Yes, again, the Darlings did know of Lord Frederick Fitzclarence. They sat back, astounded.

Grace slid her silver teaspoons into the goblet. "I'm much obliged."

"I should think you are. Those goblets are highly exclusive. Now, have you received enquiries from any artists yet? I've taken the liberty of advising one or two to contact you directly."

William had visions of Smeddle exhorting artists throughout the county to head for Longstone, disregarding the fact that it was the Darlings' place of work. "As it transpires, Grace has already sat for a local sculptor, David Dunbar. Two painters, Henry Parker and John Carmichael, are arriving soon."

An aside from me: David Dunbar was a Scotsman, born in Dumfries, who travelled widely and at this time was based in Newcastle. To enhance his reputation, he staged exhibitions of other artists' works as well as his own. In his elegant marble bust of Grace, which was more than two feet tall and heavier than granite, she had her hair up, parted precisely in the centre.

"That's wonderful." Smeddle scratched his back. "I'm surrounded by painted portraits in this castle," he said, his gaze roving from William to Grace and back. "Please bear in mind that these images will be frozen in time. They will form part of your legacy, dare I say it, your legend, for years, perhaps for generations, to come."

Grace shuddered, felt the twitch in her eye.

"Thank you as ever for your counsel," William said appreciatively.

Smeddle's words played in his mind the following week when Parker and Carmichael arrived. They had paid four fishermen to row them to Longstone, without ever knowing that two of them – Tommy Cuthbertson and Bill Swan – were members of the Robsons' crew that reached Big Hawker on 7 September. At first, William was wary of these sophisticated city characters, but he and Thomasina were sure to extend the Darlings' customary comforts and courtesies.

"I must say, you come highly recommended," William told Henry Parker. "I received a glowing letter of introduction from John and Albany Hancock, who clearly admire your work."

"They admire yours, too," Henry responded. "Your passion for the natural world, and the samples you have sent over the years, have been a source of inspiration to them."

"We were enchanted by the grey seals we observed on our ride over here," said Carmichael. "I saw one emerge vertically from the sea with a large fish flapping in its jaws. It took a bite out of the middle, then played a game of tag with the tail section. It was almost as though the game was for our amusement."

William watched Grace smile and she caught his eye. Father and daughter recognised the charm offensive. William got directly to the point.

"How can we assist you, gentlemen? Do you know exactly what you want to illustrate?"

Henry stroked his beard, which helped him to concentrate. "I'd like to start with some pencil sketches, then paintings in watercolours. I'll keep the number of sittings to an absolute minimum," he assured Grace. "Do you have the clothes you wore during the rescue?"

"I do," Grace answered, warming to this man who had come prepared and seemed eager to start work. "That's fine."

"While Henry gets scribbling on his portraits," Carmichael said, "I intend to plan some scenes of the rescue itself – the coble on the stormy sea, the wrecked vessel, the survivors on the rock. May I have a look at your coble for reference, please? I've already arranged to be taken to Big Hawker to see what remains of the *Forfarshire*."

He was right to say, 'see what remains'. Fishing smacks had stripped the site of as much cargo, comestibles, furniture and potentially useable debris as they could carry, after the pick of the salvage had been auctioned off.

"Splendid!" William shot back.

"One further application," said Henry. "Have you ever had the chance to see a panorama?"

Although neither William nor Grace had seen one, they knew what they were: popular, often spectacular, forms of instruction and entertainment. Hundreds of panoramas with a great variety of themes toured theatres in the UK and overseas.

This is how they worked. Huge reels of painted canvas, hundreds of feet long, were mounted on two vertical cylinders, turned by concealed machines. Each scene had a rolling backdrop behind a narrator, centre-stage, who described the action as it unscrolled. A live musical accompaniment heightened the audience's emotions.

"We believe that a shipwreck and a sea rescue are perfect material for a moving panorama," Henry declared. "A supreme example of a humans-against-nature story. Numerous artists would have to be involved because of the sheer size of the backcloths, but I'd like to produce a panorama of the *Forfarshire*'s story to incorporate some of our new work. We hope the tour will start at the Theatre Royal in Newcastle."

William did not break the confidence, but he had already received word from another artist, Robert Watson, who intended to create a moving panorama show bringing the very same action to life. Watson had engaged Daniel Donovan, a survivor of the wreck, to narrate his version, which he hoped would open on Boxing Day in Sunderland, then move on to Hull and theatres elsewhere. He would display centre-stage on a plinth the marble bust of Grace sculpted by David Dunbar.

The Darlings were aware that, within three weeks of Dunbar making his sculpture in October, plaster-casts of it were advertised for sale at a guinea each. They had already politely declined an invitation from Watson to attend his panorama show and to be reunited with Mr Donovan; they would not attend Henry Parker's presentation, either.

In the event, Henry stayed on Longstone for a week, partly due to some inclement weather thundering in from the North Sea, but nothing like the Great Storm. Carmichael returned safely to Newcastle with the drawings he made on Big Hawker and began to sort the paints he needed in his studio.

Henry had a warm feeling about this project. It had started well, and he struck up an excellent rapport with Grace during her sittings. Hair up, trying not to giggle, she sat facing him and then with her head turned to the side. He said he wanted to capture a bright young woman who faced life in the present, as it came, which she rather liked.

Henry hoped zealously that his paintings would revitalise his flagging career, as his daughter Mary had suggested. He told Grace about Mary's encounter with the smugglers and they both laughed – as you can in hindsight. He ended up producing multiple sketches of Grace, William and Thomasina, as well as working with John Carmichael on a bigger, exhilarating representation of William and Grace rescuing the survivors.

Despite enjoying Henry's visit, Grace felt increasingly uneasy during these autumn months. She would wake up at the dead of night when she wasn't on watch, her heart racing, muscles tense, brow bathed in sweat. Crowds were gathering around her… scrutinising her… inventing stories about her… mimicking her voice… smothering her…

She tried to move on but was stuck fast. She would find herself short of breath, twitching, dreading what might come the next day. She did not confide in her parents, but discovered through trial and error that, by taking deep, regular breaths, she could better manage her anxiety – at least until the next time.

— 31 —

Rosa Victoriana

Wafting away a wasp, the woman who had been dead-heading flowers stood up straight.

Past her fiftieth birthday, she was as slender as ever. Crow's feet ran from the corner of her eyes but the skin on her neck and hands was firm. A quality in her genes, if you ask me. Her thick brown hair, hanging in ringlets with barely a hint of grey, was the envy of many friends, but it was her wide eyebrows, neatly trimmed, that gave her an unmistakable air of authority.

As the youngest daughter of the Earl of Powis, she had been titled the Honourable Charlotte Clive – Lady Charlotte – since birth. Her lifelong passion for horticulture had continued to deepen, and she was seldom happier, or more relaxed, than when planning new sections of her vast garden. She always tried to make time for it among her panoply of other duties.

She was thirty when she'd married the aristocrat, Hugh Percy, two years her senior. That was in April 1817, the same year he succeeded his father as the Duke of Northumberland. They lived in the Percys' ancestral home, Alnwick Castle, on which construction work commenced at the end of the eleventh century. Like so many fortifications in the region, it was part of England's line of defence against Scotland. An icon of Norman power, Alnwick Castle's moat was dug twenty feet deep.

It was a Norman baron, William de Percy, who established the House of Percy in England in December 1067. Notwithstanding a bitter rivalry with the House of Neville, the Percys were northern England's most influential noble family in the Middle Ages. Early in the fourteenth century, Henry de Percy purchased Alnwick Castle from the Bishop of Durham and greatly enhanced the property.

The present line of Percys, with a freshly granted dukedom, had occupied the castle since the eighteenth century. Hugh's father had been the second duke, so Hugh himself became the third and she, Charlotte, the duchess.

She had immersed herself in public life, realising and relishing opportunities as they arose. She wrote a history of the castle and founded a school for girls in Alnwick town centre.

In her own right she had a top-drawer circle of friends and acquaintances, including Sir Walter Scott, Earl Grey and the king, William IV. With his patronage, and that of the Duchess of Kent, Charlotte became a governess of Princess – future Queen – Victoria in 1831. She retained this role for six years. In 1837, just before the then eighteen-year-old Victoria's ascension to the throne, she fell out of favour with Victoria's mother and the household controller, Sir John Conroy. She was not alone in that.

Charlotte thought of happier times with the teenage Victoria when she came to a special section of the garden – past the begonias and fuchsias – reserved for roses. Among the numerous rare varieties was a cluster of bushes tagged *Rosa Victoriana*. They were perennial wildflowers, reddish pink, now turning orange and light brown in the autumn. She believed that her Alnwick Castle garden was the only place in the north, and perhaps farther afield, where it grew. She had been delighted when the transplanted gift from Princess Victoria adjusted well to the soils and weather conditions of Northumberland.

Today was beautifully bright and sunny, albeit cool, and the garden was a riot of seasonal colours. Glorious.

"Ah, there you are, my dear."

She turned to see her husband holding out a tall glass of lemonade, from which she gratefully took a long drink.

He looked around, wishing that more people could see the special garden she had nurtured in the castle grounds. Although there were capable gardeners on the castle's staff, he knew how much pleasure Charlotte derived from her garden and he admired the expertise she had acquired. He was sure their American guest, arriving tomorrow, would be impressed with the spectacular display. There were blooms, shrubs, palms and plants from many countries and climates. Several had been brought back by intrepid – or so they claimed – plant hunters, acting on commission.

"Our dinner will be served in about an hour," he said, "and I have some correspondence that I'd like to discuss."

"Thank you," she said, thirst quenched, and kissed him.

Hugh was as charming as he had always been, she thought cheerfully as he retreated. Perhaps slightly thicker around the midriff, but only slightly. He was very much the same fair-haired, clean-shaven beau who had swept her off her feet more than twenty years ago.

After Eton and St. John's, Cambridge, he had entered parliament in 1806, initially as the Tory member for Buckingham but switching constituencies after a year to represent Northumberland. In 1812, he was elevated to the House of Lords. She recalled that they were given the honour of representing the UK at the coronation of King Charles X of France.

Later, in 1829, with Arthur Wellesley, the 'iron' Duke of Wellington, as Tory prime minister, Hugh was appointed Lord-Lieutenant of Ireland, the land of Wellesley's birth. The post of Lord-Lieutenant, an ancient title akin to Governor General or Viceroy, meant representing the PM in all aspects of Irish affairs at a most sensitive time when mass rallies agitated, successfully, for the lifting of restrictions on Catholics.

She enjoyed their time living in Dublin Castle, and came to love the people and the city itself with its Parisian-style wide streets and seductive squares. After a year, they returned to England and Alnwick Castle. The government had collapsed, the Whigs had taken office.

Looking back, she was certain that the year in Ireland had made Hugh more socially conscious, and she loved the greater sensitivity and responsiveness in him. Although he retired from front-line politics, he remained committed to supporting citizens of all classes to improve their lives, and turned his attention to the people of Northumberland. When he agreed at an early opportunity to increase labourers' wages, she had said she was proud of him.

They were both excellent administrators. Recently Hugh had been made High Steward of his *alma mater*, Cambridge University, a prestigious role which he hoped would lead to the chancellorship in a few years' time. They had so much to look forward to, she reflected, so many deserving causes and individuals to promote.

An hour later, washed and changed, she was wearing her favourite diamond necklace, a present from Hugh in Dublin. There were just the two of them at dinner and they ate in the small dining room, as they called it, a side room with double doors opening off the castle's main dining room.

They used the blue and white china he had bought to commemorate their twentieth wedding anniversary. The table's centrepiece was a magnificent African candlestick with a colourful display of dried fruits around its base. Before the soup was served, Twizell, their long-standing butler who only ever went by the one name, poured them each a glass of sherry, and deftly swapped the half-full silver salt cellar with an identical, polished one that was full.

"My dear, the matter I wish to discuss relates to the wreck of the *Forfarshire*, a few weeks ago."

She had thought so. Among his other interests, Hugh was a Vice-President of the National Institution for the Preservation of Life from Shipwreck, as well as Vice-Admiral of the Coast of Northumberland. He and his brother, Algernon Percy, were deeply engaged in issues of maritime safety, never more so than now, when its profile among politicians and the press was riding high. All three of them were regular visitors to the county's hard-working harbours.

"The young woman involved in the rescue has been catapulted to national fame, hasn't she?" Charlotte said. "I've heard of at least one new ship that's to be named after her, which is rather special. I'd be most interested to meet her, but then it seems everyone would." Just so.

"We're thinking along the same lines," said Hugh, reassured. "I've received a comprehensive report of what happened on the night of the wreck, drawing on first-hand accounts and the two inquests. It has been written by reliable hands – Messrs. Smeddle, Maddison, Embleton and Scafe, residents of Bamburgh. Mr Scafe is a fellow member of the National Institution."

"Good. May I read the report?"

"Please do, I'd welcome your thoughts." Hugh's soup bowl was removed by a white-gloved footman. "It's curious how the fates come full circle, isn't it? I visited Longstone when the lighthouse was being built and I met the heroic lady in question. As I recall, she was just nine years old."

The following evening, the Percys entertained their American guest to dinner: a Samuel Morse, who had been experimenting with telegraph systems, which allowed messages to be transmitted without them having to be physically carried. He seemed to be calling his method 'Morse code'. Hugh was eager to discover more about its potential applications, especially at sea.

That afternoon, before Mr Morse arrived, Hugh and Charlotte discussed the contents of the report from Bamburgh. They agreed that Hugh would forward it, with a cover letter and recommendations of his own, to his friend, Arthur Wellesley, Duke of Wellington, in London. Last year, 1837, the former PM had been elected Master of Trinity House. Charlotte, meanwhile, to Robert Smeddle's subsequent delight, would craft a letter to a young woman in London whom she had known for years as a princess.

Now she was queen: Queen Victoria.

The Edinburgh debacle

"I am so sorry, George, would you excuse me for a moment?"

Grace relaxed her pose, looked up.

"Duty calls?"

"Duty of a kind. If they only knew, these visitors have become my persecutors."

She exited the lighthouse, went down to the boatshed and waved at the steamer from North Sunderland that had been clanging its bell, summoning her presence. The deck full of passengers waved back lustily, awestruck that the nation's idol had personally acknowledged them. Just wait until they got home and told the neighbours. The boat's skipper grinned widely but managed to stop himself rubbing his hands together as he pulled away from Longstone.

Within a minute, Grace was back, out of the bright November chill. She sat by a window on the ground floor, a lantern beside her casting a bit of extra light and shade. Thomasina had finished a long session spinning wool and was upstairs, leaving Grace and George Smith alone. He was a twenty-five-year-old artist living in Newcastle but previously, she thought, from Yorkshire. He was introduced to them by the sculptor, David Dunbar, and due to the choppy sea last evening, he had stayed overnight.

"Please do say if I'm being overly intrusive," George said, feeling mortified that he too might be her persecutor.

"No, not at all," Grace hurriedly clarified. "I've enjoyed your company – even if I hadn't expected to before you arrived."

He smiled, a lovely warm smile using his hazel eyes as well as his mouth, and she gazed at him while he concentrated on sketching her. Unblemished skin, dark hair, unruly eyebrows. To what extent was he flirting, and should she be enjoying it quite so much?

"How many paintings have you sat for?"

She rewound the last few weeks and reeled them off in her head: Henry Perlee Parker, John Wilson Carmichael, Edward Hastings, John Reay, James Sinclair, Catherine Sharpe, Horatio McCulloch, Thomas Musgrave Joy from London, George Shield from Wooler, a parade of others.

"Well, there has been quite a variety, but you're unique."

Had she made him blush, falter for a moment?

"How so?"

"Well, all the others have made their artworks to exhibit, to sell, to copy. You're the only one who has come and offered to give your painting away to us, privately, for our family home. You yourself stand to gain nothing."

"Well, I've been able to spend time with you," George said, holding her eyes in his. "That's my reward."

Now Grace knew that she had blushed, and her toes curled.

"But I've seen the newspapers in the last two months. You must feel torn to shreds. Everyone wants a piece of you, don't they? I can't conceive what that must be like, but I know, through all the bewildering turmoil, you're being hailed as a gift to the nation. It struck me as an odd expression, a gift to the nation. I reckon you're the same person you were, just with a lot less time to yourself."

He paused. Was he talking too much? She seemed to be listening.

"I read that it's your birthday later this month – is that right? – and that's when I decided to offer my painting – showing you strong and resilient – as a gift for you."

How well this sensitive young man could read her heart and her soul. He saw through the so-called perfect maiden to the conscientious yet troubled woman underneath. He understood how she was feeling and simply wanted, in his own way, to help her and her family.

And he was right: Grace would celebrate her twenty-third birthday on 24 November. She already knew that her sister Thomasin was making a dress for her, but the style and colour would be a surprise.

She asked George what he thought about her attending William Batty's circus. They discussed it without reaching a clear conclusion.

That afternoon, she and George kissed hands farewell, after which they kept holding hands by their side. If only every sitting were as enchanting, every artist as considerate.

One day last week, she'd had so many letters to write – thank you notes, and declining invitations as she was too busy on Longstone to attend – that she'd pleaded with her sister Betsy, visiting for the day, to pass herself off as 'Grace' for one artist whom they had not met before. He'd given no indication of noticing the substitution. Betsy and Grace shared a good long laugh afterwards, as Betsy shook out her hair and returned the shawl Grace had worn during the rescue.

Grace told Betsy she hoped they would be able to spend more time together. They agreed that they hadn't seen enough of each other since Betsy moved out to get married and start work.

These bursts of enjoyment were much needed. They helped to dispel the dark cloud that enshrouded Grace by day as well as by night, although she masked it well to avoid over-burdening her family.

It was the way in which her involvement with William Batty played out that intensified her gloom and sadly caused a rift with her father that cut them both deeply.

After their meeting, Batty had kept in contact by post. He had sent a clipping from the *Caledonian Mercury* of an 'advertorial' article promoting the instructive benefits of his Circus Royal, such as pony rides on the Earthen Mound and a chance to watch the wild zebras – from a safe distance – at feeding time.

Still Grace refrained from giving any commitment, but she discussed Batty's proposal at length with William, who had, exceptionally, come down in favour of her attending the circus.

How did he justify his view? Well, she had never visited Edinburgh, reputedly a beautiful, fashionable city where Rabbie Burns, his poet of choice, spent fourteen months as a vital contributor to the Scottish Enlightenment. Her paternal grandfather, Robert, hailed from Duns, before he moved to Belford in Northumberland. Duns was a small Scottish Borders town, fifty miles from Dundee, thirty from Edinburgh. There was Scottish blood in her – it was a part of who she was.

On Monday 5 November, an enlarged advertisement for the circus was placed in the Edinburgh papers. It took pride in announcing – you can hear the fanfare – that the proceeds from the performance on Thursday that week would be donated to the one and only Miss Grace Darling, whose name and achievement were still touted frequently in those same columns.

The charming Thomas Sylvester made a return trip to Longstone to deliver the proceeds of £20 "on behalf of William Batty and all the people of Edinburgh". The payment came in the form of a pre-printed banker's cheque with the amount handwritten in words and figures. An intricate lattice design ran down the left-hand side to impede forgery.

Naturally, Sylvester took the opportunity to restate their invitation to the circus – simply as an audience member if this were her preference. Which was quite a compromise from the original proposal.

"If you're unsure who to trust in the slaughterhouse of public opinion, Grace, rest assured that that's our stock in trade. You can trust us unreservedly."

Grace would – did – trust her father above any professional showman. Nevertheless, that clinched it. On Sunday 11 November, she wrote to Batty, with William owlishly at her shoulder, promising to visit the circus in person "shortly".

So far, so good. It was Batty's triumphant, self-promoting act of having Grace's letter published in the Edinburgh papers that spawned so much angst.

She had declined the recent invitation from the Edinburgh Ladies to attend a lavish dinner. Now, unsurprisingly, the

Edinburgh Ladies felt affronted. Gravely so. Miss Catherine Sinclair was detailed to write a stinging letter on their behalf, urging Grace not to incur "the greatest injury to her well-earned reputation" by attending "such a low form of entertainment". The pros and cons of her promised appearance at the circus were even debated in newspaper opinion columns.

A media storm was raging. What to do?

William took it upon himself to write to the editors, saying that Grace would not be going to Edinburgh after all. She had not sought, nor did she want, the popularity foisted upon her. Which only made her sound callous and ungrateful for the many gifts she had accepted.

Yet the gifts did not stop coming. More and more money, too, the proceeds of appeals and collections held in tribute across the country.

She could not remember the last time she'd had a serious disagreement, let alone a blazing argument, with her father, and she was bitterly upset with herself as well as with him.

William was her safe harbour; she placed all her trust in him. He hated letting his daughter down, it felt like he had betrayed her. Of course he had not intended to, but they were ensnared in a head-spinning dance of politics and networks and egos, of which he – they – had no experience. He was utterly ill-equipped to lead her through, and he knew it.

Early that evening, when William and Thomasina were in the lantern room, working together, Grace lay on her bed, taking slow, deep breaths. She never did go to Edinburgh, except in her dreams. And now, even her sanctuary was crumbling.

She thought she heard banging sounds, opened her eyes and looked out of her little window. Nothing. She stretched out on the bed again. Had she dreamed it?

Moments later, more banging.

She grabbed a light, hurried downstairs and opened the lighthouse door. Pitch dark. No one there. As she closed it, a shadowy figure flitted across the bottom of the steps.

"Hello?" Grace called. "Who is there?"

Slowly, someone, a man, ascended the steps. He had a black coat, hat, beard. As he approached, she could see little of his face, but she was certain she'd never seen him before.

"Good evenin', ma'am." His accent was local. "Do I have the honour of addressin' Miss Grace Darlin'?"

— 33 —

A dragon reawakens

Third time lucky, surely.

At midnight that November night, Robert Smeddle was sitting at his desk in his Bamburgh Castle apartment. He was alone, just one lantern burning for him to see through the blackness. The empty bottle of ruby port in his hand was cumbersome and he needed three goes to stand it upright.

With a slurred voice he cursed it and jerked open a drawer, from which he took out a full one. The palm of his hand was sticky with blood where, during the last hour, his fingernails had dug into the skin. He didn't seem to realise.

A dragon was writhing inside him, dominating him, controlling him. A dragon of rage.

He had first encountered it during his adolescent years, when other children, including his own siblings and relatives, mocked and shunned him for his abilities. Yes, for the very skills, the intellect, that defined him.

They were jealous, of course, those nasty, petty kids, that was all. But their cruelty at excluding him was unremitting. His excellent memory, neat handwriting, fine attention to detail had scared them, he reasoned, made them feel inferior. And so he took their punishment.

Yet he had virtually no redeeming sense of humour to make people like him, rather than despising him. He still had to work on that.

He had never quite slain the dragon, but he was now its master, he was sure of that. It came less often and for shorter black-out periods. He had always hated it, felt its possession of him revealed a weakness that should be private. He must keep it secret from his employers.

He loved being the centre of attention, listened to, heeded, obeyed. Every time this happened, he knew he'd beaten his childhood detractors. His intellect had won, raised him to a position of authority, responsibility, respect.

He swallowed a glug of port. His mouth was fiery with the taste of spices and berries, while his head felt cloudy and light. He wiped away a bloom of sweat from his upper lip while wriggling to scratch his back, hairy and eczema-riddled, against the chair. Then he sat up and tried hard, so very hard, to focus on the papers in front of him.

The enterprising producer of a newly scripted melodrama, intended for the Adelphi Theatre, London, had written to Miss Grace Darling, proposing to enlist her services for a run of five weeks.

The play, entitled *The Wreck at Sea*, would re-enact the loss of the SS *Forfarshire*. Grace would appear for fifteen minutes of each performance, that was all, sitting in a small, flat-bottomed boat. It would be winched across the stage, simulating her rowing to the survivors, accompanied by percussive wind and rain effects. The producer had offered a weekly fee of £10 plus expenses with an option for a five-week extension.

When the wretched Darlings declined, the producer had contacted Smeddle and asked him to wield his influence. How ineffective he appeared when the proposal was rejected again.

It was not just that the Darlings themselves came across as vain and vulgar to any sophisticated person, Smeddle ranted, massaging his grey temples until they hurt, stoking the inner dragon. It was the embarrassment they heaped upon *him* that stung most of all. The way the Darlings behaved, anyone would think it was blasphemous to seek the praise of strangers!

All right, they were gracious when they wrote to their social betters, but why, why on Earth, did they spurn every single opportunity? Some of them he had set up himself, with a word here, a letter there, using his connections. But their responses, always negative, betrayed a lack of ambition, a lack of respect, which infuriated him.

They would say they were preoccupied in the lighthouse. Well, they should try *his* workload for the Lord Crewe trustees or, for that matter, any occupation other than lighthouse keeping, which had made them so insular, detached from reality.

Smeddle took a long pull on the port. The liquid spilled down both sides of his mouth, dripping on to one of his letters from the Adelphi. He scowled and mopped it with his sleeve, smudging the ink.

At least he had managed to make a few arrangements amidst the deluge of proposals and requests. The Darlings did not need to know about them yet, certainly not if all they did was raise objections and decline.

He had sanctioned a public exhibition of paintings and sculptures inspired by the sinking and the rescue. A member of Hugh Ross's family was securing copies, models, early drawings, anything he could lay his hands on from the artists and printers. Smeddle had suggested broadening the display to include wall-mounted poems, ballads and even newspaper articles that mentioned Bamburgh.

He had also authorised a set of commemorative Staffordshire pottery using the painted images on public display.

And he had approved another panorama. This one, focusing on the destruction of the *Forfarshire*, would be shown four times a day at the Egyptian Hall on London's Piccadilly from January. Its finale would be a showcase for the latest life-saving equipment available to packet operators. He had asked for the booming sound of the gunshots from the castle ramparts to be accentuated, too.

Ultimately, Smeddle hoped to build a portfolio of initiatives and souvenir merchandise with which to impress the Lord Crewe trustees. It was not self-aggrandising, as some might claim. All he was doing was working pro-actively to satisfy public interest and promote the village of Bamburgh, whose tradespeople could only benefit from an influx of visitors.

Surely, at the very least, he would earn a commendation. He allowed himself another generous glug of purple fuel and toasted himself in the spluttering light. But you didn't always get what you deserved, he suddenly thought, which irritated him further.

He yanked open his drawer again. No more bottles of port. If he made a mental note to have a case brought up from the cellar, he did not remember it the next day.

But there were numerous gifts that he had yet to pass on to Grace Darling. Tins of soap, a pretty scent bottle, boxes of jewellery, though she seemed seldom to wear the stuff, more bibles and other books. At least three copies of the same Jane Austen novel had arrived last week alone. Under his desk was a cast-iron coffee grinder with a jar of dark beans purporting to be – perhaps they really were – from a farm in Brazil.

Stuffed in a folder were the latest bankers' cheques sent as tributes. What would they do with all the money rolling in? There seemed to be no plan, just as there had been no expectation of any donations in the first place. How they'd misread the national mood, despite him spelling it out to them in this very room.

The Bamburgh agent for Lloyd's, Bartholomew Younghusband – oh, if only he'd attended the first inquest in October – had forwarded a financial gift on behalf of a group of underwriters in London.

The folder bulged with other contributions. He really must enter them into the account book that he maintained for the Bamburgh Darling Fund. He hated falling behind in his record keeping – that wasn't like him – it was only when this spiteful dragon reawakened...

A violent smash interrupted Smeddle's hazy reverie. The empty port bottle had rolled off his desk and shattered on the parquet floor.

Cursing, he scraped back his chair, let himself fall forwards to his knees and picked up the shards of glass. He crashed back into the chair and found himself staring at a small white shape on his desk.

It was oblong. A card. Gradually, the handwriting swam into focus: *Grace Horsley Darling.* It was the only one he had left from the stack that Grace had signed. On reaching for it, he noticed that his index finger had been nicked by glass. He swallowed hard as his stomach suddenly heaved.

He turned the little card over, leaving bloody smears on each side. Then he tore it into shreds, which he dropped on the heap of broken glass.

34

Alnwick Castle

"Here, take my arm. Gently does it."

Having climbed out of the stagecoach, William Darling turned to give Grace a helping hand. She was wearing the blue dress that Thomasin had presented to her on her birthday three weeks ago, and a bonnet borrowed from Betsy. William, carrying a small box, was in his finest Trinity House suit and neckerchief.

It was a cold Wednesday morning, 12 December 1838.

The bearded man dressed in black who had startled Grace at Longstone last month turned out to be the Duke of Northumberland's secretary, Silas Armstrong. He had a conversation – in retrospect, she thought, a surprisingly brief one – with William and Thomasina about the night of the rescue which had made their daughter famous and how the family had managed since the upending of their lives. They had not pulled their punches.

Soon after Armstrong's visit, an invitation arrived for the Darlings to join the duke and duchess for tea at Alnwick Castle, twenty miles south of Bamburgh. Thomasina stayed to keep watch at the lighthouse and to tend to Ann, Laddie's wife, who'd suffered a bilious attack and had spent the last few days on Longstone. Note: she would be fine.

The coach dropped them at the end of Narrowgate, a cobbled street lined with overhanging shops that curved from the town centre to the castle entrance. In the doorways and windows, faces peered, fingers pointed, voices whispered.

"Is that Grace Darling?"

"That's Grace Darling!"

"I've never seen her in the flesh before."

"That shade of blue really suits her!"

"What's happening?"

"She's going into the castle!"

"How long do you think she'll be?"

"Let's come back later!"

Through an archway in the castle wall, William and Grace entered a dark passage with a huge wooden portal blocking the space at the end. William yanked an iron bellpull and no sooner had the clang faded than a small door, hewn into the portal, creaked open towards them.

A uniformed guard held the door with a gloved hand and stood aside.

They stepped through into a grassy courtyard surrounded by high stone walls with occasional doors and fewer windows. The nearest doors Grace saw were marked: Stewards' Room, Laundry, Kitchen.

The guard pointed them towards a door on the far side of the courtyard, which led to a second, larger, courtyard. They paused to scan the vast space. Grace was transported back to her first visit, as a young girl, to the castle at Bamburgh, but this edifice was altogether bigger and in a better state of repair.

"Good morning, Mr Darling, Miss Darling."

They had not seen him approach, and as there were no other doors nearby it wasn't at all obvious where he had sprung from. He too was clad in a uniform but with more gold braid on the epaulettes. He must have been in his fifties and had a rather staid manner.

"I'm Edward Blackburn, the duke's resident commissioner. It's a pleasure to meet you both. Please follow me." As you'd expect, it was more of a command than a question. "We'll be out of the cold in just a moment," he added with a kindly wink.

William and Grace lined up behind Blackburn, who marched them through an archway out of the second courtyard into the inner ward. Here was an entire village in its own right, Grace thought, with stone buildings in a horseshoe layout. First a chapel, then a library, then a storehouse for wine and ale, then a great hall.

Most impressive of all were two octagon-shaped towers. Blackburn marched them to the first one, where a plaque by the door read:

PRIVATE APARTMENTS

This door must have been unlocked as, oddly, neither Grace nor William saw him use a key. Inside, it was immediately warmer. They were standing in a large vestibule with its own stone fireplace, deep carpet and picture rail from which hung a series of sombre portraits.

Grace turned to her right as the Duke of Northumberland swept in.

"Ah, splendid, thank you, Blackburn. I'll take it from here."

Her first impression was that he was a prince from a fable – tall, handsome, immaculately dressed, black shoes so polished that they were mirrored, a magnificent figure of authority from another realm.

He was shaking her father's hand. "I'm so pleased to see you again, Mr Darling. I recall with great affection my visit to your home under construction – most impressive it was – and how generous you were with your time."

"That was thirteen years ago, sir." Where does the time go, eh? "You came in the *Mermaid*, a beautiful craft."

"And your wife is in charge at Longstone this morning?"

"Indeed, sir, alongside one of my sons."

"Please extend my finest regards. And now, Grace." The duke held out his hand. "Welcome to Alnwick Castle, thank you for coming."

The hand felt soft and smooth as she shook it, curtseying in front of him.

"Good morning, sir."

"I gather you have sat for a number of esteemed painters and sculptors these last three months." She felt the duke's gaze pinning her to the wall like a butterfly. "I've never cared for those sessions, I'm afraid. Always seemed to take too long. Afraid I'm too much of a fidget."

He beamed at her, revealing the straightest rows of teeth she had ever seen. She felt charmed by his steps to put her at ease and smiled back. She had spent hardly any time in his company when he called at Longstone all those years ago, but she was sure he had not had such a spellbinding effect on her back then.

"This upstanding fellow is from another branch of the Percy family tree."

The duke was pointing to the subject of the largest of the paintings surrounding them. He saw at once the lust for knowledge in Grace's eyes.

"He's Lord Henry Percy," the duke revealed. "Three hundred years ago, in the court of Henry VIII, he was the accepted suitor of a lady called Anne Boleyn."

Grace's curiosity flooded with the light of recognition.

"They were, I believe, deeply in love. But on the king's instruction, Cardinal Wolsey prevented the marriage they both longed for from taking place. We all know what happened next."

"Do you think the king ever loved her as deeply as Lord Henry did?"

"The king was infatuated with her at first, I don't doubt that. He would see her every day in his court and yearn for her. She was clearly from an ambitious family, but then the king was always striving to prove himself, too. They married in secret – Anne was his second wife. Alas, the infatuation fizzled out and the king's eye wandered. When Anne famously produced a female, not a male, heir, he had her arrested for betrayal, witchcraft, you name it. Just three years after their wedding, she was beheaded in the Tower of London. And less than a fortnight after that, Henry VIII was married to Jane Seymour. Love is complicated, isn't it?"

"And your relative, Lord Henry?" Grace had never heard of this wronged man.

"Utterly broken. I think Anne Boleyn breathed in his heart forever."

The double doors leading out of the vestibule swung open. A man in butler's garb and greased-back hair bowed to the duke. It was only then that William and Grace noticed that Blackburn had vanished as silently as he had appeared.

"Thank you, Twizell," said the duke. Turning to the Darlings: "Please would you join my wife and me for tea?"

They walked through to an opulent sitting room with its own large fireplace and more portraits commemorating members of the Percy dynasty. The mantlepiece had matching bone china vases bursting with spectacular bouquets.

The Duchess of Northumberland was sitting with a basket in her lap. She set the basket down and smiled at Grace.

"Hello, I'm Charlotte. How are you?"

Grace curtseyed, feeling awkward but pleased that she'd remembered to do so. The duchess wore a dazzling diamond necklace, the largest Grace had ever seen.

As soon as Charlotte had introduced herself to William, they sat, and Twizell brought Earl Grey tea. William hoped self-consciously that no one would notice as he put his box down beside his violet armchair, which he sank into, almost spilling his tea into the saucer.

Twizell gave a bow, took his leave. The duke, crossing his legs, cleared his throat.

"There is much for us to discuss," he began. "We have some items that I shall be immensely pleased to present to you. And I have a proposal – no, that sounds overly official at this stage – a small suggestion, to put to you, which you may like to consider in your own good time."

William thanked the duke, taking care that his family's reputation for courtesy was upheld in this remarkable place.

"We were aware, of course, of the sad loss of the *Forfarshire* and your rapid rise to fame. But it was a report on the entire case, with several testimonials, that I received from Bamburgh that prompted me to set certain wheels in motion."

There was that devastating smile again. Grace held the arms of her chair and glanced at her father, who also seemed to be hanging on the duke's every word. Here comes his first piece of news.

"Trinity House, of which our good friend, the Duke of Wellington is master, has awarded each of you an extra bonus of £10."

"Congratulations!" From the duchess. "We know you have been well regarded by Trinity House for a long time."

"Thank you indeed," William said and took a sip of tea.

"There's more, much more."

The duchess watched thoughtfully as Grace blushed at the prospect of more rewards for having simply done what she was there to do. Charlotte and Hugh had no children of their own – the dukedom would pass in due course to Hugh's brother, Algernon – but she saw something child-like in this courageous, selfless woman. For all that she was idolised as a heroine, Grace was defenceless in the face of unprecedented intrusion and stress. This was a woman who had done the right thing – helped strangers – and felt oppressed for it.

"You'll have come across humane societies, I'm sure," the duke was saying.

William nodded. If you're uncertain, they were networks of volunteers, concerned with safety on rivers and waterways. Through their interventions over the years, many lives were saved from drowning.

"Well, the London Committee of the Royal Humane Society, of which I'm president, has awarded a gold medal for gallantry to each of you."

"I have them here for you," said the duchess, tapping the basket at her side. "They are beautifully engraved gold discs with your names at the centre. You can be very proud of them, treasure them. Yours, Grace, is the first such gallantry medal ever awarded to a woman."

"Hear, hear!" said the duke. "I should add, I'm happy that the North Sunderland fishing crew, who provided a lifeboat service in those appalling conditions, will receive a gold medal, too. That seems fair and proper, yes?"

"Definitely." William agreed without hesitation. He trusted William Brooks and the Robsons would feel vindicated.

"In addition," the duke continued after a spot of tea, "the humane societies specific to Glasgow, Edinburgh and Leith have, all three of them, bestowed a silver medal on you."

"Those are here, too," the duchess assured them, her hand still on the basket, "alongside one further medal."

The duke took his cue. "The National Institution for the Preservation of Life from Shipwreck, with which I'm also involved, has awarded you its silver medal for gallantry. Believe me, Grace, I exerted no influence at all, the honour was swiftly agreed, entirely on merit." True enough.

"Thank you, sir."

"And once again, you're the first woman to receive this medal. I couldn't be more thrilled," said the duchess.

"You're a Vice-President of the National Institution, aren't you, sir?" William sought to check his facts, believing that the duke was more than just 'involved' with the charity, as he had modestly claimed.

"I am, yes. Its reach doesn't yet extend far into Northumberland, but I have every confidence that it soon will."

"In the year the institution was formed, you organised a competition, didn't you, dear?" the duchess prompted.

"It was 1824," the duke recalled. "Not long before I visited Longstone. Sir William Hillary finally got his long-standing vision for the institution off the ground. The founding principles were agreed at a public meeting, a very well attended one, in a tavern in Bishopsgate, east London, in March of that year. My little competition was for a standard design of a lifeboat that might one day be used all around our shores. Fellow named Plenty, William Plenty, won it. He was from Berkshire, a designer and plough-maker, primarily, as I remember. Died about six years ago. Of course, the design and fit-out of lifeboats have greatly evolved since then, and I'm sure there's still a long way to go."

"One has to start somewhere," the duchess said. "And thanks to you, Grace, the spotlight on maritime safety shines brighter than ever before."

"I believe there's a new lifeboat in the south of England that's going to be named after me," Grace noted quietly.

"It won't be the last."

The duchess rummaged in her basket and took out something light in weight, wrapped in yellow tissue paper.

Handing it to Grace, she said: "This is a little gift from us, my dear. As winter approaches, we thought you might like it."

Grace opened it with slightly trembling hands. It was a beautiful paisley shawl with a teardrop motif that glinted as she placed it around her shoulders. It would be lovely and warm. She thanked the duchess extravagantly and meant every word.

"While we're exchanging gifts," William said, seizing the opportunity, "may I offer this."

He handed the box he had brought to the duke, who opened it in his lap. Inside was an ink stand which William had fashioned out of the slab of marble from the *Forfarshire*.

"In the sincere hope that we may keep in touch, sir."

"Our paths have crossed twice now, and I have no doubt they will do so many times in the future. Thank you for this, I'm delighted to accept it."

Twizell returned, bearing fresh pots of hot Earl Grey and hot water. He loaded his tray with the first set, gave his customary short bow and left.

"Let me share our proposal – our suggestion – with you," the duke said. "Charlotte and I discussed it both before and after we heard from Armstrong, my secretary, whose – what shall I say? – laconic report really helped to shape our thoughts. You see, my family shares with you an abiding interest in the safety of seafarers. And if there are ways for us to help you, well, we'd very much like to do so, provided that you consent."

"We have no intention to interfere where we're not wanted, or God forbid to impose any further encumbrance on your lives," the duchess elaborated. "Quite the reverse, in fact."

"Our idea," said the duke, "is simply this. I become a sort of guardian to you, Grace, entirely complementary to your parents, naturally. You would be my ward. I could do two things for you. First, I could advise on any approaches or requests that you wanted to refer to me. What the advantages and disadvantages might be, the wider picture, how you might respond, that kind of thing."

"We're aware," the duchess cut in, "that you don't have a secretary or assistant at your disposal, yet out of the blue you're one of the most talked-about people in the country. You're constantly showing kindness to others, but perhaps we can help you to be kinder to yourselves, too." I'm sure Grace recalled Batty and Sylvester expressing similar sentiments to her on Longstone.

Now, William and Grace glanced at each other, exchanged smiles. Much of the lingering embarrassment they had endured over the Batty affair and the aborted trip to Edinburgh dissolved. The duchess's words triggered the longed-for reconciliation. Grace looked into her Papa's eyes and knew, once again, that everything would be all right.

"And second," the duke continued, "I could manage the financial donations you're receiving. We would need to decide on a proper structure of governance, if you will, so that everything is above board. But it struck us that rather a considerable sum must be accumulating from ad hoc donations and collections and so forth."

"Speaking of which, I have received a new contribution from London," said the duchess. "It has arrived in the form of a cheque for you to cash at Sir Matthew Ridley's Bank here in Alnwick. The amount is £50."

Grace and William felt giddy and humbled at the same time.

"The cover note reads 'as a mark of my gracious approbation of your conduct'. It was written by the sender of the cheque herself, Her Royal Highness, Queen Victoria."

Grace was stunned.

"Well, that's our suggestion. As I said, please take your time to mull—"

"We'd like to accept, sir," William jumped in. He gulped, nearly pinched himself. What a surreal day this had become.

"It's so kind of you, both of you, to support us like this. I confess that, ever since your invitation arrived, Thomasina and I have discussed over and over what might lie behind it. You have offered so much more than we could ever have hoped or prayed for, but it is certainly what we need. I'm extremely grateful."

Grace spoke up, almost addressing her Papa privately for a moment. "Mr Smeddle at Bamburgh Castle. He may not–"

"Mr Smeddle has provided written evidence to support a number of the honours that have been awarded to you," the duke countered. "You and your mother are children of Bamburgh, and Mr Smeddle will do his best by you. If you have any doubts, please leave Mr Smeddle to me."

At this, Grace breathed a sigh of relief. She said nothing, but the duchess as always observed her reaction.

"Never be afraid to ask for help," the duchess told her gently. "It's a sign of strength, you know, sound judgement, doing what's needed. It's not an admission of weakness."

Grace pondered this for a moment. It was easier advice to give than to take, but I'm sure it rang true in her mind. Across the room she mouthed a heart-felt thank you.

When Twizell re-entered, it was to remind the duke of his next appointment, for which he had some freshly delivered papers to read. The duke jumped to his feet.

"I have something to show you, then I must go," he said, and led the way out of the sitting room. William took the basket and the royal cheque, but Grace kept her new shawl around her shoulders.

They walked through the main dining room into a side room with a circular table in the centre. On its white cloth had been laid two slim metal tubes, each about a yard long, with coils of rope at one end, and a set of attachments that could be clipped on to the tubes.

As the four of them gathered round, the duke issued his challenge. "What do you make of these? They're prototypes, but I believe the inventor has come up with a splendid solution to a long-standing problem."

"The ropes indicate that they're rescue aids of some sort," William said. "I'm not sure... what exactly are they?"

A pause, which the duke relished.

"Life-saving rockets!"

Grace and William stared at the paraphernalia on the table.

"When the trigger, the firing mechanism and the handles are slotted into place, you can shoot the rope out of the cylinder to reach people who are shipwrecked or in danger of sinking."

"I've never seen a device quite like this," William said, "but I've heard of something similar, where the rope was fired by a mortar."

"The Manby Mortar," said the duke. "And other such apparatus."

"That's it, Captain Manby, George Manby, made them, didn't he?" The memory clicked into place.

The duke nodded. "Captain Manby himself is supportive of this new equipment, which replaces his mortar with a small rocket to fire the rope further and more efficiently. Fellow called John Dennett – he made these ones – kindly loaned them to us for a few days."

"Well, thank you for letting us see them," said William. "I imagine there'll be a lot of interest."

"I hope so," said the duke. "Robert Smeddle is looking into them on behalf of the trustees at Bamburgh Castle, so let's see what happens there. We need a manufacturer to tool up and take them on."

Grace became aware of someone standing close to her. She stepped aside to see Edward Blackburn, who had silently rematerialised from goodness knows where.

She gave the duchess a friendly hug, regardless of any protocols she ought to have followed, and was glad to find it reciprocated. The duke shook hands with William, promising to be in touch "within a few days, I hope" with more detailed proposals for the stewardship of their affairs. William emphasised what a weight had been lifted off their backs.

Blackburn took them through the castle the way they had come in, retracing their steps to the door that led on to Narrowgate.

"We should walk along to Ridley's bank," said William, "straight away."

"Papa, I'm not sure we'll be able to walk anywhere in the town this morning," Grace replied, looking out.

She lowered her head so that her bonnet obscured her face and drew the paisley shawl tight across her shoulders. Her mouth felt dry, despite the tea she had just drunk, and she could feel her level of anxiety rising as if she were a tank filling with toxic liquid.

Narrowgate was lined with people of all ages, as far as her eye could see. The hum and hubbub grew louder as word spread like wildfire that – *yes, it's her!* – she had emerged.

She felt a tug on her arm. William pulled her inside a well-stocked greengrocer's shop next to a firm of solicitors. The shopkeeper gasped when she saw who had entered, but they were not there to buy.

"Are you all right to carry on?" William demanded of his daughter, holding her arms. The meeting had been an overwhelming experience for them both. "You're sure you're up to this? It'll be an ordeal, and no mistake."

"Thank you, Papa, but let's go to the bank, collect the donation and hail a coach back home. It has to be done, so let's get on with it."

"Very well," he said, and apologised to the shopkeeper before marching into the street.

Bedlam. They jostled their way along Narrowgate towards the sea of faces flooding the market square. Above the din they thought they heard a reporter from the Newcastle *Journal* shout their names and ask for a comment, but they pressed on.

William never let go of Grace's hand, which was sore afterwards, but he was her rock. He knew she was breathing deeply and avoiding eye contact with the swell of well-wishers, bombarding her with hand after hand to shake or notepaper to autograph. It was an excited, well-meaning mob, but a mob none the less. People were crushed so close to her, she could smell their breath. She tried to force a wave, but she struggled to feel safe, especially when heavy hands ripped the bonnet from her head.

This turned out to be the one and only public appearance, as such, that Grace Darling made after the sinking of the *Forfarshire*.

35

The lucky charm

Phweeee!

Immediately the whistle blasted, the ewe darted off the sleeper and rejoined the other sheep nibbling the trackside grass. Thank goodness, in the nick of time.

Five hours after William and Grace parted the surging mob in Alnwick market square, Henry Perlee Parker was en route from Shields back to Newcastle.

The railway line connecting the city with the coastal settlement – an emerging suburb – was brand new. Ten trains a day thundered in each direction, some serving commuters, others for goods, predominantly fish, destined for customers in the city and beyond. Next year, 1839, there would be twenty trains a day, he estimated, and the number would go on rising. Extensions to the line were already planned out to Tynemouth, Whitley Bay and Blyth.

Henry had travelled to North Shields for the day to see Sarah and Jesse Dawson. They were on their way to Dundee. North Shields was the most convenient meeting place – and it gave Henry a perfect excuse to try out the railway.

Grace Darling had explained the horrifying loss of James and Matilda Dawson on Big Hawker. As a favour to Grace, he offered to paint a portrait of Sarah and Jesse – a token, a unique gift, at the end of the most dreadful year imaginable.

They sat very quietly for him, holding hands, their children's deaths reflected in their eyes which remained dark, lifeless pools. Considerable periods of the sitting took place in a cold silence, but he had resolved to use light, when he applied his oils to the canvas, to suggest the possibility of a new dawn, of hope for a brighter future.

Although the session was not easy for any of them, he'd been happy to agree to Grace's request. His work on Longstone had revitalised his career, just as Mary, his daughter, had envisioned. Reproductions of his portraits of Grace were in high demand, and his refreshed profile had already helped him to secure new clients, more commissions.

He shivered in his first-class seat, and pulled his coat tight, sparing a thought for the driver and his fireman up front, totally exposed to the elements. At times they must be terrified! Named the *Wellington*, the steam locomotive had been built at Robert Stephenson's Forth Street site in Newcastle, where, I should add, his ground-breaking *Rocket* was also constructed.

Out of the moorland, the train clattered past a pair of lanky chimneys, reaching high above a cluster of factories and incinerators. The smoke spewing out was flattened by the sharp wind.

The first stop after North Shields was Percy Main, a village built to house the families of men who worked in the local coalmines and on the river. Its name was taken from the land-owning Duke of Northumberland. The station's two platforms, east- and westbound, were linked by an iron footbridge whose central point was almost as high as the nearby signal box.

What a boon this railway was to the region, he reflected. It had been raucously opposed by the owners of stagecoaches and steam packets, who feared their businesses would evaporate. But finally, it had been voted through parliament, MPs no doubt mindful that Newcastle was the beating heart of the nation's Industrial Revolution.

Not long after returning from Longstone, Henry had received a letter, asking whether he would consider taking up a post as drawing master at a new Wesleyan grammar school, on which construction would soon begin in Sheffield. His Methodist faith had remained an important underpinning in his life, and he sensed that a teaching role would bring his career full circle.

Having discussed the opportunity with his wife, Amy, and with Mary, he wrote back expressing great interest. As the building work progressed, he would be happy to advise on the optimal light conditions and eventually the materials needed for the students' art classes.

Grace Darling was a lucky mascot for him – yes, another one, like Mary. It was beyond dispute that Henry's circumstances had been transformed for the better since he met Grace.

Most recently he had taken enormous pleasure in writing to her, letting her know that Amy had given birth to their latest child, a daughter, whom they had named Grace. He knew it would be some time before Grace Darling was able to reply, as she would feel duty-bound to do, but he imagined her joy at reading the news and sharing it with her family – especially, perhaps, her mother.

The train rattled over the Willington Dene Viaduct, a hugely impressive achievement of design and construction, Henry thought. Nearly a thousand feet long, with a high row of timber arches supported by deep masonry pillars. Its twin, the Ouseburn Viaduct, had been built a couple of stops further along the line, shortly before the train pulled into Newcastle's Carliol Square station.

From there it was a short walk to Pilgrim Street, where Henry lived, and he had only his slim portfolio case, containing today's sketches, to carry.

Inside the apartment, he kissed Amy, who was cradling baby Grace, and checked on his other children. Henry Raphael, ever a ball of energy, was kneeling at his little bed, which was bestrewn with pencil drawings of sea monsters.

Henry was looking forward to celebrating Christmas with his family. The festivities seemed to get more elaborate year on year. With his money worries behind him, he and Amy were planning a roast beef dinner with plenty of dried fruits and nuts to pick at all day long.

He poured himself two fingers of gin, went up to his studio and lit an extra lantern. He had agreed to meet a reporter at home at six that evening. The man had already interviewed John Wilson Carmichael and was eager to follow up with Henry. It was John who had revealed to the reporter that Henry had spent a week on Longstone and remained in contact with Grace Darling herself. The hook had proved irresistible.

Punctually at six, the reporter arrived, middle-aged, dressed snugly in a grey frock coat with black lapels. As Henry hung the coat up and signalled to him to sit down, the man knitted his fingers together and cast an eye around the studio, admiring the oil paintings in progress. Looking at one easel, he tried to analyse how the brush strokes were made. After a moment, none the wiser, he introduced himself with a flourish of a card.

His name was Vincent Atkins.

— 36 —

Dickson, Archer & Thorp

Three storeys plus a cavernous basement.

The offices of Messrs. Dickson, Archer & Thorp, solicitors, at 31 Narrowgate, Alnwick, were originally a townhouse built for an army general. The partners had acquired the premises when they established the firm at the end of the previous century. Now they were widely respected as the county's leading attorneys at law.

This was Grace's first visit to Alnwick since the extraordinary meeting in the castle and the subsequent encounter with the crowds.

William accompanied her again. His arm around her, he ensured that the stagecoach dropped them at the rear entrance. There was a courtyard with sycamore trees that would have served as a pleasant back garden for the townhouse residents, trapping the afternoon sun. He had also refrained from telling Robert Smeddle about this trip, so that it remained as private and confidential as possible.

They were greeted by Thomas Thorp – "call me Tom" – who was probably older, William decided, than his youthful complexion and elated demeanour suggested. He led them to a large meeting room at the back of the ground floor, far away from any potential prying eyes at the front.

Already installed at the head of the conference table was the Duke of Northumberland. At the other end was Miss Rook, a secretary from the firm of solicitors, in attendance to take the minutes of the meeting.

One wall was lined with wooden shelves, six rows reaching almost to the coving, laden with folders and files. The opposite wall had three dusty windows with discoloured, originally white-painted shutters at either side.

The duke opened proceedings. "I thought it best for a variety of reasons to hold this meeting here. Let me first ask Tom to introduce his firm."

"Very good, sir," said Tom Thorp, who addressed William and Grace directly. William was pouring a glass of water from a jug in the centre of the table. "The Thorp in the name of our firm is actually my father, Robert, who remains a senior partner. We handle all legal matters, from marriage settlements, wills and probate, through to criminal cases at trial. For a pleasingly broad clientele, I might add. We are privileged, of course, to represent the duke himself. The Lord Crewe charity, up at Bamburgh, is also a client, as are numerous county families and many others who may have more modest means but are equally valued."

Tom had a sip of water. Miss Rook finished a sentence – although why she was minuting her employer's credentials, I'm not sure – and looked up expectantly.

"The firm's partners play a community role, too," Tom continued. "We may be asked to assist the justices at their quarter sessions, and we are often involved in governance issues affecting the county. We're always eager to sit on local boards responsible for implementing new laws – the Overseers of the Poor, for example. My own family has been working closely with the Alnwick Working Men's Dwelling Association, which seeks to improve accommodation for working people. Alas, much upgrading is still required."

"Well said, Tom," the duke lauded him.

"Does your firm occupy the whole building?" William enquired. He thought he remembered that, just before Dickson, Archer & Thorp bought it, the large house was home to multiple families.

"We do," Tom replied. "The top floor rooms, mind you, are mostly used for storage. There are trunks of client correspondence, sales and purchase ledgers, copies of wills and laws, heaven knows what else – we keep practically everything, always have done. I imagine that record-keeping in your line of work is just as vital."

"That's true," said William, his eye on the groaning shelves. "I hope you don't run out of space."

"There's always the basement."

"Grace, my proposal to you today," the duke said expeditiously, "is that we create a trust to oversee your financial affairs. Well over five hundred pounds has already come in, from generous organisations and individuals, subscribing to petitions to honour your bravery and character. I believe we should consolidate as much as we can into a single investment fund, overseen by a small board of trustees working to terms of reference drafted by my legal friends here. Everything to be clear and accountable."

The duke let that sink in and waited for Miss Rook to stop writing.

"It sounds perfect," said Grace, who would be only too pleased to have no subscriptions or donations to deal with. I bet she was thinking: Let the trustees handle the lot – I just want my old life back.

"I'm sure that not only your family, but the public at large would expect the accumulating fund to grant you a safe, secure future." The duke refreshed his mouth with a swig of water. "So, the formal deed we draw up will set out how your fund will be disbursed in various circumstances. Should you have children, Grace, I propose that she, he or they inherit the fund first, rather than everything passing to a husband."

Miss Rook, a look of approval enlivening her face, scribbled away in her own brand of shorthand and drew more blue ink into her pen.

"Should you die without issue and your mother or father or both survive you, then the inheritance would pass to them. These and other eventualities will be included categorically for you to confirm. Now, Grace, there should be a sufficient capital sum for you to receive a regular income for the remainder of what I hope will be a long, fulfilling life. As a first step, we shall consolidate the funds into a trust in your name. Is that acceptable?"

Grace's head was beginning to spin. She was content for the duke's experts to manage the investment, grow it if they could. She still felt that all this money belonged to the other Grace Darling, and she had no intention of withdrawing any of it, whatever happened.

"Perfectly, sir," she said calmly.

"We'll start on the necessary paperwork straight away." The duke gave a nod to Tom. "Now, moving on to the next item. I have three nominations for your board of trustees. I know each man well. They are clergymen or academics, and I believe their standing, their judgement to be beyond reproach."

Miss Rook's pen hovered above the minute book as the duke consulted a note on the table before him.

"First, the Reverend Thomas Singleton. He's a year or two older than me, but he was a pal at school. Ordained thirty odd years ago, he was chaplain here in Alnwick for a while. Twelve years ago, he became Archdeacon of Northumberland. Continues to serve us well in that capacity."

The duke rattled through this part quickly. The table stayed silent, respectful.

"Next, the Reverend Dr Charles Thorp. A student at Newcastle's Royal Grammar School. By his early twenties, had been made a fellow and a tutor of University College, Oxford. Archdeacon of Durham for seven years. And six years ago, when Durham University was founded, he was named its first warden and master of University College. All of these roles he continues to occupy today with, I'd say, great distinction."

"You will have noticed, no doubt, that Charles and I share a surname," said Tom Thorp. He was right, they had. "We are cousins. Charles comes from a line of distinguished Church of England clerics, but he's a passionate advocate of 'education for all', as he puts it. He's also deeply interested in seabirds and concerned with the protection of endangered species. I'm sure you'll appreciate those issues far better than I."

So saying, he turned to Grace, who let a smile play across her lips.

"Thank you, Tom," said the duke. "Third, the Reverend William Darnell, also an alumnus of RGS and Oxford. In 1809, none other than Charles Thorp brought him back home, so to speak, to the north-east by offering him the post of rector at St. Mary-le-Bow's in Durham. A six-year stint there, since when he has served as vicar at various other churches in the region. Incidentally, I know he would love to work at St. Aidan's in Bamburgh, so you might see more of him in the future."

"I should declare an interest here, too," said Tom. "The Darnells are family friends. William's eldest son is married to my cousin Charles's eldest daughter. It's a tangled web," he added apologetically.

"I said three nominations, but I have a fourth and final one for you." The duke folded his note, slipped it into a pocket. "I am putting myself forward, too. I've discussed it with Charlotte, of course, and we agree that I have the time as well as the desire to be a trustee. I believe my three esteemed colleagues and I would ask probing questions, and expect robust answers, concerning any aspect of your affairs. But the point is, we would all pull in broadly the same direction, which is essential for a board to work well."

William and Grace exchanged glances. Imagine their thoughts on such a distinguished panel.

"Sir, we'd be thrilled with all four trustees," William said. "As you know, I'm immensely grateful, and humbled by your proposal."

"It's my pleasure to offer some support," said the duke. "Our interests are aligned in making a great success of these arrangements."

"Thank you, sir, for all the trouble you've gone to on my behalf," Grace said. "May I ask how we are to deal from now on with Mr Smeddle?"

"We've given that some thought," the duke replied. "My three nominees, Thomas, Charles and William, also happen to be trustees of the Lord Crewe charity, which employs Mr Smeddle. They are well aware of his prodigious abilities, but I think it's fair to say they also have a measure of the man as a whole. I shall say no more, I've probably said too much already, but you'll get my drift."

Tom said quietly: "Please omit those remarks from the minutes, Miss Rook."

Understanding the sensitivity of the arrangements for the Darlings, the duke went on: "I propose that Mr Smeddle remains your point of contact at Bamburgh Castle, where no doubt some of your mail will continue to be delivered. It's important that that line of communication functions smoothly, which I'm sure it will. Please refer any requests or donations to me care of Mr Thorp. We'll offer advice, and implement your wishes, as speedily as we can."

"We realise that you both have many other commitments," William said. "We're only too delighted to proceed on this basis."

By way of next steps, the duke said that he would liaise with his three fellow trustees, and a deed setting out the trust's aims and protocols would be drafted. I can imagine Miss Rook putting down her pen, flexing her aching fingers.

While they awaited a stagecoach, the duke chatted to William. Grace thought she overheard the name of William Brooks but caught nothing more. She stopped listening and instead asked Tom what other work was filling his plate.

Tom thought for a moment. "We've been defending two neighbours from Rothbury. Both charged with stealing – one a coat, the other five pounds of mutton. I'm afraid the trial did not go their way. As we speak, they're being transported to Australia for a minimum of eight years."

Appalled, Grace demanded: "That is justice?"

"Well, it may be a deterrent to others, at least," said Tom. "There was much wailing and weeping in court, I can tell you. I have another case which is troubling in a different way. See what you make of this. It's coming to trial now, although the alleged offence was nine months ago. A lot of pitmen and agricultural labourers convene in Alnwick for what's called the March Hirings. A big annual tradition, you'll know the sort of thing. This year, a miner had been drinking heavily in one of the inns along the road and the landlord fetched a constable to throw him out. A crowd gathered and the constable was blocked from entering the inn. During the skirmish, he was knocked to the ground, kicked and trampled. His toughened hat, his truncheon, his whistle – all gone. While this was happening, the miner who'd been drinking slipped out, was lost in the crowd and has not been seen since. No one seems to know his name or where he came from. But the poor constable – by the time he was carried back to the police station up the hill, he was dead. Left a wife and five children."

"How sad," said Grace. "Who is being put on trial?"

"Well, eventually there were enough eyewitnesses who described the two men who kicked the constable to death, so they were identified and arrested. They both had steel-capped hobnail boots, which were confiscated. But they are claiming that in the melee, with much alcohol consumed, they were jostled themselves and couldn't even see the ground, let alone know what they were supposedly treading on."

"I think they'll be found guilty," Grace proclaimed.

Tom smiled thinly. "You may be right. Ah, here comes your coach."

Next morning, a pristine leather case was delivered to Longstone on the daily provisions boat. Grace flipped it open eagerly. Inside was a card with the ducal crest and a note which read: *Wishing you all a merry Christmas, looking forward to working with you in the New Year.*"

For William, Thomasina and Grace, the duke had sent newly invented waterproof outfits, capacious enough to fit over their clothing.

For his ward, Grace, there were extra gifts: a book of common prayer 'for her welfare and happiness'; and a silver-gilt timepiece with a gold seal around the face. Grace referred to it always as her precious 'gold watch'.

Meeting Jane

To Felton.

The village lay ten miles south of Alnwick and seven inland from the coast. A brisk sea breeze bent the bare trees and dried the ground as William Brooks Darling walked the last few yards, having enjoyed a lift on the cart of a farmer friend for most of the way.

This was Saturday 12 January 1839, a little after noon. William Brooks had been invited to the opening of The Saddler's Arms, a coaching inn built by a crossroads in the centre of the village on the increasingly well-used stagecoach route from London to Edinburgh.

Felton already had two inns, where coaches switched teams of horses and let passengers refresh. With the advent of mail coaches, the village was self-evidently expanding. Strolling along the main street, he counted blacksmiths, saddle and harness makers, joiners, bakers and butchers.

The new inn was larger than the other two combined. At the rear stood a theatre where, it was hoped, troupes of travelling players would present shows to audiences buying drinks at the public bar. One facility not installed in The Saddler's Arms was a cockpit, even though it might have attracted punters from all over the county. The landlord's solicitors, Alnwick-based Dickson, Archer & Thorp, who had advised on everything from the purchase of the site to dealings with suppliers, had counselled that cockfighting would soon be outlawed. Thankfully in my opinion, they were right.

Even before he reached the wooden door beneath the inn's freshly painted sign that swung in the wind, William Brooks heard the hum of voices bursting out from inside. The launch party, with a mix of locals and invited guests, was under way.

Zelda Miller, a well-known solo violinist from Ashington, was standing on a corner podium, playing up-tempo Northumbrian folk songs. They reminded William Brooks of the ditties his father played on the fiddle.

Amidst the crowd jangling coins and glasses at the bar counter was Peter Collingwood, the lookout at Bamburgh Castle, making the most of a weekend off. He was clinking tankards with a farrier, Ben Liddell, who was celebrating winning a prize at a local agricultural show. Cheers!

As soon as he spotted them, William Brooks made for Tommy Buchanan and Robbie Knox, his fishermen friends. They were chatting over their ales to a man whom he instantly recognised from the back of his head: his twin brother, George. They had not seen each other since family drinks at New Year.

"Hello stranger, how the devil are you?" Vigorous backslapping. "Great to see you!"

As he embraced his brother, William Brooks's eye was distracted by a young woman his own age, standing apparently on her own further along the bar. He thought she was beautiful, radiant. She seemed to have noticed him, too, but looked away when their eyes met.

Even as a young child, William Brooks had been plucky and fearless. Some, his parents included, would say rash and exasperating. Auspiciously, his courage did not fail him now.

Excusing himself from George and his friends, he pushed his way towards her, nonchalantly, hoping that she did not walk off. The intensity of his interest in her surprised him – he simply had to find out who she was.

Bless her, she stayed rooted to the spot. But as he was about to speak, two older adults, a man and a woman, appeared and stood beside her. From the facial resemblance, the woman could only be her mother. But he was past the point of no return.

"Hello," he said confidently, ignoring the butterflies in his stomach. "I saw you didn't have a drink and wondered whether I could offer you one."

Thankfully she smiled, a warm, kind smile that touched his heart. She took in the clean looks, eagle nose, unruly fringe, mischievous eyes that pleaded with her, and she decided for once, to her own as well as her parents' amazement, to go easy on this bold young man.

"I'd like that, Mr–"

"Darling. William Brooks Darling."

"Darling, did you say?" Her father cupped his ear and shouted above the racket. "Would that be any relation to–"

"Grace Darling? Yes, she's my sister." William Brooks spoke quietly, while trusting that he was still audible. He did not think her father had heard, but before he could say anything, the daughter took charge.

"I am Jane Downey. May I introduce my parents, Margaret and Thomas."

William Brooks shook their hands, pressing hard.

"Now, I believe you were going to provide me with a drink."

Before William Brooks knew what was happening, Jane had hooked her right arm through his left elbow and was marching him towards the bar counter, leaving her parents in her wake.

"Actually," she said to William Brooks, "you might have just saved me."

"From what?"

"Tedious hours having the same old conversations with the same old neighbours. I was born in Felton, just up the road, and as happy as I am to see the village expand, there are other places I can think of to… have a drink."

"Oh, yes." William Brooks made a quick decision. "Follow me," he urged, and led Jane through the bar, past Zelda Miller playing in ascending tempo, and on into the theatre.

The stage ran the full width of the room. In the open space facing it, a few benches were placed haphazardly on the oak floor.

William Brooks invited Jane to sit on a bench at the back, and he sat next to her. Not too close, he told himself. Be polite. For a moment they simply sat still, enjoying the peace and quiet of the large auditorium.

"We still don't have a drink," she said in mock-exasperation. A beat. Yes, he was sure she wasn't really vexed.

"I've promised myself and my family that I won't drink too much this weekend," he said. Not what she'd expected to hear.

"Well, to be honest," she confessed, "I was never a big drinker. But I was really put off alcohol by an incident last year."

"Oh, what happened?" he asked, keeping eye contact.

"A cousin of mine, a parish constable in Alnwick, was killed. It happened when a drunken brawl at the March Hirings got out of hand. Two men were convicted of the killing last month. I was very fond of him, he'd have made a decent policeman."

"Sorry to hear of that."

Let me quickly shade in a bit of background. Since the Metropolitan Police Act of 1829, London had a police force with seventeen divisions, no less, headquartered at Scotland Yard. The service answered to the Home Secretary, Robert Peel, who had steered the act through parliament. Now, a decade later, the roll-out of police forces around the land was still proceeding slowly as the national plan to improve law and order took time to win public trust.

It was clear to William Brooks that Jane Downey had faith in a fledgling police service, just as he himself had in a lifeboat service. He admired her for it and felt there was already a bond between them.

"What's your excuse?" she asked.

He looked blank, still half-lost in his own thoughts.

"Your excuse for not drinking?"

"Oh, that. Sorry. There's a meeting on Monday morning with Trinity House, the seafarers' charity responsible for lighthouses."

"Is it to do with the light on Longstone?"

"No. My father is the keeper there, and Trinity House rightly thinks the world of him. It's just, there may be an opportunity for my eldest brother to run a smaller light, which is going to be built soon. A brand new one. I think they want to sound him out, measure the cut of his jib. A couple of us will go along to show the family back-up, give character references if needed."

"Moral support, eh? Good for you. How old is he, your brother?"

"Early thirties. Name's Laddie – or William. He works as a joiner at Bell's firm in Alnwick."

"And where will it be, this new light? In Northumberland?"

"On Coquet Island, a mile off the coast by Amble. Very small, mainly pastureland, with colonies of seabirds – including roseate terns, an endangered species, so Grace informs me."

William Brooks was enjoying this fluent conversation. He felt as though he had known Jane Downey for years, rather than a matter of minutes. He felt he could say anything to her, and that made him happy.

Fittingly, Jane had a big grin on her face. "Does anyone live on Coquet at the moment?"

He shook his head. "Given the increase in shipping, I think the Boulmer rocks to the north and Hauxley Point to the south are simply too hazardous to leave without a beacon."

"So he'd be the first keeper of the new lighthouse?"

"Yes, but it's a long way off."

What William Brooks did not mention was that Coquet Island was owned by the Duke of Northumberland. He had committed personally to funding a lighthouse there, working to the designs and technical specifications of Trinity House's engineers. The duke was also recommending that Laddie be appointed keeper when construction was finished in another year or two.

It was a further example of the duke acting as a benefactor to the Darling family. Quiet, unassuming, but a force to be reckoned with in the background. Both Hugh and Charlotte Percy had made private payments into Grace's fund, now governed by his formidable board of trustees, who never failed to acknowledge the bravery of the North Sunderland boatmen, William Brooks included.

"You referred to your sister just then," Jane said thoughtfully. "How is she?"

"One of the most feted people in the country," William Brooks replied. "What's happened is extraordinary. But I'm worried about her, deeply."

Jane watched him, said nothing, waited.

"You see, the rescue that she and my father carried out, against all odds, so captured the public's imagination that Grace no longer has any privacy. Practically every day, even in winter, visitors sail by, expecting to see her whatever she may be doing. Letters pour in, gifts, requests, more gifts, more requests. I don't know… for someone as selfless as she, it's a form of torture and she finds it hard to bear. Then there were the deaths…"

"She saved nine lives, didn't she?"

"Yes, she and my father, William, rescued nine survivors. That's all who lived. More than forty were swept away. There were sixty-three souls on that steamer. And my father is still referred to in the press as 'Grace Darling's father'. He says nothing but you can tell it irritates him sometimes. Despite his own bravery, he's become nameless, exiled from the record." Maybe, but not from my version of events.

"Wait a minute, didn't you row out to the wreck, too? You were one of the lifeboat crew, weren't you?"

He was impressed by her memory for detail. "Yes, that's right. But by the time we arrived, no one was left alive. It was shocking, dreadful. Two young children died on the rock before anyone got there. Grace gets panicky, I think she finds that particularly tough to deal with."

"How could she not?"

"It's four months since the wreck. It's not getting any easier."

"So, this is where you disappeared to!" A familiar, if slurred, male voice.

George, William Brooks's twin, plonked himself down next to him.

William Brooks touched Jane's hand. She did not pull away and he realised that his heart was thumping.

"Do you know the legend of St. Henry of Coquet?" Jane asked. George rapidly lost interest in the couple's conversation and returned, slightly unsteady on his pins, to Tommy and Robbie in the bar.

"Daft as a brush," he muttered on his way, shaking his head. William Brooks shrugged.

"He was a Danish man of noble birth. Twelfth century. I think his name was Henry – perhaps not – but he was definitely a saint. Anyway, he sailed single-handed across the North Sea, landed at Tynemouth and asked the Prior if there was an island where he could live as a hermit."

"Why? To serve God?"

"To escape an arranged marriage."

"Oh. Seems rather extreme. As legends go, that's not much of one, is it?"

And not applicable to Laddie, either, who was happily married to Ann, now six months pregnant with their first child.

Jane smiled, squeezed his hand.

"I should go and talk to my friends," said William Brooks. "They invited me and I haven't even said hello properly yet. But it's been lovely – I can't tell you how much – to meet you."

"You, too. My parents will be wondering what's happened to me."

"Would you consider not having a drink with me again some time, Jane? I'd really–"

"Yes."

William Brooks seemed genuinely surprised, which pleased her, fulfilled her.

"I'll give you our address before we leave," she said, reading his expression. "Next time, let's rendezvous outside Felton."

"That's wonderful, it's–"

"Yes," she said. "It is. Now giz a kiss and be off with you."

William Brooks would have been mightily excited had he known then that he would marry Jane Downey in North Sunderland the following year, 1840, the same year that Queen Victoria married her cousin, Prince Albert.

Furthermore, before that year was out, Jane would give birth to a son, the first of their nine children. And soon his own career with Trinity House, as well as Laddie's, would reach new heights.

— 38 —

The trustees convene

Crisp and clear dawned the last day of January 1839, a Thursday.

Just after 8 a.m., Grace pushed the coble off Longstone, heading for Brownsman. She feathered the oars as she rowed across the placid water, her eyes on the eastern sky.

Sunrise.

The blacks and browns of night-time melted in the orange glow that passed overhead as swiftly as it had emerged over the horizon, leaving behind a bright blue canvas tainted by barely a wisp of cloud.

Grace had taken to watching the sunrise, from either her lighthouse window or the coble if she had an early trip to make. Thomasina would be there at her spinning wheel, watchfully seeing her off: she'd never had the luxury of a long sleep.

Every sunrise, glorious and uplifting, reminded Grace that every morning was a fresh start. Nothing stagnated for long. Anxious as she was about the mound of letters she had to write – particularly when so many ended up being sent on to local papers to publish – the sunrise gave her hope, at least, that her current predicament was transitory. Soon, a clean sheet. A relapse into obscurity could not come a day too soon.

Not far off, two trading schooners, each showing three white sails, passed in opposite directions. It was a lovely daybreak to spend at sea. Unlike most children, Grace had not grown up playing in the countryside or on the streets. Her upbringing had been on or beside the water, and venturing out in the coble, with a purpose to achieve, made her happy.

She had received no word recently from George Smith, the artist from Newcastle with whom she had corresponded joyously for a few weeks after his visit. Then nothing, which had hurt her. Where was he? What could she have done to upset him?

Thank goodness Thomasin was always there for her. So much more than a shoulder to cry on, her sister was her confidante in the outside world – even if only a few miles away in Bamburgh. But it was the outside world that had let Grace down so badly that part of her spirit had still not recovered.

She appreciated Papa was not to blame for the Edinburgh debacle. He had wanted to help, of course he did, but this time he'd been as much in the dark as Grace herself. Thomasin knew how she felt, week by week. Usually, the very act of expressing herself in her letters made Grace feel a little stronger, better able to face the rest of the day. It helped to diminish the fear that corroded her well-being.

Some guillemots, six or eight, peeled off the top of the Pinnacles nearby, screeching and squabbling. They made a wide arc over the coble and hovered above the Pinnacles before dropping back into position.

A rowing boat was approaching – fast. There must be half a dozen oarsmen, Grace estimated at first glance. Had it launched from one of the schooners, or the mainland? Grace wondered whether they needed help, but an instinct warned her they did not. She pulled harder on the oars and the flat-bottomed coble responded immediately, surging across the glassy sea.

"Wait!" came the cry.

Wait?

There were six of them, all men. Yes, she could see them now, the reddening cheeks, the torrents of breath at their mouths and nostrils. They were not sailors, nor were they seasoned rowers.

"Come here, lass! You're Grace Darling, ain't you?"

Oh.

Grace quickened her pace, leaning further into each stroke, pulling hard when she stretched back. Unlike the chasing pack, she had not broken a sweat.

"Come about! Come and save us!"

Grace did not engage with them but shot a glance to her left as she skimmed by the little islands. She knew immediately where she was. Past the Hawkers and approaching the Wamses. The tide was at its lowest. Every piece in the chain of the Farnes was now exposed, nothing submerged.

The six men had closed to within twenty yards. She'd had an idea – but could she realise it before they caught her?

Off South Wamses was a nameless rock with a tiny cave indented in its west side, the side out of the rowers' line of sight. At high tide, it filled with water, leaving just the tip of the rock protruding. Grace lifted her right oar out of the water and pulled on the left. Instantly, the coble turned to port. But had her pursuers seen her change of direction?

Expertly, she manoeuvred the coble into the frosty cave, using her oars as hands on the fissured rocks. It was just deep enough to swallow the coble, though not wide enough to turn around.

Where were they?

"We're coming, Grace!"

The chilling words sounded close – very close. This was no game. They could only be a few yards away, one or two more strokes.

Abruptly, a maelstrom of rasping, hissing and flapping filled the air.

"Hey – what's that?"

"Where did they come from?"

"Ow! Aargh!"

Grace knew what had happened. A flock of shags, probably males, had swooped on the six stalkers, to within inches of their heads, warning them off with their green eyes and hooked, razor-sharp bills. Resident on the Farnes in all four seasons, they defended aggressively the nests they began to build on the ledges at this time of year.

A loud splash.

A groan.

One man cursed as he let go of his oar, raising both arms to protect his face from the aerial attack. He couldn't prevent it dropping into the water. Alongside him, he was aghast to see a crony wiping his lacerated forehead with the back of his hand.

"You wazzock! Let's get oot of here afore we lose another one!"

"Aye."

"That Darling lass thinks she's a legend, but legends aren't real, they don't exist, do they? They're *nada. Nada, nada, nada.*"

"Howay, cut the blather, let's stop wasting time."

Another man sniggered. "*Nada,*" he repeated.

The others aped him, but without mirth.

Keeping silent, Grace heard them turn and pull away. Holding her breath, she let the sound of their oars splashing in the water fade completely before she moved. She pushed the coble out of the cave, using the walls for leverage and keeping a sharp eye out for the pursuers. They had gone.

On Brownsman, fifteen minutes later, Grace weeded the family's walled garden and trimmed the goat's dirty hooves. As she walked over to the vegetable patch, she was struck by the pure tranquility of her surroundings – a massive relief after her nasty encounter.

She stopped for a moment. Not a sound except for the gentle lapping of the sea as the tide started to turn. She was alone, another schooner sailing near the horizon the only other sign of human life. And yet, the other Grace Darling, the larger-than-life imposter whose identity she had helped to create by posing for portraits, would be mobbed if she set foot in any town in the land.

Two books had recently been published, one in Newcastle, the other in London, each purporting to be biographies of Grace Darling. She and her parents had been disgusted by the absence of facts and truth in both. The accounts of the rescue were fabricated nonsense. They should have been published as fiction, if they were published at all. But now they were out, on sale, and the frustrating thing was that they would form part of the record of her life, and stoke the more fantastical versions of her legend, for many readers. God help us all, she murmured.

The inaugural meeting of the trustees assembled by the Duke of Northumberland had taken place last week. There was a full house – the duke; his solicitor, Tom Thorp; Reverend Darnell; Archdeacons Thorp and Singleton. Grace and William attended, too. This time, Tom took the minutes himself.

The meeting was in the library at Bamburgh Castle – a spectacular cathedral of books. Why not in Alnwick? Well, perhaps there'd been a session of the Lord Crewe trustees earlier in the day.

Robert Smeddle did not attend, but he was aware of the meeting. He left the castle just as William and Grace arrived, dressed ready for a journey on horseback. This time he would be riding a three-year-old colt, Spirit, who had just had new steel shoes fitted by the freshly appointed farrier, Ben Liddell.

"Off to a tenant's review on the other side of the county," he announced breezily, without stopping. "Good day!"

Since the duke's new arrangements took effect, the Darlings had seen less of Smeddle. He thought about them a lot, more than they knew, and deep down he admired their endurance and mettle. His manner was always pleasant, matching their courtesies to him – but probably, they sensed, out of obligation rather than affection.

The duke called the meeting to order with a reminder of the trust's objectives, namely, proper recognition for Grace and the North Sunderland boat crew; and prevention of unworthy exploitation, if I may put it that way, including by potential suitors, who seemed to write asking for Grace's hand in marriage with daily monotony.

Tom summarised the trust's finances. He circulated a sheet with four columns:

DATE – DONOR – SUM – RUNNING TOTAL

The top entry was the Queen's contribution of £50, collected from the bank in Alnwick on 12 December last. Each entry was shown in pounds / shillings / pence as appropriate.

Various municipal authorities, especially in north-east England and southern Scotland, had raised funds by public subscriptions. Received from Newcastle: £150. Alnwick: £114. Glasgow: £100. Dundee: £50. Birmingham: £15.

The London Exchange had contributed £50, while the philanthropic Coutts family of bankers on the Strand in London had donated £30. Numerous individuals, including the Duke and Duchess of Northumberland to whom William proposed a vote of thanks, had sent private donations.

A further letter had come from Catherine Sinclair of the Ladies of Edinburgh. Despite the Batty fiasco, and Grace not attending their tribute lunch, the ladies had magnanimously arranged collections in her honour at a range of events. From the hefty total they sent – £84/10/07 – they expressed the desire that Grace should receive an annuity of £5.

Grace's preference was for the ladies' donation to be added to the capital sum already invested, and that the interest earned be reinvested rather than paid out. Every new deposit was recorded by Dickson, Archer & Thorp. The running total was £767 and counting.

Grace regarded this fortune as a burden of responsibility now shouldered by the duke. The trust was a construct of the duke and his solicitors; the money was not her personal property and there would be no change to her lifestyle.

"As you wish, my dear," the duke noted, "but we shall keep the finances and all other matters under review."

One matter Grace referred to him that day was an invitation to attend a bazaar in aid of the Port of Hull Society, to benefit sailors' orphaned children. It was hoped that her presence would spur the 2,000 guests to raise a humongous sum. The organising committee, which included a plethora of titled ladies, refused to take no for an answer. Can you believe it, they pestered her with not one but four, five, six letters, each more insistent than the last.

It was a great help to Grace to be able to declare, truthfully, that her ducal guardian stroke principal trustee was dealing with all such requests. Mind you, it did not eliminate her obligation to write to every correspondent, advising them accordingly. She yearned to be free from the drudgery of posting keepsakes – although everyone agreed that not one more lock of hair should be cut from her scalp, with immediate effect. It was written in the minutes.

And yet an inner voice berated Grace whenever she undertook family duties in the lighthouse instead of writing to donors. At times throughout that year, 1839, and the year after and the one after that, the same torturous voice would not be silenced.

The Aberdeen Angus breed

Picture perfect.

From a snowy hilltop on his Perthshire farm, Glen Ritchie regarded the spire of Ruthven village kirk, far below. From this distance it was a miniature model, brushed with white dust. Yet throughout his life, the kirk's beauty, constancy and ability to bring a community together had impressed and comforted him, just as it did now.

The bodies of his aunt and uncle had not been among those recovered last September from the wreck of the *Forfarshire*, so a traditional funeral was not possible for them as it had been for some other families left bereaved by the disaster. But the parish minister had readily consented to a service of thanksgiving for their lives, and Ritchie commissioned Fraser McCarthy, a local mason, to create a joint memorial stone, for which a prominent place in the churchyard was secured.

When the *Corvette* put all nine of them from the quarter-boat ashore, he headed at a gallop for Bamburgh, seeking news of his relatives with whom he'd had a heated exchange – how he regretted it to this day – shortly before the *Forfarshire* slammed into Big Hawker. He could not remember how many endlessly frustrating days he spent in Bamburgh – his recollection of much of what happened at that dreadful time was foggy – but eventually he shared stagecoach passage north to Berwick, from there to Dundee, and then finally home to Ruthven.

His late father had successfully diversified the enterprise from arable to a mix of arable and animal farming. On the arable land, he now sowed potatoes, spring barley and winter wheat. On the grass land, more than 180 sheep and some cattle grazed. The animals' manure helped to break down and enrich the soil. He had installed a dairy with a growing base of customers that he hoped was safe from cheaper overseas imports. The whey extracted from his cows' milk could be sold to pig farmers as feed.

He had stayed in contact with Jas Hall, the *Forfarshire*'s coal trimmer, whom he had helped to board the *Corvette*. When the only joiner in Ruthven had succumbed to consumption, Jas put him in touch with the ship's carpenter, Johnny Tulloch, who, fortunately, was only too pleased to travel up from Dundee for a week. The eight crewmen with whom he'd escaped the wreck had mostly resumed their careers at sea. Allan Stewart, chief engineer, and James Duncan, first mate, were reunited on a steamship plying the east coast, although Ritchie could never remember its name. Was it the *Genesis*? The *Pegasus*? Yes, that could be it.

Between sailings last October, Tulloch had helped him construct the dairy, and repair gates and fences. Tulloch seemed fine, but he confessed that he was still haunted by the sight of the aft section of the *Forfarshire* shearing off, and Ritchie thought he had aged appreciably in the weeks since the wreck. The experience was scored into the lines around his eyes and mouth, but they hardly discussed it.

Tulloch teased him about the scythes and pitchforks that the labourers who shared the farm's tied cottages still used. If he acquired modern, steam-powered machinery, he'd not need as many horses or men and could expand the farm into the bargain. Looking to the south and west, there was plenty of bordering land for him to acquire.

Tulloch's points chimed with Ritchie's own ideas about the development of the business. The farm appeared more outdated by the day. With Tulloch's encouragement ringing in his ears, he invested in a new machine, intending to run it for a while side by side with a manual operation. So, Ritchie hired a steam-driven plough to tackle the late October harvest.

When a large twig jammed the rotor blades, he managed to break it loose but did not withdraw his hand in time. The little finger of his left hand was sliced clean off. Despite the shock and throbbing pain, he bandaged the wound, determined to keep it free from infection. Good thinking.

It was in the kirk the following Sunday, when the bandages were at their bulkiest, and sympathy at its most abundant, that he met Brenna. She was the daughter of Fraser McCarthy, the mason who had carved the memorial stone, and he found her admiring his handiwork after the service. She had been staying with an aunt in Dundee when he dealt with her father, but they arranged to meet again and bonded over drams of Islay malt – "strictly for its curative powers, ye understand."

Now, with Brenna in his life, Ritchie no longer had to remind himself not to act recklessly. He thought of her first thing in the morning and last thing at night. Acting responsibly, reliably, felt natural, even noble, rather than conduct to adopt forcibly.

Remembering his late aunt and uncle, as he frequently did, he knew they would be pleased with the calming influence Brenna was having over him. He had at last decided on a plan. He would increase the firm's income by doing more with the land he already occupied, by being more efficient, rather than by expanding his acreage.

The adjacent land seemed fertile enough – but was the soil the same? Were there issues with weeds or drainage? With spreading his resources too thinly? The Glen Ritchie of a few months ago would have dismissed such considerations, if he had thought of them at all. He had given himself a year, then he would judge how his plan was working, and reassess whether the farm needed to be extended.

As he crunched through the snow, back down the hill to the farmhouse, Ritchie hoped Brenna would accompany him to an agricultural show at the end of March. It was an annual regional gathering, where farmers could recruit apprentices and labourers, test the latest machinery – under supervision – and trade their produce and livestock.

As part of his plan, Ritchie had decided to invest in selective breeding, to raise the value of his cattle. He liked the look of the Aberdeen Angus breed, glossy black, very muscular, and hardy enough to survive the toughest winters. A female could weigh twelve hundred pounds, a male eighteen hundred or more, yielding the premier beef for which demand from far and wide was enticingly fast-rising.

Ritchie felt more excited about the future than he could ever recall. Yes, the agricultural show could be a positive turning point for him. But the irony in its location, he reflected, opening the farmhouse door, was palpable. It was to be held on a large field just outside the village of Forfar.

— 40 —

Coquet Island

How could anyone not love him?

The black Labrador puppy bounded up to Grace, his tail rotating like the blades of a windmill. He licked her hand with his hot tongue and ogled her as if she was all that mattered to him.

"Yes, Buddy, I love you, too," she said, caressing his head. He rolled over on the rug, panting, and waved a front paw, imploring her to stroke his belly, which she was happy to do.

Grace had grown attached to Buddy in the weeks since William Brooks brought him to Longstone. He was a stray, found wandering, scrounging, in the village of Felton after a troupe of acrobats had spent a night performing there en route to a festival in Edinburgh. Grace had named him Buddy, partly for his companionship and unconditional love, and partly in memory of Cuddy, the eider duck that had meant so much to her as a youngster. He'd put on some weight and had settled in well.

William and Thomasin were relieved that, as they'd hoped, the newest member of their family had restored a sense of playfulness to the home. Over time, they trusted this would help assuage the anxiety that was so reluctant to release their daughter from its jaws.

Despite Buddy's arrival and the high-powered support of the Duke of Northumberland, Grace remained more reclusive, more fatigued than she was before she became famous. She just wasn't herself. William wanted to know how much intrusion was too much but found it impossible to judge. He was pleased that Grace confided in Thomasin, and he made a point of talking in person to her sister in Bamburgh as often as he could. He was desperate for Grace to feel right again but was unsure what more he could do.

He and Grace were touched to receive a letter from a Mr Henry Strachan, congratulating them on their silver medals from the National Institution for the Preservation of Life from Shipwreck. More than a decade ago, in December 1828, Strachan and his son had saved five men – a tide surveyor and four crew – from the befouled, freezing River Tyne when their Custom House boat capsized. The Strachans' dinghy was only a dozen feet long, but the five men would undoubtedly have drowned had they not gone to their assistance. Henry Strachan himself had been one of the first ever recipients of the National Institution's silver medal. It was kind of him to write, wasn't it?

Without reference to the duke, Grace turned down an invitation from the mayor of Newcastle to tour the new city centre and to receive in person a donation as a further tribute. Having already declined similar invitations from civic dignitaries elsewhere, she felt it would be impolite, improper, to do anything other than the same with this one. For a lengthy period, the five miles from Longstone to Bamburgh Castle was as far as she travelled.

Two trustees, Archdeacon Singleton and Reverend Darnell, asked her to join them at the castle to discuss religion, morality, love, compassion, forgiveness. It was heady stuff and at first she felt intimidated. Although the learned men were kind, she was amazed when they invited her back.

The sessions became an occasional fixture. Thomasina and William said nothing, but knowing that the trustees sought only to restore Grace's self-belief, they encouraged her to attend. When Archdeacon Thorp invited her to the castle, it was, thankfully, to discuss seabirds, plentiful and rare species alike, and she felt more of an equal partner in that conversation. He seemed particularly to enjoy hearing about Cuddy.

Dozens of ballads were composed to sing of the bravery of Grace Darling as her name embedded itself deeper and deeper into national folklore. Grace herself tended to recoil from each new one that was drawn to her attention, sensing that they were further examples of the doppelganger disrupting her life.

A copy of one ballad, set out in admirable calligraphy, was sent to her with an amusing cover note by its writer, George Linley. He was a Yorkshireman, now in his forties, who lived in London, having earlier worked in Leeds and Edinburgh. Known for his quick-witted, humorous style, he had composed hundreds of sings and he hoped she liked this one. Grace was secretly delighted when Buddy reared up on his hind legs, snatched the pages from her table and ripped them to shreds.

Early in 1839, Grace received a series of gifts from admirers in Scotland: silver teaspoons, silk, a Methodist hymn book, volumes of poetry by Rabbie Burns and James Hogg, storage jars, fountain pens, another bible. She had to collect some of these from Bamburgh Castle, where Robert Smeddle stayed mercifully concise and unfailingly courteous in his dealings with her.

When Scottish admirers also mailed a donation of £30, she sent the cheque on to Tom Thorp to be deposited in her fund. The trustees reminded her that she could draw down the interest, or take a lump sum, if she so wished. She did not.

That summer, nearly a year after the *Forfarshire* was wrecked, boats sailed past Longstone daily, bulging with visitors who would point and wave and shout. Occasionally one landed on the island, offloading passengers to run amok. Grace deeply regretted the disturbance to the birds and seals and would stay in her room, longing for them to clear off.

Once, her father cajoled her into coming down and greeting the visitors outside the lighthouse door. It triggered a stampede on the rock, leaving an elderly – by which I mean in her sixties – woman with a twisted ankle.

One Saturday in June, a fishing smack overloaded with sightseers ran aground on Little Hawker. Buddy at her side,

Grace observed the incident from her bedroom and alerted her father. He was in the lantern room with Laddie, who was visiting that weekend, and had not only seen the fishing smack run aground himself, but was certain, from her speed and course, that it had been a deliberate manoeuvre designed to force a rescue by the famous Darlings of Longstone.

William and Laddie rowed out to Little Hawker and refloated the boat with their long pikes. This earned thunderous applause from the deck and a sheepish nod of appreciation from the bridge. William's record of that coble outing in his logbook did not run to a second line.

Now, at this point, I'm shifting into fast-forward mode for a bit. The weeks turned into months, the months into years… In the summer of 1840, the same pattern of sightseeing boats sailing up to the lighthouse played out, with Grace steeling herself to acknowledge at least some of the well-wishers.

Robert Smeddle had been right to think that seismic reform of the postal service was in the offing. Across the country from January 1840, a postage rate of one penny applied to all letters up to half an ounce in weight. As the charge was pre-paid, delivery of the mail speeded up – a smart move, yes?

Not only that, Grace was convinced that the sheer amount of mail multiplied. The replies she had to write climbed day by day. In May, penny black stamps were introduced, showing Queen Victoria's head in profile. They were despatched to the post office in Bamburgh in printed sheets of 240. Every morning the clerks cut them into strips of twelve. The adhesive on the reverse was dextrin, made by boiling starch, and it tasted revolting on Grace's tongue. Nevertheless, millions of these little squares were printed every month. Officially, they could be used on letters from 6 May, a Wednesday, but Grace noticed a few slipped through postmarked the weekend prior.

On top of the incessant letters and cards, the post brought more clothing and jewellery than she could ever wear. More proposals than there were days in the year. More books and bibles than she could ever read. She loved to share the gifts with her brothers and sisters and, where appropriate, little nieces and nephews, too. She remained close to her family and was relieved that they seemed to need her as much as she needed them.

For the duke's new lighthouse on Coquet Island, a square design by James Walker, a Trinity House engineer, was approved. At a cost of £3,268, it was constructed in 1841. Sandstone walls, three feet thick, seventy-two feet high. The lantern was surrounded by a turreted parapet, which Grace felt made the lighthouse look more like a fortress.

The light from its oil-fuelled lamp was concentrated via a set of mirrors into a large lens, supplied – credit where it's due – by Isaac Cookson & Company of Newcastle. A clockwork mechanism, which enabled the beam to revolve, periodically shaded the beam from view, creating the illusion of it flashing off rather than on. The range of the beam was nineteen nautical miles. The lantern room was also equipped with a foghorn, calibrated to emit a three-second blast every thirty seconds.

Laddie was immensely proud to be confirmed as the first keeper of the Coquet Island fortress, and naturally the Darling clan was proud of him, too. Trinity House issued new blue suits to all their keepers; those for William and Laddie were delivered to Longstone and Coquet Islands on the same day.

Grace and her sister Thomasin arranged to visit Laddie and his family for a long weekend in March 1842. The sisters shared a chilly room on the second floor of the fortress, from which they could see the mainland village of Amble, where a harbour was under construction to serve the spread of coal mines.

By this time, Laddie and Ann had two young boys, aged three and fifteen months, so an uninterrupted night's sleep was a treasured rarity. Nevertheless, Ann took her sisters-in-law on hikes at low tide, starting with one along the River Coquet to Warkworth, where a medieval castle crowned a hilltop overlooking the river. In the fourteenth century, Grace told them, this castle was home to Sir Henry Percy, a knight who earned the nickname 'Harry Hotspur' for repelling invaders from north of the border.

Grace kept her hair up, a bonnet on and her head down, and did not seem to be recognised by any passers-by. She was delighted to be able to go incognito, but the wariness of being out in public never quite left her in peace.

Winter should have thawed into spring by the time of their visit; they'd manifestly hoped so when they planned it. Unfortunately, the icy rain and bitter winds were unrelenting, and both Ann and Grace caught colds.

Usually, Grace reflected, while the water might be clearer and the air cleaner on the Farne Islands, it was always a degree or two warmer on the mainland. Well, not this week. Unlike many people, Grace had enjoyed continuous good health, but this cold hit her hard. Aching muscles, lost senses of taste and smell, pressure building in her ears and a rasping cough that hurt her whole chest, not just her throat.

With Grace laid low in bed for two days, Thomasin extended their stay until the end of the week. Ann's cold had cleared up by then; against expectations, Grace's had not. Thomasin put it down to Grace's fatigue and anxiety rendering her more prone to infection than she might otherwise have been, but was sure she'd feel better soon. Privately she was not so certain.

At the weekend, the sisters hugged Ann, Laddie and the boys, and took an open coach to Alnwick. Thanks to a torrential shower at just the wrong time, they got soaked yet again, but they had arranged to visit some cousins and enjoyed the free-flowing news and gossip from another branch of the family. There was concern over Grace's persistent coughing and sneezing, but she waved it away as the tail end of a nasty bug.

From Alnwick, Grace returned to Longstone and Thomasin to Bamburgh. She had been away from her shop for longer than intended and the backlog of orders would not design, cut and stitch itself.

"Oh, angel, you don't look well."

The moment her daughter entered the lighthouse, Thomasina stopped the spinning wheel, suddenly apprehensive. Grace put down her suitcase, kicked off her heavy shoes and folded herself into an armchair by the fire. The movement irritated her chest and she coughed deeply while patting Buddy who was making a big fuss of her.

"I'm fine, Mama. I just need to shake off this wretched cough, that's all. Don't fret. And it's lovely to see you, too, Buddy, have you missed me?"

Buddy retracted his little ears, wagged even faster, licked Grace's hand and scampered off with one of her shoes.

Grace updated her mother with the news from her cousins in Alnwick and from Laddie and Ann in their family fortress. Laddie wore his blue suit from Trinity House as exultantly as any soldier a new uniform. He was taking his responsibilities as seriously as his father, William, had taught his offspring to do, and was determined to reward the faith placed in him by Trinity House and the duke.

Thomasina, who had expected nothing less of her unflappable son, nodded and smiled. She was always a good listener. She had prepared a beef stew and asked Grace to put it on the stove.

"A goodly portion for you, angel. You look like you've lost a bit of weight, have you?"

While the meal was cooking, Grace took her case up to her bedroom. Before the third floor, she was gasping for breath on the stairs, and Buddy charged past, ears flapping, unaccustomed to the slow pace.

The next day, William rowed Grace and Buddy over to Brownsman. She offered to take an oar; he would not hear of it. Dozens of birds scattered, squawking their annoyance, as Buddy lolloped up the path to the walled garden, where he sat and waited impatiently for William and Grace to catch up.

William told her that Trinity House would soon start work building two cottages on Longstone, at a cost of more than £1,000 each. William Brooks and his growing family would move into one: Jane was expecting their second child, not long after the first, a son named William Swann Darling, was born. The other cottage would be reserved for the use of shipwreck survivors as the original builders' barracks were so ramshackle.

Grace could see her father was excited that the island was to be developed in this way and she welcomed the investment.

"Lots of new friends for you to make while the cottages are built," she promised Buddy, who wagged his approval as usual.

After an hour's light gardening, William grabbed a bucket and took Grace for a much-needed break, down to the edge of Brownsman, close to where the coble was roped up. The tide was out, and a large rock pool had formed just off the island. It was an aquarium, lined with a palette of seaweeds, red, yellow, orange and green.

He dunked the bucket in the water, pulled it out a few seconds later. The array of species inside never failed to impress them, however many times they had seen it before. Hermit crabs, sea anemones, hairy worms, even a tiny starfish, along with kelp, barnacles and whelks.

Buddy tried to sniff the contents of the bucket, but it was salty and he bolted, enthralled by a new spoor. Grace plucked out a whorled shell and inspected it closely: surprisingly thick, it had been made by a mollusc as armour for its soft body. She kept this souvenir when they emptied the bucket back into the aquarium.

That spring, William, Grace and Buddy made many more rock-pooling trips to Brownsman. They left much unsaid, cherishing instead the carefree times, enjoying what John Keats described as 'the songs of spring' all around them. Once, Buddy chased a stick that had washed up until their throwing arms were worn out.

But when the days grew longer and warmer, William became ever more concerned that Grace's coughing and breathing only got worse.

— 41 —

Consumption

"This way, please, and watch out!"

Edward Blackburn ushered William Darling into the rose garden, sidestepping a Griebel garden gnome made of clay. He left William seated on an oak bench, admiring some bushes of a reddish pink variety that he had not noticed before.

It was a warm summer's day with just enough of a breeze to freshen the air. William shut his eyes and basked in the sunshine. His nostrils wrinkled with the soothing perfumes of the rose blooms, and for a sublime moment his worries dissolved like grains of sugar.

"Good afternoon, William, lovely to see you again."

At the Duchess of Northumberland's voice, William got to his feet. When they'd shaken hands, she sat on a second bench, facing him. There was a low oak table between them, upon which Twizell the butler placed a tray with three glasses, a pitcher of water and a dish of lemon and orange slices.

"Many thanks, Twizell," said the duchess.

"The duke will be here momentarily, ma'am. His meeting with Algernon has overrun. He sends profound apologies."

Algernon Percy, Hugh's younger brother who was excelling in his Royal Navy career, had never much liked the designs to which the castle was rebuilt seventy years ago. He was probably suggesting a fresh round of improvements.

The duchess leaned forward, looked William in the eye.

"You mustn't breathe a word of this." It was so quiet that the rustling of the leaves almost drowned out her words. "Queen

Victoria and Prince Albert will be taking their first holiday in Scotland in September. We're very much hoping they'll make a stop here on their way back."

Suitably impressed, William promised to keep the secret. He wondered how the royal entourage might travel. He had read in a newspaper sent by Robert Smeddle that the twenty-three-year-old queen had made the first steam train journey by a British monarch, a few weeks ago in June, from Slough to Paddington. He returned his focus to the duchess.

"We wondered," she was saying, "whether Grace might wish to meet Her Majesty?"

A frown clouded William's face.

"That is so kind of you…", he started, but he spoke with far less enthusiasm than the duchess had expected, and his voice tailed off. That was the moment when she knew beyond doubt that Grace's health was dwindling away. She sat back on her bench, ill at ease.

The brief silence was broken by the duke's arrival. He apologised again for not being there to welcome their guest and poured a glass of water for each of them.

"Help yourself to a slice of fruit, don't stand on ceremony."

"Thank you, sir."

The duke sat next to his wife and took a long, refreshing drink.

"How are the new buildings on Longstone?" he asked. "Must be finished, or very nearly?"

"Yes, sir. We had twenty-plus workmen for a while, the island was overcrowded. Now, the two stone cottages are finished, the roofs are on, and Mr Duncan has left. They're really lovely inside." Mr Duncan was Trinity House's agent who supervised the works.

"I imagine," said the duchess, "that the noise and dust can't have been easy for our dear Grace?"

William's face darkened. He took a sip of water, the two faces opposite watching him sombrely. The duke put an arm around his wife's shoulder.

"I'm sure you'll know, this is why I requested to see you, and thank you so much for making the time. Thomasina and I – all of us – we're very concerned about Grace's state of health."

It came as a relief simply to have said it. Perhaps he had bottled up his concerns for too long. Everyone in the family was distressed, fearing the worst. Buddy was acutely aware that Grace was not herself and persisted in trying to lick her better.

"Some days are better than others, but over a few months we fear she's been going steadily down. During the worst of the construction works, she stayed with a sister in Bamburgh." When he'd last spoken to Thomasin, she could bear only to say that Grace was "in good spirits".

The duchess perched on the edge of the bench. "It began as a cold that never cleared up?"

"As far as we know, yes. Then she seemed to develop a form of influenza – the aches and pains have been so debilitating at times, in her head and body. And now, well, we're just not sure."

"It must be painful for you, too," said the duchess with compassion, "to see this happening."

William nodded, dismal face, said nothing.

"You told us, I think, that Grace was to spend a little time in Wooler," the duke recalled. "How did that go?"

"She wrote to us once or twice from there and said she was feeling better," William replied. "But Thomasin, that's her sister, who has been a marvellous support all through the illness and couldn't have done more, told us privately that she was putting on a brave face. Actually, they both are."

"As you'd expect of dear Grace," the duchess said dejectedly. Strange as it may seem, she'd had a certain empathy with Grace Darling from the start. She knew that Grace had been comfortable in her own skin, had known herself well, and hated being powerless to prevent her world being torn apart.

"I was keen for Grace and Thomasin to pass some time together in Wooler," William continued. "They've always been close, and we know their host – he's been to Longstone and was more than happy to receive them. George Shield is his name."

"I know of him," the duchess clapped her hands. "Very clever with his hands, yes? A master tailor, like his father, and an artist. Excels at birds of prey, I believe. Hawks, buzzards and the like." Well, that saved me from inserting a snapshot of him.

"That's the fellow," said William. "Generous, thoughtful, did his best to help. Took the girls walking and riding, fed them well, nothing too much trouble."

"Is Grace still in Wooler?" asked the duke. "Or back on Longstone?"

"She's back, but actually she's lodging with some relatives again, here in Alnwick. I'm a great believer that a change of air is a tonic in itself… sometimes."

The duke and duchess swapped glances. They had read William's facial expressions, in which they could find no vestige of optimism regarding Grace's well-being, only the deepest paternal concern.

The duchess stood. "Come with me, William," she enjoined him. "I want to show you around my garden. Today is one of those idyllic days when it looks its best."

William followed her away from the roses into a spectacular Japanese garden with ferns and fiery-leafed maples, azaleas and quince. The borders overflowed with forest grass that whispered in the breeze. She halted under an arbour of wisteria to pick off a few side shoots that had grown out. They chatted about the plants, bursting back after a harsh winter, sustaining other lifeforms in the garden.

"It's superb, your garden, it really is," William complimented her.

She brushed it aside. "Look, I know you're very worried," she said suddenly, close to him. "Of course you are. But please, don't get distressed. You have so much to think about at the lighthouse, so many family considerations. Hugh and I will do everything we can to help Grace, be sure of that, at least."

William thanked her, examined his hands. "I read all the time that Britain is the world's leading power, on the back of the Industrial Revolution. But what sort of progress is it if a father can't help his own daughter to get better?"

"She'll be – what – twenty-seven in November? She has youth and general good health on her side."

When they returned to the rose garden, the duke drained his water, leaving just lemon peel in the glass.

"This is what I propose," he said solemnly. "I have to spend a few days in London. Sir Robert, the PM, wants a word about a couple of rising stars in the political realm. Both supremely able, lots to give, but with sharply conflicting policy ideas. On a personal level, they can't stand the sight of each other. Literally, when one of them enters a room, the other walks out. Exasperating! Mr Gladstone and Mr Disraeli, they're called. Anyway, before I leave, I'm going to chat to our private physician. Another William, I'm afraid, Dr William Bamfather. Excellent fellow, well read, at the forefront of knowledge. Let's get him to have a good look at Grace, shall we, see what he suggests."

"Where is she staying in Alnwick?" asked the duchess.

"Close by, in the centre of town. Not far from your solicitors' office."

"Does she know you're here?"

William shook his head. "But I'll pop in before heading up to Longstone, see if there's been any change."

"Well, I think we should relocate her, if possible," the duchess recommended. "How about this. We — that is, the estate — have a property in Prudhoe Street, just beyond the centre of Alnwick — do you know it? There's a splendid church up there, and a railway line will run by, once they get round to building it. But it's on quite a steep hill, you see, and the air is purer than in the centre. The house is clean, warm and dry, and Grace can have it to herself."

William felt a lump in his throat. "That sounds too good to be true."

At 2 p.m. the following Friday, a slim man in a black coat, carrying a battered leather medicine bag, mounted the stone steps of a townhouse in Prudhoe Street. With a gloved hand, he rapped on the front door.

It was opened by Thomasin Darling, who had been watching through a downstairs window.

"William Bamfather, at your service," the caller announced. "The doctor. I believe you were expecting me?"

"Do come in, doctor." Thomasin hastily introduced herself before standing aside. As he swept past, she caught a milky, vanilla scent.

"Straight upstairs?"

"Please, yes. Grace's room is at the far end of the landing."

Thomasin gathered her black, taffeta day dress and headed after him. When she reached the room, Dr Bamfather was already examining his newfound patient, gloves off, fingertips probing her swollen neck. Sitting up in bed, Grace looked pale and exhausted and was coughing frequently. On the bedspread, a heap of screwed-up handkerchiefs, blotted with sputum and blood. On the floor, a scattering of unopened letters.

"Have you been experiencing night sweats? Convulsions? Any other symptoms? How is your appetite?"

Grace was breathless, could manage only short sentences. A bead of sweat trickled down her forehead into her left eye. Thomasin mopped Grace's brow. She looked so upset to see her sister in this state that the doctor called her back to the door.

"Please fetch me a bowl of hot water – boiling, if you can," he said. He took care to look her in the eye, and not let his gaze stray to her cleft lip.

"Can you treat her?" Thomasin blurted out. "Do you know what's wrong? We just don't seem to be able to do anything to help her…"

"From her symptoms, my diagnosis is that your sister has consumption, an infection of the throat and lungs."

Thomasin's eyes were swamped with tears, which she dabbed with a clean handkerchief. She had not allowed herself to dwell on it, but hearing the doctor say the word now felt like a knife twisting in her chest. She knew that consumption was often fatal; there was no cure.

"As you've observed, it's a progressive illness that leads to a lack of appetite and weight loss, hence the term 'consumption'. Within the last decade, a more precise medical name has been coined – tuberculosis, from the Latin, indicating a swelling, especially in the lungs."

Thomasin began to sob. She stepped on to the landing so that Grace did not hear.

"I'm afraid that the disease has been with us a long time, and it remains all too common. I've treated many other cases, the symptoms are clear."

"And how are your other patients?"

Dr Bamfather sighed. "Please be aware, Miss Darling, I shall use every treatment at my disposal. Then, we must pray that Grace's body is able to fight off the infection."

"Oh, she's fierce," Thomasin said adamantly. "She's been through a lot these last few years, but her spirit is even stronger than she knows. Let's hope that providence allows her body to be just as strong."

"Quite so. Now, the water, please."

"Right away."

While Thomasin was downstairs, Dr Bamfather busied himself with the contents of his leather bag. He selected some glass vials and laid them out on Grace's bedside table.

Thomasin soon returned with a large glass bowl, three-quarters full of steaming water, which she carried with a red towel.

"Perfect, thank you," said the doctor, indicating to her to lay the bowl on a dresser by the wall.

He tipped a little substance from each vial into the water – crushed leaves, weeds, bark, a pinch of seeds, some burned roots, and finally plenty more crushed leaves. With a long-handled spoon, he stirred the concoction thoroughly. Lifting the bowl across to the bed, he asked Grace to lean over it, as close as she could. He draped her head with the towel and urged her to inhale the vapours, which she did gallantly, despite the attempt to breathe deeply inducing a renewed fit of coughing.

Thomasin encouraged her from the sidelines and mopped her brow again when she'd had enough. She noticed, but ignored, the twitch in Grace's eye. There was enough to worry about.

Dr Bamfather said he was pleased with this first session and promised to return tomorrow. He replaced his vials in his bag and wiped his hands on a cloth.

At the front door, he told Thomasin that he would want to administer herbal treatments for at least three weeks, subject to constant review.

"I'm not an advocate of bleeding and purging," he said. "It seems to me that there are at least as many serious risks as potential benefits, although not every physician concurs."

"How has Grace caught this ghastly disease? It has made her melt away like snow."

"I believe it is through close contact with an infected person. Could have happened anywhere. It's a type of plague, very widespread. It's been suggested that not everyone who catches consumption develops symptoms or gets ill, but I've yet to see proof of that."

"Can anyone get it?"

"As far as we know, anyone at all. It knows no bounds, no social strata. I realise this will be difficult but try not to hug or touch Grace while she's in the grip of the contagion. And if I were you, I'd wash my hands after being in her bedroom."

Thomasin's eyes filled with tears again. "I'll do that. Is there anything else I can do for her?"

"Give her plenty to drink."

"I can certainly do that. Thank you for coming, it's much appreciated."

Dr Bamfather was as good as his word. Between two and three every afternoon for the next three weeks, he visited Grace and gave her a herbal inhalation.

During a visit in the second week, there was a knock at the door. Thomasin opened it to an authoritative woman, dark eyebrows, immaculately coiffed and dressed in a summer blouse and skirt with white court shoes.

"I'm Charlotte," she whispered, stepping inside. "The duchess. I've come to see Grace. You must be Thomasin, it's a pleasure to meet you at last."

"Oh, yes, and of course you too. Thank you for letting us stay here," Thomasin said, flustered, unprepared.

"I've heard a lot about you." The duchess was gliding upstairs. "How helpful you've been."

She had no sooner entered the bedroom and smiled at Dr Bamfather than her good humour evaporated. At first sight, the duchess was shocked at how emaciated the bed-ridden Grace had become. All her strength had decayed, like the leaves on a tree.

Shine bright, my angel

Dear Father and Mother,

As I cannot write you a long letter this time, please God in a little time I will write a long one.

Your loving daughter,

Grace H Darling

It said nothing; it said everything.

It was to be the last letter, of so many, that Grace wrote.

When they received it on Longstone, William and Thomasina could bear it no longer. Leaving William Brooks to run the lighthouse, William made haste to Alnwick, to the townhouse in Prudhoe Street, where Thomasin had nursed Grace throughout the summer, into the autumn.

Dr Bamfather had completed three separate courses of herbal remedies, each time with his mixture tweaked. Grace felt stronger on some days than others. She would sit up in bed and chat to Thomasin about the places and people they might visit when she'd recovered.

She grew to like the doctor, and felt immensely privileged when the duchess popped in to see how she was. The doctor insisted that there should be no other visitors until further notice, that Grace should rest in isolation to battle the infection. Sadly, he knew, just as Grace herself did, that over the course of those weeks her health steadily declined. The family physician, Dr Thomas Fender, who had overseen Grace's birth, was consulted regularly, but knew of no more efficacious treatment to recommend.

William discussed the next steps with Dr Bamfather, who had tried every remedy he knew – plus a few others that he had read up on, such as cod liver oil and stretching exercises. No joy.

William thanked him and arranged for Grace, with Thomasin, to make the journey from Alnwick to Bamburgh. An uncle now lived in Grandpa Job's cottage, where Grace was born. If his daughter was not going to recover, William wanted her to spend whatever time she had left in familiar surroundings, closer to her parents. There were no complaints from Grace, who seemed serenely reconciled to her fate.

William wrote to the duke, reassuring him that Grace was as well as could be expected after the bumpy, twenty-mile journey to Bamburgh, yet she remained gravely ill. She could not sign any documents or discuss her funds for the foreseeable future, but she was most grateful for the trustees' on-going efforts on her behalf.

The duke replied promptly to say that he and Charlotte very much hoped to hear news of improvements in Grace's condition soon.

Letters addressed to Grace continued to arrive. William himself brought those delivered to Longstone on his daily visits to her. Robert Smeddle went out of his way to drop off her mail from Bamburgh Castle, particularly at weekends. Members of the castle staff did so when the agent was away. But Grace unsealed none of them.

Monday 17 October. Gasping between bouts of heavy coughing that stabbed her weakened chest, Grace asked her father to distribute her many gifts among the family. With a heavy heart, he agreed. Grace insisted that her gold watch went to Thomasin. Her paisley shawl with the teardrop motif was earmarked for Laddie's wife, Ann.

On the Wednesday morning, doctors Bamfather and Fender visited Grace together. Having conducted an examination, mainly checking that the patient was as warm and comfortable as possible, they proposed no further treatment. On their way out, they confirmed to Thomasin that there was simply no more that could be done. Nature had to take its course. Grace was ailing and in all likelihood – please prepare yourself – the consumption would claim her within hours, not days.

Thomasin collected her mother from Longstone. They sat at Grace's bedside while she dozed, her breathing shallow and laboured. The only sound that reached William, sitting downstairs in a rocking chair, was his wife's sobbing. Each sob came as a blow to his heart. Many families had been racked with bereavement after all the recent wars and with so many incurable diseases. But today it was his own daughter up there, her life draining away. Nothing else mattered, nothing else would be in focus for some time.

Grace opened her eyes and gazed up at her mother who was gripping her hand.

"Don't cry, dear Mama," Grace gasped.

Her voice had become such a husky whisper that Thomasina hardly recognised it.

"The bible has always told us," Grace continued, "not to fear the next world, and I don't. Thank you, thank you for all your love and kindness. Soon, I think, I'll be reunited in heaven with my brother, Job. I know he will cherish every memory of you, as will I."

Grace suffered a coughing spasm. Her mother released her hand so she could wipe the phlegm and blood spurts from Grace's nose and chin. She took hold of Grace's hand once again, and the words tumbled out of her.

"My dear angel, you are so beautiful, so mighty and courageous, and you are loved deeply. You know that, don't you? I've been so lucky to have had you, to have known you, and you'll always be here in my heart. I know you'll be safe in heaven and loved there too. So, when you are ready, off you go, my angel, and God will go with you."

Thomasina collapsed on to Grace's bedspread. With Dr Bamfather's advice ringing in her ears, Thomasin put an arm around her shoulders and guided her away.

"I'll take Mama home," she said to William downstairs. "Will you–?"

"Yes, of course. I'll stay here until the end."

Thomasin supported her mother out of the cottage to the far end of the village green, where a four-horse coach was waiting.

"Shine bright, my angel. Shine bright, my angel," her mother repeated under her breath.

William heard Grace coughing and spitting, and forced himself, his heart and mind clogged with dread, to trudge upstairs, one at a time, to her room. He must have been more fearful now than when he left Grace to handle the coble alone while he was on the Big Hawker rock.

His stricken daughter was lying flat in bed, her face white, her chest barely rising as she inhaled. She half-opened her eyes when she heard him enter.

"Is there anything at all I can do for you?" he asked, his loving, weathered face inches from hers.

With a supreme effort, Grace sat up. He turned a pillow to bolster her back.

For a moment, her mind was outside her body and she saw herself from above.

She gasped: "Although my life is to be cut short… I've lived the life I wanted to live… the life I was born to live. Thank you, Papa… When we rescued the survivors that night, you put your trust in me, didn't you… had faith in me… I was… I am… afraid of failing you, letting you down… I have never wanted to be… it sounds ridiculous… a hero, but you… you are… always have been… my hero."

William wrapped his arms around his daughter's body. Dear God, how emaciated she was. Hollowed out. He hugged her as tenderly as he could.

Downstairs he had been thinking of all he wanted to say – that he was immensely proud of her, that it was she who had inspired him with her dedication and strength which had been such a credit to the whole family. He was accustomed to writing the briefest of notes in his logbooks, but now, for once, he wanted to let his emotions rip, his heart sing of his eternal pride, admiration, gratitude, love.

All these thoughts swirled in his head like seabirds over the Farnes, but where to start? He had not put them in any order, and–

"Oh, my dear, dear girl…"

William never got to voice those thoughts. He leant back and gazed at his daughter, peaceful and serene, through misted eyes. He had felt her go completely still, and knew immediately that she had gone. He removed the pillow from her back and let her body down ever so gently on to the mattress.

He fully closed her half-closed eyes, pushed the curls from her face and folded her arms across her chest.

At that moment, William despised himself with an intensity that scared him. Why had he not been able to protect her, save her? Had the fame thrust upon her contributed to her health breaking down? Had her family, and other acquaintances exploiting her name, let her down, to the extent that her life was intolerable too much of the time? Could they not have better respected the firm principles with which she'd framed her own life? Had she, in part, been pestered to death, yes, on his watch? Dear God, in the final reckoning, what sort of father had he been?

Grace Horsley Darling died in her father's arms at 8.15 on the evening of Thursday 20 October 1842. It's all the more horrifying when you think she was just twenty-six years old.

Four days later, her funeral took place in Bamburgh. I've seen diary notes recording that the air itself in the village was sorrowful – although there was little wind, the trees were bowed, restless, disturbed. The village green and the streets either side of St. Aidan's church were crammed long before 3 p.m. when the hearse arrived, drawn by a quartet of coal-black shire horses, the front pair with snow-white lower legs.

The coffin was borne into the church on the shoulders of four men: Dr William Bamfather from Alnwick, Dr Thomas Fender from Bamburgh, Mr Robert Smeddle from Bamburgh

Castle and a Reverend Taylor from North Sunderland. William and Laddie led a ten-strong procession of family members who followed the coffin through the parted, respectful crowd. Many tears were shed that day, a public lament for the distressing death of a young woman whom the region, the whole nation, had taken to its heart.

No one noticed him, but standing silently at the back of the crowd, close to the cottage where Grace died, was a young man in his late twenties, wearing a pressed black suit and a black armband, tears in his hazel-coloured eyes. His name was George Smith. He was the artist who had given Grace his painting of her and briefly stayed in touch. It had pained him when his whole family moved to Seville, where his *Yaya* – Grandma – Juliana still lived, and where incentives were offered to settle as so many locals had emigrated for new lives in South America. Most of the family had fitted in, but George never really did. He was lonely. He had returned to England last month, after another admittedly gorgeous Andalusian summer, but when he tracked Grace down, it was too late. Now he was alone. But, he resolved to himself, having got to know the woman behind the fame a little, he would do his best to feel happy about her life, rather than sad at her death.

Curiously, Buddy, who was with William Brooks, wagged frantically when, for the first time, he saw George and gave his hand a sniff and a lick as they passed.

Grace's tragically premature death was front page news. It served further to enhance her fame, her reputation for self-sacrifice. The iconic image of her, alone in the storm-lashed coble off Big Hawker, was frozen for all time, as Robert Smeddle, and no doubt others too, had predicted. For years to come, it continued to be reinterpreted on household products from soap tablets to glassware, toy ships to tins of chocolate.

In 1843, the poet laureate, William Wordsworth, composed 'Grace Darling', immortalising her bravery on the night of the rescue:

"The natural heart is touched –
Inspired by one whose very name bespeaks
Favour divine, exalting human love;
Whom, since her birth on bleak Northumbria's coast,
Known unto few but prized as far as known,
A Single Act endears to high and low."

More paintings of Grace the icon were made posthumously. The acclaimed portraitist Thomas Brooks, who trained in London and Paris, produced one, as did Charles J Staniland, a prolific illustrator of marine scenes. Both men were born in Hull, whence the *Forfarshire* began her final journey.

Promptly after Grace died, planning for a memorial began. In 1844, a substantial stone monument with a carved figure of Grace lying on a plinth beneath a three-arched canopy, was unveiled in St. Aidan's churchyard, where it could be seen by sailors out to sea. Its architect, Anthony Salvin, born in County Durham, would later undertake restoration work on Alnwick Castle. There is also an effigy of Grace inside the church – part of an earlier monument whose stonework crumbled.

For many weeks, when Thomasina woke up after a restless night, it felt as though Grace had only just died. At times, she wanted to shut herself away somewhere – anywhere – in the winter darkness, but she never succumbed. She sat like a wounded lioness at her spinning wheel, unseeing, sustained by a rich, if brutally curtailed, store of memories.

She and William received sacks of cards and letters of condolence. Archbishop Thorp, representing Grace's trustees, penned a glowing eulogy. The Duchess of Northumberland, signing herself simply as Charlotte, wrote a heart-warming tribute on behalf of herself and the duke – which mentioned that Queen Victoria herself had expressed how bereft she'd felt on hearing of Grace's passing.

There were messages of sympathy from Henry Perlee Parker, George Shield, George Smith, James Kelly, Johnny Tulloch, Thomas Buchanan, William Batty, Catherine Sinclair for the Ladies of Edinburgh, the directors of the Dundee & Hull Steam Packet Company, the partners of Dickson, Archer & Thorp, the Robsons of North Sunderland, Glen and Brenna Ritchie, dozens of others.

William was particularly touched to receive a thoughtful letter from Sarah and Jesse Dawson. Although he and Thomasina had already lost one child – their son, Job, aged nineteen – and youth mortality was not uncommon, neither of them had ever experienced sorrow or grief such as they suffered when Grace passed away. Long afterwards, when William rowed out in the coble, she would be there alongside him, pulling an oar, keeping him safe and steady.

Before I sign off, what about me? You may have been wondering for a while who I am, where I fit into this saga? If you have, thank you. So, at last, for the record:

My name is Ethan H Darling. No relation, as far as I can ascertain. I'm a present-day archaeologist, contracted to work in Bamburgh. My project team is excavating burial grounds containing a vast number of plots – about 1,500 in all. They were recently unearthed – or at least the first few, in multiple layers – by builders digging up a field behind St. Aidan's church.

For more than a year, we've been using carbon dating techniques to establish that the earliest graves date back to the sixth century A.D. but we're not sure of the range yet. We think it's wide, which is exciting.

You'll know that every living creature absorbs carbon from the atmosphere. Some of it is radioactive and, helpfully, this type of carbon goes on decaying long after the body itself dies. By measuring the proportion of radioactive carbon to the non-radioactive types in the remains, we can work out, reasonably accurately, when the host body died.

Anyway – and I promise that was my last little digression – I've been spending a lot of time in Bamburgh, in clear sight of the Darling family cemetery. It soon became a magnet, compelling and fascinating. I was drawn to learn more about who these people were. What was the story behind the monument? I was not clued up at the outset.

As you know, I'm fascinated by history, most of all for its uncanny ability to light up the present and the future – because, of course, human beings, brimming with ideas and emotions, are there in every century we measure.

I scoured a lot of archives, physical and digital, read some great stuff, and spent too many evenings and weekends – there, I've confessed it – assembling this version of events. But I've loved doing it. Honestly, the experience has nourished my soul.

As a child, you adored stories. We read them together and you made up lots of your own. I hope this one inspires you, my amazing twenty-six-year-old, especially now that you are well again, to go on in life, be the most brilliant version of you, and be happy. That's all I've ever wanted for you.

I am delighted that Grace Darling's star shone brightly, just as her mother prayed it would. Grace went through some dark times. She was blessed with stamina and resilience, tempered with a human vulnerability, inner doubts and nervousness that crept into social anxiety. She struggled to accept that she was worthy of the acclaim and rewards showered upon her – what might now be diagnosed as a form of Imposter Syndrome. Undoubtedly today we would be more concerned about the potential impact of sudden fame upon mental health. Back in Grace's day, the modern concept of celebrity had yet to emerge.

Nevertheless, Grace showed us that you can accomplish anything, against all odds, if you put your heart and mind into it. She achieved as much as anyone, man or woman, could possibly have done – at a time, in the nineteenth century, when all too few women seemed to triumph at all.

Among those whom she inspired were two British women from strikingly different backgrounds: one born in Kingston, Jamaica, in 1805; the other in Florence, Italy, in 1820. Contemporaries of Grace, they came to prominence after she had blazed a trail for female public figures. Both these women were celebrated for tending to sick and wounded soldiers in the Crimean War of 1853–56, when a coalition including Britain and Turkey fought the Russian Empire. They both passed away in old age in London, having led transformative lives and become icons in their own right.

Their names, respectively, were Mary Seacole and Florence Nightingale.

Epilogue: Aftermath

For someone who lived practically her entire short life on the Farne Islands, Grace Darling's legacy was colossal. It endures today.

Much as Grace herself detested it, the media circus that ballooned after the rescue of the SS *Forfarshire* survivors focused the nation's attention on many issues of maritime safety, including the relative lack of rescue facilities around the UK coast.

Grace's death from tuberculosis, aged twenty-six, boosted the public fervour for reforms to benefit sailors and shipping, driven at least in part by a desire to honour her life.

Lloyd's of London strengthened the safety measures required for marine insurance cover, and more inspections took place. Improvements to steamship engines continued apace throughout the nineteenth century, until they were superseded by diesel models. In the 1840s, screw propellors began to replace paddles. In the following decade, lifeboat crews – increased in number – were issued for the first time with lifejackets. Made of cork, they were bulky but effective.

In 1852, an official lifeboat station was established in North Sunderland harbour, although for many years before that the local fishermen had provided an unofficial service supported by the Lord Crewe trustees. The first official lifeboat, thirty feet long, needed a crew of ten oarsmen. It cost £150. Records show that the service has saved hundreds of lives. Other RNLI lifeboat stations were established and remain, at Amble and Craster for example, further down the Northumberland coast.

By the way, the settlement around North Sunderland harbour has been known as Seahouses ever since a branch line (long disused) brought trains the extra half-mile beyond North Sunderland station, stopping at the coast itself. Seahouses is now a bustling resort, while North Sunderland village is not to be confused with the Wearside city, Sunderland.

A telegraph-based weather warning service for sailors – the Shipping Forecast – was introduced in 1861, the brainchild of Vice-Admiral Robert FitzRoy. He was a founding father of the UK's Meteorological Department – now known as the Met Office – and coined the weather-related term 'forecasting'. He is also remembered as the captain of Charles Darwin's ambitious voyages as ship's naturalist on the tiny vessel, HMS *Beagle*.

In 1854, the National Institution for the Preservation of Life from Shipwreck, then thirty years old, changed its name to the Royal National Lifeboat Institution (RNLI). Blessed with a royal charter, it was, as always, run as a charity. Grace Darling was the first woman to receive its prestigious gallantry medal, but more than twenty women have since been awarded one. Today, hundreds of women serve among the RNLI's volunteer crews.

By the time of the RNLI's name change, its president was Algernon Percy, the fourth Duke of Northumberland. He had succeeded his elder brother, Hugh, in the dukedom in 1847, amidst a long and distinguished naval career. Four years after his succession, he promoted a design by the boat builder James Beeching for a 'self-righting lifeboat', made of wood, which became the RNLI's standard model. The fourth duke and his wife, Eleanor, maintained contact with the Darling family.

Thomasina, Grace's devoted mother, died aged seventy-four in October 1848, six shrunken, broken-hearted years after Grace.

Thomasin, Grace's beloved sister, gave up her dressmaking business and moved in with her parents on Longstone. She died in 1886. Her twin sister, Mary Ann, died prematurely aged thirty-five in 1843, a further hammer blow to the family still grieving the loss of Grace.

In their own way, the Darlings packed quite a punch. Two of William and Thomasina's children became lighthouse keepers: Laddie on Coquet Island and William Brooks, whom

Trinity House appointed as his father's assistant on Longstone. In 1859, the brothers swapped positions, as Laddie prepared to succeed his father on Longstone, and William Brooks, Jane at his side, took charge in the 'fortress' on Coquet Island. Both men were inordinately proud to prolong the family tradition.

Laddie and Ann named their third child – their first daughter – Grace Horsley Darling. Born in 1843, the year after Grace's death, she married Thomas Hall in Belford at the age of twenty-one, bore five children and lived into her seventies.

Grace Darling did not make a will. Her trust fund passed to her parents, and on her father William's death aged seventy-nine in May 1865, the sum was divided equally among the surviving siblings. True to her word, Grace never dipped into the fund to enrich herself. William is buried in St. Aidan's churchyard, Bamburgh, alongside Thomasina, Grace and other family members.

The Farne Islands, forever linked to early Christianity, remain a world-renowned habitat for seabirds and seals. Thousands of them colonise the islands every year.

Much of the *Forfarshire* was washed out to sea, with debris landing on beaches along the coast in the days and weeks that followed. Heavy objects, such as brass handrails, steel ladders and air ducts, were strewn across the seabed. Fragments of her sunken aft portion still lie on the seabed off the tip of Big Hawker – better known today as Big Harcar.

As divers attest, however, precious little of the wreck is visible – some timbers and iron plates, perhaps, silent witnesses to the dreadful disaster – mingled with material from other shipwrecks. The best time to dive the area is at low, slack water, on a spring tide.

The Longstone light, which has warned ships off the rocks for two centuries, was automated by Trinity House in 1990. It is necessarily among the brightest such lights in Europe: there remain some of the most dangerous waters of the British Isles.

Today, safety standards in UK coastal waters are carefully regulated. Under the auspices of the Department for Transport, the Maritime & Coastguard Agency co-ordinates HM Coastguard's search and rescue service and administers the UK Ship Register. Every year, the MCA's marine surveyors conduct thousands of inspections on UK-registered ships, among many other responsibilities.

In the nineteenth century, the shape of life continued rapidly to evolve. In July 1841, a Baptist preacher from Derbyshire named Thomas Cook arranged his first excursion on the Midland Counties Railway. Having chartered a train, he charged a shilling a head for a day return from Leicester to Loughborough, eleven miles each way. Later, he pioneered visits to London, and then his first holidays abroad, enabling tourists to see the world and experience a shared humanity.

For many years after Grace died, the Darlings' coble was displayed at public events and exhibitions UK-wide. Today, it properly resides at the dedicated RNLI Grace Darling Museum, facing St. Aidan's church in Bamburgh.

The name 'Grace Darling' retains its salience in the travel and tourism trade. It brands hotels and holidays in Northumberland and farther afield. More figuratively, its connotations of selfless courage, integrity and loyalty endure. As one of the most famous Britons of the early Victorian era, Grace's story is also a cautionary tale about the challenges inherent in a rapid rise to media celebrity status.

For all these reasons, Grace's life and its aftermath resonate in today's world. Grace Darling should be, surely will be, immortal.

Author's Note

For more than a hundred years after her death, Grace Darling remained famous, a popular icon.

But today, if Grace is known at all, only the rescue of the SS *Forfarshire* survivors is likely to be recounted. This book seeks to redress the loss, refresh the balance, for modern-day readers, embracing the complete arc of her brief but extraordinary, impactful life.

It does *not* purport to be a text-book account. It is a *dramatised version*, with some invention of characters, personalities, events and timelines along the way. But I hope and believe that it is fundamentally faithful to Grace's true story.

Among the writers whose books about Grace Darling I consulted are Richard Armstrong, Hugh Cunningham, Jessica Mitford, and Constance Smedley. Also, the beautifully illustrated book by John Harper, John Pagan and Moira Pagan; the informative website gracedarling.co.uk; and the publications of the RNLI Grace Darling Museum. My admiration and appreciation go to them all – Grace's spirit lives in each of them. Numerous physical and online reference works on the splendidly rich history, geology and ornithology of Northumberland were also invaluable. Any unforced errors in this book are mine alone.

I should also like to acknowledge Gareth Howard and his team for their time spent guiding me through the dynamic world of publishing; and Geoffrey Macnab for being so open to collaboration on *his* recently published books. Thank you.

A parting thought to bring *Grace* full circle, in an age of global warming and rising sea levels. It is self-evidently impossible to know, but given her appreciation of the natural world, I think it's likely that Grace Darling would welcome the switch we are making in the twenty-first century from fossil fuels to cleaner, renewable sources of energy. Don't you?

About the author

Mark Batey was born and raised in Newcastle upon Tyne.

As a student at Pembroke College, Cambridge, he chaired the college film society and, after five years working in advertising, he forged a career in the film industry.

This included three years at the BFI and two decades running the trade association for UK film distributors – the companies that acquire, promote and release films to audiences.

He wrote stories from childhood. Throughout his career he scripted articles, speeches and reports, and is thrilled to have turned recently to longer-form narratives.

Grace is his first published book.

He lives in London and Northumberland.

Visit www.markbateyauthor.com

CPSIA information can be obtained
at www.ICGtesting.com
Printed in the USA
LVHW090015150122
708530LV00005B/143

9 781914 498374